A Spiral of Echoes

By

Barbara M. Hodges

And

Maggie Pucillo

Coastal Dunes Publishing

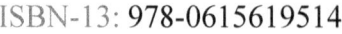

ISBN-13: 978-0615619514
ISBN-10: 0615619517

Cover art by Jay Dismas
artfulimage.com

Author's Note

Dedication page

This book is dedicated to everyone who believes in the magic and power of love.
Barbara M. Hodges and Maggie Pucillo

Acknowledgements

I couldn't have written this book with anyone but Maggie Pucillo. Thanks for sticking it out with me.

My local writers group, The Santa Maria California Word Wizards, your feed-back is priceless.

A big shout out to Jay Dismas, cover artist extraordinaire, next to the word patience in the dictionary, they should have his photo.

My mom, who taught me to love words and stories at an early age. And my husband Jeff who makes it all possible.

Barbara M. Hodges

Mentor and excellent writing partner Barbara M. Hodges. And many thanks to the Hoppers for their tour of the islands and the hours of Internet access.

Maggie Pucillo.

Also by Barbara M Hodges

The Blue Flame

The Emerald Dagger

The Silver Angel

Magical Stew

With Randolph Tower

Ice

One Last Sin

With Darrell Bain

Shadow Worlds

The back of the Jeep held branches and small cuts of three different kinds of wood - piñon, roble, and madera de salvia - all stacked separately as Magdalena had ordered.

Andres climbed in, started the engine, and in moments they were on the beach, at the chosen place.

The sand stretched before them. Andres unfolded a chair and draped a down comforter over it. Magdalena climbed from the Jeep, seated herself, and arranged the corners of the comforter around her shoulders.

"I'll bring a few more rocks and have the fire started soon."

Magdalena, deep in her thoughts, didn't respond.

She remembered the sad day and those who had drowned. It was April, with a strong east wind, water temperature in the 50's. The search continued for days, but they never recovered Patricia Mullins' body.

"It's possible," she murmured as she watched her grandson feed the small fire. "Do you have the proper wood?" she called out to him. "I want the piñon to begin. It is most important."

"Yes, Grandmother. Then the roble, and the madera de salvia. I will be most careful. Do you wish a bite to eat?"

"Perhaps later. I believe I am ready. Thank you for the tea. Rest now, and stay near, tend our fire." She reached for her bag, passed the strap over her head and shoulder, then stood.

Magdalena stopped often to pick up small, sea-smoothed pebbles as she walked toward the top of the berm. Three times she brought thumbnail-sized pieces of the herbs from her bag, to her mouth. Time slowed, the pebbles in her pocket warmed as she reached outward, searching for her guides and the answering awareness of the Other.

Near the small fire, Andres watched his grandmother. He became entranced, forgetting for a moment everything but her measured steps. She was only the width of the beach away, but he knew where her soul journeyed he could not follow.

A log settled into the fire and he jumped. Andres released a shuddering breath, then stood and reached for a piece of wood on his right. He stirred the fire and carefully added the small cut.

Magdalena walked in a circle, creating a path in the sand. The spiral she traced led to the core of her heart, the place where she would rendezvous with those from the other side.

Every few paces she dropped a pebble. The first sounded a mere whisper, yet she knew by the time her pocket emptied, each would reverberate in her bones, a screech, an echoing boom, as grains of sand landed in new resting places. They scattered outward from the opaque glow of the mother stone, a spiral of echoes.

The tide crept in, bringing a salty resonance to the air. The breeze came alive as the spiral grew. When Magdalena reached the center, the last pebble thundered as it hit the sand.

Andres watched her arms rise from her sides to meet over her head, palm to palm. A glow traveled from the middle of her body, up her arms to her hands. The top of her head began to pulse with light.

A dulcet call filled his ears. He looked beyond his grandmother to the shallows. Bottle-nosed dolphins had gathered. He watched in astonishment as they swirled and leapt, circling and dancing on their tails.

Swaying, Magdalena faced the tumbling assembly. She sank to her knees. The dolphins calmed and began to rock in time with her. The glow moved from Magdalena's body, onto theirs, until it shrouded all.

Their vocalizations became less random. From the dolphins' minds and into hers the experiences of those on the small boat became known.

Tears running down her cheeks, Magdalena fell back onto the sand. As she watched, the dolphins rose from the water as one, then turned and headed out into the bay.

The wind roared, and Magdalena felt her spirit leave her body. She saw her small beach camp from the top of the island's volcanic crest. The wind increased, blew spray through her.

The wind and water cried, "Why hasn't he come for me?"

Then Magdalena was once more on her beach. She heard her own voice, pleading, "Why hasn't he come for me?"

"Grandmother, I have come. I am here."

Hands lifted her. She felt the warmth of the fire. Magdalena opened her eyes and looked into Andres' face for a moment.

"I think we must invite Isabelle to my house soon. There is much I would speak to her about."

Isla Santa Maria
Baja, Mexico

The woman sitting on the rock shifted, rubbed at her chilled arms. Above the island the sun rode high in the sky, but its rays did nothing to soothe the constant cold inside her. A sharp cry made her look up. Two ravens rode the currents in a dance of love, the sun reflecting from their blue-black wings. She saw them often, felt as if they watched and waited; for what she did not know.

The woman bowed her head.

"I have a love. Why doesn't he come for me?"

The man she remembered, tall, sandy-haired, with an ever ready smile; a veil across her mind blocked all else.

I am to stay. I am to wait. He will return for me. I must be here. If not he will never find me again.

The women knew she had a life before her time upon the island. She dropped her head onto her raised knees, sought again to shred the barrier, but it held fast and trapped her in a misery of loss.

She straightened, stared across the sea toward the other beach. A cluster of houses stood there. When the woman had first awaked upon the sandy beach, she hoped her love was among the homes. Yes, he had told her to wait on the island, but if he were so close.

At first she feared she would have to swim. She did not want to venture into the sea again, but the woman found she could ride the wind, like the butterflies she loved to sculpt. Deep, in a distant part of her mind, she knew she should not be able to do this, but she had pushed the thought away.

I am different now. I am reborn. He will understand. This experience has changed me, but my love still burns strong.

When she had landed upon the far beach and walked upon the sand, it was to find her love was not there. In a panic she had raced back to the island. What if he'd come for her while she was gone?

The woman stood. Was that it? Is that what happened? He came for me and I was not here? She wrapped her arms around her stomach.-

I should have stayed as he told me to. But he will come once more, as he promised he would. Until then I will wait. I will never journey so far that I cannot return to my island. Never. Not until he comes for me.

A movement to her right caught her eye and she turned. On the sand below, a snake slithered. It slowed, flicked out its tongue in her direction and came onward. The woman still marveled at the lack of fear the inhabitants of the island showed toward her, it was if she did not exist. The only ones who paid her any mind were the two ravens and the dolphins.

She lifted her hand to shade her eyes and searched the sea. Yes, the dolphins were there, two of them swimming back and forth. The woman felt as if they also watched. At first they had come closer, danced upon their tails, and chattered at her. She did not understand them, but felt they urged her to action.

Once in frustration she had screamed. "What? What do you want from me?"

They chattered louder, leaped higher and in a rage she had sent a stone flying toward them using only the power of her mind. The flying rock had shocked her, but the spark of warmth her anger ignited had filled her with joy.

For the rest of the day she'd picked up rock after rock with her mind, tossed them here and there. But she could not summon the anger to bring her the warmth. Yet, she craved the heat and used what memories she had, even at times allowed her wrath at the man to grow. He who had left her on the island with an urgent command.

"Wait for me. I'll come back for you."

Yet the woman feared to give in to the need too often. What if anger swallowed the memories that remained?

The dolphins still came but kept further from the beach.

The woman stood. "When he comes for me, this numbness will vanish. I will feel again."

She turned to look down at the sea. The various shades of blue and green called to her. In her heart she knew she'd once formed such beauty, but she couldn't remember how or when it had been.

"Come for me, my love," she whispered to the waves. "Come for me. I am so tired of waiting."

Chapter One

Isabelle Allen stared down at her husband's blue-tinged lips and lifeless eyes. He sprawled on a bed in the captain's quarters of his cabin cruiser. The old cliché, *he looks asleep,* came to her, but she shook her head. Donald didn't look as if he slept. He looked like what he was, dead, and by the grimace on his face, it hadn't been a pleasant experience.

The boat dipped, rose beneath her and she heard sobs. They rose in volume, bordered on hysteria.

She turned, looked across the cabin, toward the girl who wailed at the police officer. What was her name? The officer had introduced them, Evelyn, Evangeline, something like that. She was Donald's newly preferred type, brunette, curvy, young, and dumb as a rock; the girl thought Donald's heart attack was the culmination of some fantastic sex.

Isabelle shrugged. Maybe it was. God knew they used to be pretty hot together between the sheets. When was the last time that happened? Three years ago, after too much wine at some brain-numbing charity event.

Two Mum's champagne bottles stood on the table next to the bed, one full, one empty. Isabelle glanced across at her friend Sharlee. "Looks as if they had a good time."

"Ah Izzy, I'm so sorry."

"Why? He screwed around. It wasn't a secret."

Sharlee raked her fingers through her cropped, auburn hair. "But it's so...so...public. Not like you at all." She waved a hand toward the girl and officers. Her friend's southern accent drew out the words, a tip-off to how upset she was about the entire mess. Sharlee, or Sharleen Wilkerson when she wasn't decked out in short-shorts and a tank top, was an attorney. She worked hard to keep her southern roots hidden. They'd been friends for eleven years and Isabelle had yet to figure why Sharlee's Georgia birthplace was an issue. She knew from past conversations that Sharlee was adopted and was searching for her birth parents. Sharlee had discovered her paternal grandmother was Cajun, but she'd found out nothing more about her father.

"Mrs. Allen, would you like to wait up on deck?" The police officer said and glanced at his watch. "The coroner's late."

"Sure."

She waited until the officer turned his back and then grabbed the full champagne bottle, crossed to the small galley and grabbed two clean glasses from inside a cupboard. "Sharlee, let's get some fresh air."

On deck, Isabelle poured two glasses of champagne, handed one to Sharlee. She stared across San Francisco Bay toward the Golden Gate Bridge. Fog still covered its upper spans. Donald had found San Francisco's weather gloomy, but had tolerated it for all of the snobbish nightlife he craved. She loved the city with all its kinetic energy, at times it seemed an living entity. A stiff breeze blew hair from her braid across her eyes and she flicked it away with her hand.

"What now, Izzy? You know you won't make the Arthritis Fund benefit tonight. Madeline always counts on Donald."

"I'll send a check." She faced Sharlee. "You remember the rock opera *Tommy?*"

Her friend looked puzzled. "Yes."

"There's the song where the lyrics go something like, *I am free. I am free.*"

She saw when Sharlee got it. They shared a long look and a smile.

Isabelle held out her glass in a toast to the sky and took a long drink.

✳✳✳✳✳

Isabelle looked up from her loom and rubbed at the back of her neck. She had been spending more time here in the six months since Donald's death, than her bed. "Time for a break, huh, baby?" She reached down, patted the head of her basset hound, Sammi-Sue, stood and walked to the window where Longfellow bathed in the sun. She scratched the champagne Burmese cat's pale ears.

"Maybe we'll make a run into China Town for dinner. How's that sound?" She moved back to her loom. Another hour and *Baja Cortez* would be finished. Wide swaths of brilliant colors formed the abstract sunset. The bands came together, touched, and flowed apart.

Along the weaving's horizon she had worked a line of small flames, her trademark. She brushed them with her fingertips. Isabelle wasn't sure when they had appeared, she hadn't noticed until Sharlee pointed out all of her weavings contained at least one flame.

Isabelle looked over her strands of yarn. Yes, the Aztec Gold would work well for the highlight. She smiled, even as the expected tears clogged her throat. It was always the same, her passion to see an idea born, then a surge of melancholy with the last strand of color added.

14

Downstairs, the doorbell chimed.

Sammi-Sue hopped up and raced from the room, already in full voice.

"Oh, come on. Not now."

The doorbell rang again.

"Damn. If you want to clean a spot on my carpet, or sell me another magazine...."

Her flip-flops slapped against the oak hardwood floor as Isabelle marched down the hall. As she reached the top of the stairs the doorbell rang for the third time. "Your momma never tell you patience was a virtue?" she muttered.

At the front door Sammi-Sue bounced, barked and warned whoever waited on the other side. "Quiet," Isabelle said. The basset hound calmed, but stood where she was, her nose pointed at the door.

Isabelle peered through the ornate, leaded glass pane at a man with a bouquet of red flowers. Flowers? She groaned. It had all the earmarks of another fix-up attempt. How many had this been in the past six months since Donald's demise? At least twelve.

She thought she had made things clear after the last disastrous blind date. She would be the one to decide when it was time to put Donald's death behind her and get out into the world.

Isabelle opened the door. "Yes?"

"Isabelle Allen?"

"That's me."

His gaze fixed upon her clothes. Dressed for her work, she wore a droopy sweatshirt and pants. They had once been bright blue, but had faded to a dull gray. Wisps of blonde hair had escaped her braid and she didn't have on a speck of make-up. But hey, she'd remembered to brush her teeth.-

The man's gaze lingered on her breasts and her lips tightened. His appraisal rose to her face, slid to a halt as their eyes met. His widened. Isabelle didn't bother to hide a smile. Her eyes were deep violet with specks of gold; always a surprise to someone who met her for the first time. "And you are?"-

"Oh. Sorry." His face flooded with red. "Philip Collier. I work with Joshua Drake."

Good old JD. She saluted his tenacity. He never gave up. She decided to play dumb. "If you have something you'd like me to invest in you've made a useless trip."

"No...I...." He smiled. "Didn't Joshua speak to you?"-
Isabelle shook her head.-

"Talk about a blind date. More like blind-sided, huh?" He flashed his white teeth.

He does have a nice smile, maybe...but for sure not tonight. "I know JD meant well," she said.

"Well, since I'm here...."

Isabelle shook her head. "Sorry. Philip was it? Not a good time. I'm in the middle of something."

"Cynthia told me you weave as a hobby. I parasail."

She cringed at his use of the word hobby. Non-artists didn't get it. Her work was on display at six art galleries. She'd been offered a one-woman show in Los Angeles, but Donald insisted she turn it down.

Isabelle forced herself to smile. "I'm sure you didn't mean to insult me, but your comment came close. I'm a master weaver. Do you know what that means?"

"Well, no. It sounds impressive. Maybe you can show me your work sometime?"

Right. Maybe when there's a heat-wave in Siberia. "I've always wanted to try parasailing," Isabelle said. "But tonight still won't work. How about…?"

"It will be tight, but if you hurry we can still make the reservation at the *Top Of The Mark*." He glanced at his wristwatch. "On second thought, I'm sure they'll hold the table longer for me." He pulled out his cell phone.

"Please don't bother on my account and if you leave now you might make it if the traffic's light."

"What?" He looked astounded.

"Like I said, maybe some other time."

At her answer his eyes narrowed and his smile faded. "I see. Well, I promised Joshua I'd give it a try." He snapped the phone closed and put it back in his pocket.

"And I'll thank him for you. The next time I see him. You can be sure. Good night, Philip." Isabelle shut the door. "Nice try JD, but dear Philip seems to be another Donald-clone." She shook her head. "And one Donald was enough to last a lifetime."

Sammi-Sue woofed and Isabelle looked down. "Ah, princess." She patted the basset hound's head. "Our friends have exhausted my patience. We need a place where no one knows our number, and we know where that is, don't we? Baja here we come."

She climbed the stairs, walked to her work room and over to her woven sunset. Running her fingertips across the mingled lengths of silk, she sighed. How could I let Donald take this from me?

She frowned, stared into the air. Now be truthful. You promised not to lie to yourself any more.-

Okay. Fine…he didn't steal my weaving. I didn't have to stay with him. Why did I? Did I ever love him? I thought I did. He was different from the other guys, smart and worldly. And I was unlike any women he'd chauffeured around. She patted Sammi-Sue's head. "Should have been a clue, huh?"

But I never dreamed he saw me only as a challenge, someone to change, to mold into what he considered the perfect little wife.

And I let him.

She turned, walked to the mirror. A photo of the two of them at some charity affair sat on the dresser. They made a handsome couple, she in a sequined, violet gown, chosen by Donald to match her eyes. Bejeweled chopsticks anchored blonde hair, piled upon her head. He wore a black tux. He always looked so distinguished, his mouth curved into his little superior smile, as if he knew in his heart he was better than anyone else in the room.-

Isabelle studied her face in the photograph. She smiled too, but it looked forced. She turned away from the photo. Yeah, I smiled, I got so I could on command. Like any well-trained bitch. She snorted in disgust and Sammi-Sue whined in question.

"It's okay baby. Soul-searching and don't like what I found."

Sammi came and leaned her head against Isabelle's leg.

The telephone rang and she let the machine get it.

"Izzy, I know you're there." It was Sharlee.

Isabelle picked up the phone. "Not a good time."

"Uh oh, what happened?"

"Another impromptu want-to-be-date."

"Hey, it wasn't me."

"Not this time." Isabelle took a deep breath. "I'm headed to the Baja place for awhile."

"Come on, Sugar. We don't want to chase you away. No one's wants you to re-marry. Have some fun. We worry about you…"

"I do have fun. What I want now is my art, Sammie-Sue and Longie. Maybe later…who knows?"

A long silence stretched before Sharlee said. "You want some company? I'm between trials."

"Thanks, but I need some me time. Maybe in a week or so?"

"You call when you get there."

"I will."

"Give Sammi-Sue a hug and Longfellow an ear rub. I love you, Izzy."

"I know you do."

"Well. Adios, Sugar. "

Isabelle hung up the phone and looked down at Sammi-Sue. "Come on baby. Let's pack."

Chapter Two

Isabelle exhaled as she drove out of San Felipe, Baja, Mexico. She angled the rearview mirror and checked on Longfellow. He still napped and dreamed his cat dreams. "Okay, we'll have our first rest stop just south of town. How's that sound? Even if I keep it to just below forty, we'll still make the beach before dark."

She glanced at Sammi-Sue. The basset hound already seemed in her Baja mood as she stared at the scenery, alert in a mañana kind of way. Isabelle smiled as she punched the button on the CD player. The flamenco vocal grated from the Bose, filled her head and welcomed her again to the Baja reality.

*****

Sammi-Sue nuzzled her arm and Isabelle glanced at her. "You sure you can't wait?"

The basset yipped an urgent response.

"Fine."

The Suburban's tires went over a larger-than-the-rest rock and her teeth clicked together. "Well damn-it to hell," she muttered. Isabelle glanced at Sammi. "I swear I'm going to learn to fly. How hard could it be? The Judkins make this whole trip from San Francisco in less than five hours. It takes me two-and-a-half to drive the fifty miles from San Felipe to the beach."

She stopped the truck and climbed out. The sharp edges of Northern Baja's Sonora desertscape shimmered in the mid-afternoon sun. The dark volcanic rock was beautiful in a stark, dangerous way, but it held the all ready triple-digit heat, magnified it and bounced it back into the air.

"Come on."

The basset hound joined her on the dry dirt.

She tethered Sammi-Sue's leash to her belt loop and looked in to check on Longfellow. He snoozed and snored in his kennel on the shady side of the Suburban's back seat.

"Well, let's get it done."

Sammi-Sue led her on a smell-fest down a small arroyo.

While Isabelle waited, she watched the dust drift inland as the afternoon tide strengthened the onshore breeze. The complete silence was a relief after the hypnotic clatter of the Suburban's passage over the rutted road.

"Do it, Sammi-Sue."

The basset hound tossed Isabelle an insulted look, then found her required spot and gave some much needed moisture back to the Baja. Her business accomplished, Sammi-Sue pranced all the way back to the truck.

Isabelle looped the leash through the passenger side seat belt and moved to the rear of the Suburban to find the basset hound's bowl. She glanced at her watch as she leaned in to grab a three-gallon bottle of water. "We've made good time, but we'll have to make this our last stop if we're to get to our casa before Longfellow's comfort tab wears off."

She poured water in the bowl, circled back to Sammi-Sue and then froze in place.

Less than two feet away a rattlesnake traced a path across the dirt road.

The basset hound stared at the snake's blasé undulations.-

"Oh, God." She sent up a prayer Sammi-Sue would remain quiet. They both stood on point as the snake continued west. When the rattler disappeared around a rock Isabelle exhaled. "Okay baby, you're having your drink in the truck."

Forty-five minutes later they turned off the main road and headed toward their beach.

Isabelle slowed as she approached her landlord Miguel Fuentes' ranch house. The door of the family's shrine stood open. Inside, candles flickered prayers, a sure sign Magdalena Fuentes visited.

Her house came into view and Isabelle heaved a sigh of relief. Donald had taken three years to design their casa. One double-sized lot hadn't been enough for him. He'd leased two. She had called ahead and knew Elisio's wife, Concordea, would have everything cleaned, dusted and prepared for her arrival.

Isabelle backed the dusty Suburban into the garage, turned off its engine, and clipped Sammi-Sue's leash on. The two of them climbed out and walked around to the front door.

She smiled as they entered the house. The light rose and orange tones of the canterra stone warmed the large volume of the rooms and created intimacy despite the fifteen-foot ceilings. The saltillo floor tiles gleamed, and the blue and red Aztec patterned cushions on the sofas and chairs beckoned. "Not yet. I don't dare sit down, or I'll never get back up."

Isabelle walked through the living room and past the kitchen island. She unlocked the back door and crossed the patio that separated the garage from the house, unloaded what she needed for the first night, and brought Longfellow in last. She closed the outside door and opened his carrier. He stepped out, stretched, and set out to explore.

Isabelle walked to the bathroom, opened a drawer, and dumped her cosmetics and vitamins into it. Longfellow sauntered in and indicated to her with a long, heartfelt meow how ready he was to have a bite to eat. Together they walked into the kitchen.

With the cat and basset hound watching, she set up their food stations. While they munched, she unpacked the groceries and un-corked a bottle of wine.

Isabelle sipped Chardonnay as she gave Sharlee the promised call, glad when the answering machine picked up. She loved her friend dearly, but right now all she wanted was to forget about San Francisco.

The tide was at its high mark when she stepped out onto the front ramada and sank into the hammock. Sammi-Sue butted her head beneath Isabelle's hand. "Want a walk, huh? That anxious to get down on the sand and mark your territory? Let me check the windows and doors first. We can't let Longie get out."

With everything secure, she grabbed her hat and Sammi's leash and they started out on their first of many beach walks.

The Gulf of California's sedate waves splashed and gurgled. The lowering sun glinted off the water, changing the sea to the elusive and glorious vermilion color that was impossible to describe. "Okay Miss Sammi-Sue.

You're off the leash. Let's walk as far as the big rocks, then turn around and see what's for my dinner."

The basset hound bounded ahead and explored everything from shells, to rocks and sticks. Isabelle gazed across to the three islands, Isla San Simeon, Isla Santa Maria, and Isla San Francisco. They rested five miles off the beach, beautiful and calm, belying their fiery origins. She had heard from a neighbor the last time she was here that the United States Geological Service and an arm of the Mexican government had started to monitor various islands in the gulf for volcanic gas emissions and she wondered if any test had been done this far north.

I'll have to ask at the ranch house; maybe some of the family has news of the project.

She split the silence with a long whistle. Sammi-Sue stopped, turned, gave one last sniff at the remains of a dead bird and ran to her.

"That's enough for now. It's my turn to eat." She clipped on Sammi's leash and they broke into a slow jog.

As they drew even with her studio she slowed and looked inside. She loved this room. The large windows faced south and flooded the space with light. The French doors, the ecru painted walls, and tiled floors made the room seem larger than it was. Generous storage and layout-sized counters around the perimeter of the room left ample area for her loom and what she thought of as 'thinking on her feet' space.

Donald had not been happy with the expense of the added small bathroom and kitchen bar but she had calmed him when she'd pointed out she would be able to work late without disturbing him. Emphasizing his comfort had always soothed and assured him the world did, indeed, revolve around his desires.

Isabelle's fingers suddenly itched to unload her yarn and get at the loom, but she forced herself to continue toward the house. *Mañana, tomorrow is another day. I'll get started after lunch.* She pictured again in her head the sketch she'd been working on for the new piece. The silk yarn, ordered from a dealer in Hong Kong, would capture the large work perfectly. The planned weaving was a take on Venus Rising From the Sea. But in her head it was a nude man rising from an ocean of flame. The sketch was complete, except for the man's face. She couldn't seem to get it right.

"Dang, Sammi. I forgot to buy any meat and everything inside will be as hard as your head."

Macaroni and cheese with French bread and another glass of Chardonnay became dinner.

Isabelle yawned as she dried and put the last spoon away. She suddenly stopped and grinned down at the cutlery. *Whoa,* she'd just dined on mac and cheese and half a bottle of eighty-dollar wine. She knew Donald turned in his grave.

The meal had been fine for tonight, but tomorrow she'd drive to the fish camp several miles north. The local fishermen usually had some fresh sea bass and one time, even some beautiful sea scallops. If they had scallops, she'd buy a kilo or two.

She escorted Sammi-Sue out for her evening constitutional. The spoiled basset hound would not venture outside alone unless a light was turned on. They came back in and Isabelle hunted up Longfellow, who was already snoozing on the window seat in the bedroom.

Isabelle yawned. "It's some sleep for me." After quickly washing her face and brushing her teeth, she climbed into bed and turned off the lights.

Chapter Three

Isabelle squeezed lime juice on her hands and wiped them with a towel. She and Sammie had made their trip to the fish camp and she had bought the scallops. Now she was ready for some me time.

Sammi-Sue lay in front of the front door and her head came up as Isabelle neared. "Nope. You're staying home. This walk's for me."

Sammie sighed and placed her head on her paws.

"A long jog when I get back. I promise. You and Longie guard the house."

Isabelle walked out the door.

She scanned the sand as she walked, keeping her eye out for golden olives and moon snails. The shells she cared enough to keep she dropped into a canvas bag that had been a fantastic find at a garage sale.

Isabelle groaned when she saw the full estuary. By the swift flow of the water, she could tell the tide had just started to go out. The inlet would not be clear to walk across for another hour or more. Damn it, why didn't I check the tide chart? Well, a little siesta won't hurt. I'll cross when the water is lower. Isabelle untied her sarong from around her waist and laid it on the sand. She put the canvas bag under her head for a pillow, propped her hat low over her eyes, and drifted into sleep.

*****

The woman reclining on the rock bolted to her feet.

What? Who is this? They are like me. I feel their passion for creation. I've been alone so long. They are not my love, but to speak with another artist.

She turned and stared across the sea toward the campo on the beach. It comes from there.

But what if my love comes while I search? She glanced again across the water. Who are you? I must know.

The woman moved swiftly over the top of the waves. In the first house she felt only an absence of life. In the second a man drank and watched a couple have sex on a television screen. In the third a couple ate lunch. In the fourth house, an elderly man and woman sat next to each other on a sofa and held hands. An ache formed within her and her thoughts went to her own love.

Why has he still not come back for me? He promised. And he has always kept his word. Has he forgotten me? Has he found someone new?

She felt anger fill her. It brought the craved warmth, but not as much as before. A shiver raked her form. It has been so long since I've experienced true warmth. His touch and the press of his lips, that's what I miss the most. She drew closer to the couple and saw the woman rub her upper arms.

The tug came again and the woman's artist soul responded.

As she neared the fifth house, she felt the pull grow stronger. Yes. It calls from within. She entered the house. Confusion filled her as she saw only a sleeping flop-eared dog and champagne-blonde colored cat. They are not what draws me. The dog stirred, whined softly, but did not wake.

The cat lifted its head and fastened its golden gaze upon her. It senses me. The woman would have liked to stay and commune with the cat, but she felt the call become more urgent.

Outside the house she turned in a slow circle and sought the source. A small structure adjacent to the house drew her. Entering she felt the glow of creation. A loom stood in one corner. Next to it were stacks of un-opened boxes. Brown sketchbooks lay next to a drafting table. A photo of a woman, standing next to a wall-sized weaving, sat on a stand. A thank you note lay propped against it addressed to Isabelle.

Her name is Isabelle. She is who I seek.

The woman leaned closer to the photograph. In the weaving, palm trees surrounded a volcano, lava flowed over its rim and trailed to the ocean. In the smoke above the volcano a face hovered. It was the fire goddess Pele.

I know this place. I have been there with my love. We had planned to return for our honeymoon. When will I see it again? Why am I still alone? I have waited and waited as he told me to. It was warm there. The sun bathed our heads. We swam naked in the ocean.

This—this Isabelle has seen what I yearn for. It's not fair.

She glared at the photograph. It rose into the air. With a move of her head, she sent it flying across the room. It shattered against the far wall. The woman turned her glare to an unopened box. It flew upward, burst open, spewed colorful yarns into the air, as if it were a volcano. She moved on to the second, third and fourth boxes.

The woman looked at the havoc. Yarn, like large strands of confetti covered the room's floor. She felt a twinge of shame, but pleased surprise overshadowed it.

28

She had never before been able to do so much with her mind.

She moved to the shattered photograph. I should not have done this. It is not her fault I am alone. But she will understand my frustration, what it is like to go years without creating..enough of this. Where is Isabelle?-

Outside the studio she hesitated. The pull had faded.

I must find it again. She stared toward the sea, watched two dolphins leap high. I will make the spiral.

The woman floated toward the ocean. Well out from shore, she walked the pattern above the water. The waves followed her movement, rose higher with each circle she made.

"Por dios."

She turned toward the voice. It was a lone fisherman

"What is this? Perhaps big fish, feeding upon small." He looked into the sky. "But, there are no birds." He aimed his panga toward the widening whirlpool.

With a smile she watched him draw nearer. You know what happened to the too curious cat, she thought. She began to move faster.

The waves rose higher.

Her smile widened.

She felt the fisherman's fear and a spark of warmth filled her. Suddenly the panga angled to the left and swept by her. To either side of the boat she saw the dorsal fins of dolphins. They chattered their displeasure with her as they sailed by.

Interfering creatures.

The spiral now formed, she waited impatiently within its swirling spray. It came again...the pull...Isabelle is upon the beach.

The woman stood beside Isabelle.

She looks different from the photograph...older. Pain has etched lines into her face.

How do I make myself known to her? She lay her hand against Isabelle's back, and felt the artist's soul within. Oh. Yes. I know this. The burn to create. The woman smiled, pressed closer and even in the bright sun, Isabelle drew her legs up against her chest and trembled.

Anger filled the woman. Yes, I am cold. It is what I have lived with, and you quake with but one slight touch. If I leave my hand...?

She forced herself to step back. You are as I. The first to come in all this time. It must mean something. We will speak.

*****

Isabelle dreamed.

A woman walked on an unfamiliar beach. Long, wet, hair fell over her shoulders and down her back. She wore a two-piece, tropical-print bathing suit and sand covered her long, brown legs and arms.

"Where is he? Where is he?" the woman cried. "Where?"

Isabelle jerked awake. Her hands shook as she fumbled in her bag for the water bottle and took a drink. The dream had a presence, the woman a palpable air of misery. But she didn't know her, or the lonely stretch of beach.

Must have been from a movie or book I've seen or read before. I hope it had a happy ending.

She gathered her bag, tied her sarong around her waist and headed toward the inlet.

The tide had gone out farther, but still not far enough for her walk across. She could wait, take another nap, but the thought of the dream made unease inch up her spine. She shrugged.

Hey, so I'll have to swim a little. The water looks sedate enough, and it's only a short way. It's not as if I haven't done this before. One thing. The bag will have to stay here.

She stuffed her sarong into it, took another sip of water and placed the bottle inside, too.

The sun at its zenith heated her arms and legs. The tide moved swiftly through the narrow channel, stirred the sand, and made the bottom difficult to view. She knew stingrays loved this area, and looked for their telltale circular depressions. Satisfied, Isabelle stepped into the shallow water of the inlet. The sand was thick and her feet sank. The water, warmed from its stay in the estuary smelled fishy, but the temperature cooled as she waded deeper. When it reached her waist, she dove and began her crawling strokes and kicks.

She was well into the tidal flow when something brushed her legs. Startled, she looked down—and lost her rhythm. A strong rip tide grabbed her body. She stroked and kicked, but it did no good, she no longer moved across the flow, but toward the opening of the inlet.

Okay, breathe girl. Relax, Izzy. Breathe and relax, you can do this. She caught a breath, more water than air, coughed and gagged. Breathe, kick, stroke. Do it. Her world narrowed to the struggle of her will and body against the persistent tide.

*****

The woman watched the struggle against the tide. Isabelle's arm movements became sluggish.

No, I cannot lose her.

She felt the presence of another and sped outward into the sea.

Cristiano Casamiro dozed in the panga. It was good to push it all aside and drift with the current. The sun bathed his head. He breathed in and out, enjoying the smells of the bay, even the briny scent of the wet nets tangled in the bottom of the boat.

A touch, like frigid fingers, trailed along the back of his neck and his eyes snapped open. His heart pounded, even though he knew he was alone.

"Dios mio," he swore and rubbed at the back of his neck as he struggled to his knees. The panga rocked with his sudden movements and he swore again. A shrill gull's cry drew his eyes to the inlet. A woman struggled in the out-rushing current.

"Idiota," he muttered. He started the outboard motor, opened it to full throttle and sped toward the inlet.

*****

Isabelle felt a hand tug on the waistband of her cut-offs, suddenly a hard edge pressed into her stomach, her head dangled over a mound of nets and in the next instant she joined them.

She smelled fish, felt the scratch of the nets on her chilled, wet skin, heard an motor roar and accelerate. She coughed, spat water from her mouth, rolled to her side and kicked the nets away from her feet.

Isabelle pushed herself up and looked into the grinning face of the man who sat at the rear of the panga.

"Relax you are okay now." His Spanish came fluently and she was glad she understood more of the language then she spoke. "But why señorita, did you choose to go swimming in the inlet? The water is much lovelier on the north side."

"I left my bag there," she pointed toward the beach. "I planned to pick it up on the way back. My house keys are in it."

He looked at her for a moment and turned the boat toward the beach. Close to shore, he cut the engine, stood, and even as the shock vibrated through her, she could not help but notice his lean brown legs. He must spend a lot of time outdoors. Then she laughed to herself. Of course he does. He's a fisherman.

"My bag's right there. I can walk back. Thank you." Isabelle stood. Dizziness washed over her and she swayed.

He grabbed her by her shoulders, lowered her on to a seat. "No, I will take you. If you pass out you could get sunstroke before found. I will get your bag." He pulled his shirt over his head, jumped from the boat and waded through waist-deep water to shore.

"Señor, am I keeping you from your work," she asked as he returned and climbed back into the boat.

He shrugged. "It will wait. I spend much time waiting. Perhaps you should have tried it. In but one hour you could have walked across the inlet in safety." His gaze dropped to her chest. "And with your top still upon you."

Isabelle looked at her breasts. They were bare and growing pink in the strong sun. My God. She almost reached to cover them with her arms, but under the circumstances that would have been silly. She heard a smothered laugh and looked into his suddenly, politely composed face. A smile lit his dark eyes.

"Señorita, if I may?" He handed her his tee shirt. It felt warm from his body and smelled like lime.

Isabelle grabbed it, turned, pulled it over her head and then smoothed it across her chest. Her cheeks burned as she turned to face him. She raked her fingers through hair that had escaped its braid and clung wetly to her face. Isabelle took a deep breath.

"May I offer you something for your time and gas? I am grateful for your help. I misjudged the tide and. . ." Her words trailed away as she realized she babbled.

His lips tightened for a moment, but then the smile was back. "But of course. The money is of no importance, but if it pleases you."

It took her a moment to decipher his quick flow of Spanish words, and then she nodded. "My house is that way. It's not far." At least she hoped that was what she said. It must have been, because he nodded.

She watched in awe as he maneuvered the panga with ease. What is it like, she wondered to depend on the sea for your livelihood? Had his father before him, and his father's father also? Their gazes met and she looked away.

Cristiano smiled, but as she turned from him his eyes narrowed. Another rich *Americana*. Their greedy leasing and buying of the beautiful beach lots along the Sea of Cortez, displayed an attitude he had come to hate. Oh, how they liked to spread their money about. He frowned. The money was not the problem. The *campesinos* could use every peso. It was the air of entitlement that grated his nerves. The gringos seemed to feel that since they were here, the entire Baja belonged to them.

He watched as she stared across the waves, her teeth tugging at her bottom lip. God knows she wasn't the first gringo he pulled from the estuary inlet; they were such fools. Yet, when he had seen her, his heartbeat had tripled and when she had looked up, dazed, into his eyes, his stomach had knotted. Her eyes—they were like amethysts, flecked with gold, and—and—he knew them, he'd dreamed of them many times. No. Of course, he had not. Eyes were eyes. Despite his denial, the hair rose on the back of his neck.

The woman was embarrassed and that pierced his heart. He understood pride wounded by defeat. Her lips had trembled from the cold as she looked at him, and he had felt a surprised yearning to warm them with his own. When he pulled her into the safety of the panga, her nipples were puckered by the chill sea. As they had traveled toward the beach they'd warmed and relaxed and he'd wanted to take them in his mouth, tease them with his tongue, until they grew hard again. The urge shocked him. He wasn't attracted to pale American women. They were too thin and boyishly flat. He liked a dusky woman with curves to hold onto.

Cristiano glanced at her again. Yes, this one's skin was milk white where the sun had not kissed it, but she most definitely had curves. Her legs stretched from the ragged hem of faded cutoffs and were long and shapely. Her breasts full and firm, the nipples the same shade of pale-pink seen inside the multitude of empty shells upon the beaches. He felt himself harden and with a groan shifted upon the seat.

She turned back to him. "Are you okay, Señor?"

He inwardly smiled at her halting Spanish. He spoke fluent English and could have told her so, but his reaction to her made his skin prickle. She was a gringa who had taken him for one of the local fishermen. He would drop her at her beach, refuse the money she offered—and bid her adios. It was better this way. "I am fine, señorita."

She pointed. "There's my place."

Cristiano nodded and then stood in the rear of the panga. Ah, so this is her home. The house had been closed since he had accepted Institute Geologico Mexico's assignment to document the rumbles of the volcano on Isla Santa Maria. It was the first time he had been out in the field in two years and he had only accepted because it was close to his home and old friends. Friends. I have not let Andres know I will attend his Grandmother's birthday party tonight. I will stop by after I deposit my passenger. "Si, Señorita."

He had admired the house before. Its walls of canterra stone glowed a soft rose in the afternoon sun. He had always liked the deep porch that surrounded the front of the house. Before nothing but dark shadows had occupied the space, now three chairs and a round table rested there.

The panga's bottom touched sand and Cristiano vaulted into the sea. With a few tugs he had pulled the boat high enough to be safe, then turned toward her and held out his hand. She looked unsure for a moment and then let him help her. She moved out ahead of him and he followed, enjoying the fluid sway of her hips as she walked.

Isabelle realized she hadn't gotten the man's name, or given him hers. As she turned, the words froze in her throat as she saw where his eyes lingered. Her heart pounded and she felt an instant heat in her lower stomach. My God. How does he do that to me? We've just met. She had never considered herself overly sexual, although Sharlee had said that was a load of crap and for her to look at the passion in her weaving. Donald had been the problem.

The man did not look away, but instead took his time as he raised his eyes over her body, to her face. I should be insulted. Instead she felt his appraisal like a hot, physical touch. Her cheeks burned and she knew her breasts rose and fell with the quickness of her breathing. With a smothered gulp, she turned back from him and quickened her pace toward the house.

*****

The woman had smiled when the man rescued Isabelle. Now, as the emotions of the two swamped her the smile faded. Attraction she knew, the flushed skin and quick beat of hearts. She remembered the times she lay in the arms of her love, the heat of their bodies, the happiness of shared dreams. And it all had been ripped from her.

Isabelle has the beauty of creation in her soul and fingertips, and now she is to know the heat and passion of love as well? While I wait and wait for him who I fear has forgotten his promise to me. It is not fair.

Behind the man a small tornado of sand arose. It hovered, drew shells, small rocks and splinters of driftwood into its body. It began to whirl toward him. Only he will be harmed and not too much. Isabelle will be fine.

*****

Isabelle paused at the door and heard the excited greeting of Sammi-Sue. She felt him stop behind her. "I have a basset hound who can be over zealous in her greeting."

"I like dogs," he said. "At my home we have three."

Isabelle opened the door. Sammi-Sue bounced and quivered, her tail whipped back and forth. "Sammi, behave," she said. The basset hound looked past Isabelle and woofed.

The man moved to stand beside Isabelle, kneeled and looked into Sammi's brown eyes for a long moment. He stood and nodded. "We will be good friends."

"Excuse me?"

"We have taken each other's measure and both like what we have seen."

Isabelle looked from man to dog and then back again. Sammi-Sue did look quite pleased as she turned and led the way into the kitchen. Without a glance at her, the man followed. She watched them with a bemused expression. With a shake of her head, she closed the door. Something slammed against it as she turned away. Puzzled, she opened it again. A pile of shells, rocks and driftwood, lay at its bottom. She shaded her eyes with her hand and stared across the beach. Now what was that about? Must've been a freak gust of wind. With a shrug, she closed the door and walked toward the kitchen.

*****

The woman felt a rush of rage. A wave of weakness followed. It was time for her to return to the island. She stared at the closed door of the house. Isabelle, we will meet. But it has to be on my terms. You will come to me.

*****

Isabelle stopped before the center island. "Would you like something to drink? A beer? Glass of wine?"

"Water will be fine." He touched a tile on the island with his finger tip. "Very beautiful. *Sol y Luna* design, is it not?"

She looked down at the dark blue tile with its depicted half moon and half sun. "Yes."

"In my mother's house she has some of the same tile. Not on as large an area, of course."

She opened the refrigerator and pulled out a pitcher and poured him a tall glass. "Ice?"

"No, it is fine." He reached for it and their hands touched. Her eyes opened wide at the instant charge arcing between them. It was as if she touched metal after shuffling across a nylon rug. Their gazes locked. His lips parted and he licked his lips. Isabelle felt a groan begin in her stomach. God. I want him. Right now, on the tiles or on the floor, maybe both.

A disgusted yowl filled the air, followed by a length of blonde fur that landed at Isabelle's feet.

The connection broken, she released the glass and stepped back. She hadn't even thought about Longie who would of course been in his favorite sunny spot below the kitchen window. Her feline baby did not respond well to being ignored. "My cat, Longfellow," she said in a rush.

"Señor Longfellow," he said, but this time he did not kneel. Instead he waited while the cat stared at him with golden, baleful eyes. Longfellow glided forward and rubbed his body against the man's legs.

"Well you've certainly been honored," Isabelle said. "Longie doesn't take much to anybody."

"Gatos must be given the time and space to come to their own conclusions," he said and turned to stare at the floor to ceiling windows that flanked the door. "You do not find the area is more difficult to keep cool with all of the glass?"

"My late husband saw it in a magazine and thought it was classy." Her tone came out acerbic and she saw him raise an eyebrow. "The double-paned glass helps keep things cool." She watched him sweep a glance over the rest of the open floor plan.

"Very comfortable, I am sure."

She looked at him sharply. Had that been a mocking undertone she heard? His dark eyes stared back at her in angelic innocence. "How many pesos do you think is fair for the time I've kept you from your work?"

"One-hundred," came the instant reply

She did a quick calculation. The amount was less than ten dollars American. "Are you sure?"

"It will do me fine, señorita."

"Oh, okay. Then I'll be right back." She turned and walked from the room, feeling his eyes warm her as she moved away.

In her bedroom she stared at her face in the mirror. Her cheeks were flushed, her hair, now dry, wild and wind-tossed about her face. She looked like a woman who had just been made love to. The thought made her legs quiver. *He's turned me to jelly. I never felt like this with Donald, never. What would it be like to kiss him?* Her reflection frowned. *No way. Don't you go there. This is my escape from all of that. I don't need any local romantic entanglements to mess things up.* She smoothed her hair and, clutching the pesos, walked back toward the kitchen.

The man wasn't there and her heart did a queer little jump. Then his voice came from the living area. He sat upon the chocolate-leather couch, Sammi-Sue at his feet, Longfellow curled upon his lap. He idly scratched the cat's ear and hummed softly. A smile tugged at her lips, and then instant panic erased it. Whoa. No. No. No. Times like these fooled you, and before you knew it you were locked in a velvet prison. "Señor," she said, sharper then she'd intended. "I have your pesos." She thrust out her hand toward him.

His eyes narrowed before he sat Longfellow aside and stood. "Of course, Señorita." His voice was cool and remote. "I apologize if I have over-stepped by coming deeper into your life."

She forced a smile. "I just don't want to keep you any longer."

He walked toward her and she stepped back. In front of her, he stopped. "I understand quite well. Will you see me to the door?" A mocking smile followed the words.

She felt a rush of anger as she realized what he thought. It wasn't like that. She wasn't afraid of him stealing something, but before she could answer Sammi-Sue came between them and butted his hand for a pet.

"Adios, Señorita Sammi and Señor Longfellow." Then without a glance toward her he strode from the room.

Isabelle stood, stiff and mute. When the door closed, a whoosh of breath escaped her.

Longie and Sammie stared at her, and she could have sworn disgust radiated from their eyes. "Hey," she said in defense. "We don't need that type of complication anymore. Remember what it was like?"

With a swish of his tail, Longfellow stalked away while Sammi-Sue moved to the couch and lay below the spot the man had vacated.

I never did get his name. Isabelle rubbed her upper arms. *It's as if he removed some of the heat from the day.* She grimaced. What a thought. She crossed to the side-table and picked up her sketch pad. There was still enough light to work on the design for her next masterpiece.

Chapter Four

Disgusted, Isabelle ripped off the page and tossed it next to the pile of others. Everything she sketched seemed cold and passionless. How could she not find some fire here in Baja? The people, the sand, the sea, they breathed passion and life with each exhale. Fiestas, laughter, tears. They were everywhere.

She recalled the words of one of her instructors. *Let your subconscious be your eyes.* She forced herself to breathe deep, willed herself into a trance-like state. Her thoughts drifted. A touch of a cold nose brought her back. She looked down at her sketch book and then surged to her feet with a feeling of almost horror.

"Oh no. Oh no. Oh no." She shook her head. In her trance-like state she had sketched the nude man rising from the ocean of flame, but this time he had a face, her rescuer's.

She tossed the sketchbook on the end table. "Come on, Sammi. Let's go for a beach walk."

The day had cooled. The sun just an hour or two from setting. They had the smooth stretch of sand to themselves. Sammi-Sue raced ahead to protect the beach from sea gulls.

Isabelle shaded her eyes with her hand and looked. toward the blue-gray, elongated shape of Isla Santa Maria. She'd always wanted to explore its volcanic secrets, but Donald had thought it an insane idea. The talk in San Felipe had been that Isla Santa Maria's volcano had started to whisper its tales again. And there was speculation as to when its whispers would become full-fledged, fiery shouts.

A wave played out upon the sand and teased her bare toes with a wet kiss. Its retreat left behind a glistening sand dollar and with a smile she scooped it up. She had at least a hundred of these stashed in the casa, a little secret she had kept from Donald.

She took a deep breath and drew the salty air into her lungs and heart.

"Izzy."

She turned. It was Andres Fuentes, the landlord's nephew. They had struck up a friendship on her last visit. The slight Mexican man loped toward her, the sun's rays highlighted his red-streaked and severely spiked hair. The purple silk shirt with white pearl buttons he wore clung to his compact frame. In the sunlight he reminded her of a sugar-glazed grape. Andres was gay and had confided on her last trip he had just "come out" to his mother, who'd had a difficult time with the news. Isabelle realized he never spoke about his father.

He picked her up by the waist and whirled her in a circle.

She laughed as he replaced her on her feet. "You are so loco."

Sammi-Sue bugled.

They both turned in the basset hound's direction. She charged toward them with ears flopping.

Andres dropped down onto his knees and braced himself. Sammi-Sue adored Andres. "Ah, Señorita Sammi-Sue. You grow more beautiful each time we meet." The basset hound hopped like a rabbit, kicked up sand in her joy. He leaned closer. "What is this? A new collar? Hand woven, is it not?" He glanced at Isabelle. "Your creation?"

She nodded.

"Quite lovely. All the colors of a summer sunset."

"Not all."

"You are too modest." He pointed to the lowering sun. "Shall we see who is right?"

She shook her head. "Can't. I promised Sammi and Longie a meal fit for a queen, well, make that two queens and one feline king."

"Too bad I can't have dinner with you also. It would be three queens and a king." He shrugged with a theatrical sigh. "But there is a big fiesta to take place tonight at Uncle's. My Grandmother has reached the glorious age of seventy." He slapped his thigh. "Hey, you must come. She would love to see you. And there are many who would welcome your company. Especially since you are no longer with Donald."

Isabelle frowned. There had been some nasty scenes between the locals and Donald.

"Seventy? Wow." You should spend the night starting your new weaving, her voice of reason scolded.

But I haven't even sketched a design, she argued back, and seventy years of age, that's a milestone. "How formal is it. I didn't bring anything fancy."

"Fancy?" He snorted. "We don't do fancy."

She laughed. "What can I bring?"

"Your smile."

44

"No, I want to bring your, uh, grandmother a gift. And since when is it grandmother instead of abuela?"

Andres shrugged. "Magdalena has decided all the young ones, meaning those younger than she, will be bilingual as she herself is. 'Studies show', she says, 'there is a window for language learning'. So, we are to hear and speak only English when we visit with her until she deems us as adept as she."

"Well, good idea, but about the gift…?"

"She has asked for no gifts. And has threatened dire consequences for those who do not abide by her dictates."

Isabelle grinned. "Then it won't be a birthday gift. I will bring her something I've woven simply as a sample for her to show the people of Baja, and a bottle of California chardonnay. She still likes the wine?"

"Oh yes, she still loves the chardonnay. The weaving? You're selling your work?"

Andres knew Donald had forbidden her to do so, had said it demeaned her. "I accept commissions."

"Good for you. Such beauty must be shared." He looked over her shoulder. "I should be getting back. I've been charged with hanging the piñata for all of the little ones." He glanced at her, gave a wicked grin. "But they can wait. So what have you been up to?"

She sighed, and Andres pounced upon the fact.

"Ah-ha. Tell me all."

Isabelle told him of her well meaning friends, their attempts to fix her up and ended with her disastrous run-in with the fisherman.

When she finished, he patted her arm and piously said. "Ah, amigos. They always mean well." He hesitated from a moment and then said, "About tonight. I should tell

you...." A sharp whistle cut through the air and Andres turned toward the sound with a frown. "Am I a dog?"

She wisely kept quiet. Family matters, were just that, family matters. "What time should I be there?"

"Nine o'clock."

As he turned away she realized he'd said nothing of his lover. "Will Juan be there?"

"No," he shortly said. "We are no longer together."

"Oh, I'm sorry."

"Don't fret. It was for the best. Juan is not ready to come out, and I no longer wish to sneak around. Who knows, perhaps in time...but enough. I must get back. I will see you tonight."

She watched him walk away. He hid the hurt well, but having been a professional at hiding hurt, she spotted the scars. Love was such a bitch. "Come on, Sammi-Sue. It's dinner, then I have to get dressed for a party.

Isabelle saw the lights and heard the laughter before the Fuentes' casa came into view. She stopped and smoothed her cotton sundress. It was a terracotta color, with green and brown embroidery at the full skirt and scooped neckline. She had opted for low-heeled sandals and no panty hose. Andres had said casual.

She looked up. A full moon hung in the middle of the black sky, a splatter of pale stars, like specks of silver paint, surrounded it. The night was warm, no breeze yet, but she had brought a shawl with her in her canvas tote bag as well as the soft, silk sash she had woven and a bottle of chardonnay.

There was a lull in the laughter and a rich voice floated to her. The man sang of lost love. The words flowed over her like raw silk. Goosebumps formed on her arms and tears filled her eyes. My God, a voice like that should be outlawed. What did the singer look like? Probably uglier than a horned-toad. Surely God wouldn't give looks and such a voice to one man. She stood and listened until the song faded. There was a long hush and then loud applause. The sultry guitar notes of a Spanish ballad began. She smiled and started forward.

The voices and laughter rose in volume as she neared. She inhaled roasting meat and tortillas frying in oil. A few yards from the patio a bonfire lit the sky. Around it she could see a group of men. They laughed, gestured and passed a bottle freely. The teens had formed their own group farther from the patio.

Then she was among the rest of the guests. Aunts, uncles, cousins, grandchildren and great grandchildren, greeted her with hugs and smiles. "Welcome. Bring the señorita a Cerveza. Or perhaps some sangria?"

"Cerveza is fine," she said, and a cold glass, the top of the Mexican beer still foaming, was thrust into her hand.

Bright lanterns circled the patio and strands of chili-pepper lights glowed red and yellow. In a large empty area in the center, three couples swayed to the lilting sounds coming from the five-piece band nestled at the patio's far side. Two of the musicians strummed guitars. Beside them on a small table, she saw maracas and small hand-held drums.

"Izzy, you're here." She turned. Andres moved toward her. He had changed his shirt. Now, he wore a red one with large gold parrots emblazoned on each lapel. "Come see Grandmother."

He placed his hand beneath her elbow and guided her forward.

Andres' grandmother sat in a large chair decorated with lengths of braided flowers and sea grass. The petite woman wore tan slacks and a rust and white striped shirt, her auburn braid, trailed along one shoulder. Magdalena's caramel colored skin was smooth and wrinkle-free.

She looks as if she could be strolling the streets of New York City instead of overlooking a birthday fiesta, Isabelle thought. I only wish I look that good when I'm turning seventy.

Andres leaned in to kiss Magdalena's cheek. "Grandmother, look who has come to join you in the celebration of your birth. Isabelle."

"Isabelle. It is wonderful to see you again." Her voice came low and husky. If you were not facing the sprite-of-a-woman you would think a young girl had spoken.

"Señora Fuentes, it is an honor to be here."

"I am Magdalena. Señora Fuentes is my madre." Her gaze lingered on the tote bag. "You have brought me something?"

"I warned her not to," Andres said.

Magdalena made a shushing motion with her hand. "A woman knows when words are to be ignored."

Isabelle smiled as she reached into the bag and brought out the length of woven silk.

"Very beautiful." Magdalena ran her fingertips across it. She stood. "I will wear it tonight in your honor." With a flourish Andres helped her wind it around her trim waist. "And what else?" she said as she settled back into her chair.

"Grandmother, Izzy will think you are greedy."

"It is my birthday."

Isabelle laughed as she handed her the bottle of wine.

"Wonderful. We will open it and toast to your return to our beach."

The band's tempo changed to a rhythmic salsa and Isabelle faced the dance area. That was when she saw him, her rescuer. He stood next to a young beauty, his head bent toward her. The young women tossed her hair and smiled a promise.

"Who is the beautiful young woman in the red dress," Isabelle asked.

"My cousin, Paloma. That is Cristiano Casamiro with her. He is a long time friend and I believe the two of you met earlier."

She looked hard at him. "How did you know?"

"He and I spoke this morning."

"And you didn't tell me he was going to be here because?" She kept her words low.

Andres tried to look innocent. "Why would I? He is but a guest, as you are. Do you wish me to inform you of all of them. There is…."

"Okay, Andres. I get it."

He laughed. "You are too suspicious. Relax. Enjoy the party. Look, Paloma wishes to salsa, and he will not deny her, no one does. In all these years I have never seen Cristiano salsa. Let's see if he moves as well as he sings."

She almost groaned as she realized his had been the voice she had heard.

Cristiano knew the moment she spotted him. Even from here he saw her body tense. He'd seen her as soon as she arrived.

After leaving her house, he paid a visit to the Fuentes' and greeted an angry and frustrated Andres on his way out the door. He had matched his steps to his friend and let

Andres stomp in silence to the beach. At last Andres had stopped and stared across the sea.

"She does not understand me. She thinks I can be cured if I would but try to make love to a woman." Andres laughed. "As if I have not." He looked at Cristiano. "Do you think I welcomed my homosexuality? I fought it, refused to see it, and then hid it. I will no longer do so. It is who I am."

"Your mother loves you," Cristiano said.

"I know she does. It's her look of disappointment when she thinks I do not see that rips my insides." Andres rubbed at his forehead. "I know I am the only son, that she had hopes for many grandchildren. "

"That can still be," Cristiano said. "You could use your sperm to artificially inseminate a woman."

Andres laughed shortly. "Can you see me telling my mother that?"

Cristiano gave his friend a pat on the arm. "Time will help. Let her get used to this new side of her son."

Andres shrugged. "Enough of my problems. What have you been up to and will you be at Magdalena's party tonight?"

Cristiano told him of the woman he'd rescued.

"That would be Isabelle. Surprises me though, she's usually not stupid."

"Gringa idiota," Cristiano said with a shrug. "What do you know about her?"

Andres smiled. "Isabelle is a widow. Her late husband was an ass."

"How long has she been a widow? She did not seem to be in mourning."

"I said he was an ass. He treated her like shit. She's a weaver, you know. Does beautiful work. Did you meet Sammi-Sue?"

Cristiano nodded. "And Señor Longfellow, too." He smiled. "She thinks I am a fisherman. Offered me money for gas and time."

"And you didn't tell her any different?"

"It didn't seem of importance. She jumped to a conclusion, like most of her kind."

"I think you like her."

"What?" He scowled at Andres. "She's a gringa. You know how I feel about them."

"Yet, you keep looking toward her house. She interests you."

Cristiano frowned. "Maybe a little."

"Then if you see her again, don't tell her who you really are. Stay a fishermen, at least until she gets to know you."

"Why?"

"You're at least fifteen years younger," Andres said. "And you're rich. Both will count against you with Izzy."

"The age difference I can see. But the money?"

"Donald was rich. He bought everything. Even her, she says. No way is she ever going to be caught like that again."

"I will not pretend to be a fisherman. Now, about your grandmother's party, of course, I will be there."

"That's great. And Cristiano, don't hurt Izzy. She's been through hell."

"It will be fine. A couple of dates, a little fun. Right now I find her intriguing. No doubt that will change when I spend a few more minutes with her."

Andres laughed. "You just might be surprised. Now tell me of the new rumblings from within Isla Santa Maria."

And they spent the next minutes talking of the island and its belching volcano vent.

"Cristiano. Cristiano. You are not listening." Paloma's soft scolding voice jerked his thoughts back to the party. He looked into her pouting face.

"Ah, little dove. I was thinking of your cousin Andres."

She sighed and tossed her head. "He has been chosen for a difficult road. But he is much loved. So, you did not answer me. At your advanced age, can you salsa?" she said.

He grabbed at his heart."You wound me. But I will attempt to keep up with you."

She laughed as she pulled him out onto the dance floor. Cristiano let the music flow into his heart and then downward. He placed his hands on her hips and they began to dip and sway, faster and faster. She moved away from him, whirled and then leaned forward and shook her shoulders. Her breasts bounced, came near to escaping her top and he hoped her five brothers and father were not watching the two of them too closely.

He became lost in the music. Paloma moved to his right and her older sister, Natalia, stood before him moving to the driving beat. He grabbed her hips, swayed with her. In. Out. Up and down, and then she was gone and another took her place. His partners became a kaleidoscope of beautiful faces, smiles and undulating bodies.

Isabelle watched entranced as Cristiano moved. His back was to her and she flushed as his knees bent and his jeans went taut over his butt. He stood, spun his partner, laughed into her face. His dark eyes flicked to hers and then away. The emerald-colored shirt he wore flowed like a waterfall of silk. The first two buttons were open and she caught a flash of tan skin as he moved away from the girl and did a wild gyration with his hips. Another woman moved into his arms. They came together, swayed hip-to-hip. The woman leaned back, her dark hair almost brushing the floor, and Isabelle felt her own pulse drum in time with the music.

"The salsa, it stirs the blood," Magdalena said.

Isabelle tore her gaze away from the couple. "The dance is so - so - sensual. I don't think I could ever do that."

"Latin blood is hot. You should have seen me. I love the flamenco as does my Andres." She raised her hands above her head and snapped her fingers.

The music ended with a flourish and was followed by a lilting ballad.

"Señorita, may I have this dance?"

The slowly spoken Spanish words came from behind her and she turned. Of course, it was Cristiano. With her eyes at the level of his chest she shook her head. "I don't dance."

"Of course you do," Magdalena said. "You are a woman, we are born to dance. You have not had the right partner."

Isabelle looked up into his eyes and saw a challenge. He held out his hand and she took it. He led her out onto the floor.

Cristiano placed his other hand in the small of her back. The heat from his palm singed her skin and she shuddered.

"You are cold." His warm breath stirred her hair. "I will heat you up." He pulled her closer until their bodies were molded together. "Better?"

Isabelle nodded.

She stepped on his foot and felt her face heat. "This was a mistake," she muttered.

"Look into my eyes."

His hand lifted her chin. She had thought his eyes were brown, now she saw they were more like dark chocolate, swirled with rum.

"Quit thinking, señorita and just move."

His hands lowered, came to a rest on her hips. The music filled her head. His palms, branded where they rested, guided, first side-to-side and then in a slow circle. His body seemed glued to hers and mirrored every movement.

Their gazes locked, they continued to sway. Everything around her became a blur, except for him, his body, his scent, and his eyes.

The music stopped. He did not release her, but instead bent to whisper into her ear. "Let's walk."

In a trance, she let him pull her into the darkness.

The full, white moon played hide and seek with sleek clouds that cast bands of pale light upon the sand.

They walked just above where the waves ended. His hand held hers loosely, their fingers entwined.

"Listen, the waves whisper their secrets."

She realized he had switched to English - clear, precise, English. She frowned, pulled her hand from his and turned to face him. "When I was in your boat you let me flounder with my Spanish, and now…why?"

He shrugged. "It seemed expected of me."

She stepped back from him. "Oh, I see…gringa." She turned and stared out toward the dark lump of Isla Santa Maria.

"Perhaps I am wrong. I apologize." He turned to look out across the ocean. "I come from those who take their livelihood from the sea, but my mother believes in education."

"Well, good for your mother. I'm ashamed I don't speak Spanish as well as I could."

"You said earlier your husband died."

She frowned. "Yes, six months ago."

"I am sorry."

"Don't be. It wasn't a happy marriage."

"Then why did you stay with him?"

She shrugged. "I'm a coward, I guess."

"No, Isabella, you are not a coward."

"It's Isabelle, I suppose Andres told you my name."

"He might have mentioned it." He reached to touch her hair. "The moon turns each strand into white-gold."

She felt her breath catch in her throat. She lowered her gaze to his lips.

"You have such beautiful eyes. Violet, like amethysts." He reached to clasp her hands. "I am going to kiss you Isabella. Stop me now if you do not wish it to happen."

Entranced, she watched his hands slide up the length of her arms. They left behind streaks of fire. He hesitated at her shoulder, heat worked its way across into each of her breasts. She felt her nipples pucker in reaction. His fingers continued upward, cupped the back of her neck. A soft gasp escaped her and she closed her eyes as his mouth descended.

His lips were soft, warm, they teased and she rose upon her toes to press hers firmer against his. His tongue slipped into her mouth and her knees trembled. Cristiano's fingers traveled along her spine, came to rest on her hips. His lips demanded more and she pressed harder against his solid length. He shifted his hands to her backside and pulled her closer still.

She felt his ridge of arousal press against her stomach and felt heat build between her legs. With a groan, he pulled his mouth from hers, trailed his lips along her neckline, up to whisper in her ear. "Lie with me."

They dropped onto the beach. He stretched her out upon the sand, rose above her, and looked into her eyes. His face blocked the sky, there was only him. She reached for his shoulders. His skin burned through the thin silk of his shirt as she pulled him to her.

Cristiano's body pressed against the length of hers and she welcomed his strength, his hardness. Their lips met again. With a quick movement that made her gasp, he rolled and brought her atop him, astraddle his hips. The skirt of her sundress rose, leaving her thighs bare. His hands cupped her breasts, thumbs circled each nipple, and she moaned and arched against his palms. He trailed his lips across her cheek and down her neck. His hands in the small of her back urged her nearer and his mouth closed over her right nipple.

"Oh God."

Through the thin fabric of her dress she felt his tongue circle. His teeth gently nipped and she cried out his name.

She felt him touch the skin of her inner thigh. His fingers trailed upward, slowly, and flames shot into her core. He lightly teased the elastic at the leg of her panties and she moaned. Then, he was cupping her through the thin silk. A shudder began at her toes and raced upward to pool where his hand branded.

Oh God. Oh God.

A chilling cold flooded across her legs and she yelped.

For a long moment, they stared at each other. His face as stunned as hers. And then with her legs still around his waist, he rose to his feet.

His back was to the sea. Isabelle looked across his shoulders and watched as a wave flowed inward and covered his shoes. A giggle escaped her.

"Mother nature has a cruel sense of humor," Cristiano murmured.

A wind blew across her wet legs and she shivered.

Her legs were still wrapped around his waist and he slowly lowered her down the length of his body. "I still burn for you." He took her hand. "Come, your casa is not far from here."

She hung back, although her body still hummed and throbbed from his hands and mouth.

"What is it?" He took her hand, pressed it against his still rigid hardness. "I want you."

Isabelle licked her lips. "And I want you, but you've got to understand. It's just sex."

"But of course. What else would it be?" He pulled her forward again.

His quick words were as good as a frigid shower. She stepped back from him, frowned. What was she doing? She'd promised herself after Donald, it would be her head that ruled her body, not her hormones. "Let go of me, please."

He released her hands. "What is wrong? Look at me."

Isabelle lifted her eyes.

His head blotted out the light and left his face a dark oval.

"I've changed my mind. It would be a mistake," she blurted. "I don't want…I can't…I won't let it happen. Our worlds, this is yours. Mine is San Francisco."

She saw his lips tighten before he smiled mockingly. "Oh do not worry, señorita. I do not want entry into your world, just your body."

She gasped and stepped further back from him.

He shrugged. "But if you no longer wish it, then that is fine. There are always willing women to be found." He turned his back on her. "Come, I will see you home."

"I can find my own way, thank you," she choked out.

"Adios, then." And without looking back, he walked into the darkness.Isabelle's knees shook and she collapsed onto the sand. Her lips felt bruised from his kisses. Her skin still tingled. Why didn't I just go with him? Woman do it all of the time-one night stands. She closed her eyes. *I want more. I want what my parents have-forty-eight years of togetherness and still counting. Donald couldn't give it to me.* "And I'll be damned if I'll settle for anything less"

Chapter Five

Isabelle woke early after a sleepless night She lay in bed going over everything that had happened since her arrival at the casa. *Maybe my friends are right, it's the only explanation for my strong attraction to Cristiano. I need a man in my life. Just not him. He's too young. What could we possibly have in common?*

She mentally sorted through the men she'd met on the beach when Donald was alive. There weren't many…most had wives and families. There was Carl Vanderhort. The man had shown her a lot of attention the times they'd attended the same parties. But maybe he had a thing for married women and she wasn't married anymore.

He wasn't ugly, not too tall, and he had all his hair and teeth. She recalled a party they'd attended, Carl had gone overboard with the tequila, but they'd been partying since mid-day. There were some who could say the same thing about her.

Isabelle kicked the coverings off and stood. "Well it doesn't make any difference. He isn't around anyway. How about an early walk,
Sammi-Sue?"

The basset hound scrambled to her feet in happy agreement.

Outside the door of the casa, Isabelle stopped and took a deep breath. The sun felt warm upon her bare head. The beach was empty as far as she could see in either direction. It looked to be a perfect day.

She and Sammi would walk, have breakfast, and she'd get started on her commissioned weaving. She'd work on it for a couple of hours, and maybe do some sunbathing.

They were on their way back to the casa when she saw a man jogging toward them. She felt a moment of sadness at her loss of solitude, but her interest heightened when she saw it was Carl Vanderhort. Well, how about that?

He stopped in front of them. "Isabelle, what a surprise. I'd expected to be alone on the beach this time of year."

She smiled. "Me, too."

He reached to pat Sammi's head and the basset hound shied away.

Carl laughed. "She must know I'm a cat person. I was sorry to hear about Donald. Must have been quite a shock."

"Yes, it was." She turned to look across the sea toward Isla Santa Maria for a second, and when she looked back he was staring at her like she was a hamburger and he hadn't eaten in weeks.

So maybe before his interest hadn't been because she was married.

"I've got a new boat. Had her brought from San Diego. Taking her out this afternoon. Would you like to join me?"

So here was her chance. Time to put her new way of thinking to the test. "Sure, I'd like that. It sounds like fun."

"I'll head home, shower and pick you up around one. That sound good?"

"I'll be ready."

*****

As the Bayliner cut through the waves, Isabelle's eyes took in the view. Range after range of jagged mountains ran south to north.

It was mid-afternoon, the sun warm, the sky a sharp blue with no clouds or haze and Carl was on his third Tequila Maria.

The boat slowed and fell from its plane. She watched in apprehension as he fiddled with the control panel. Her unease tripled when he joined her in the bow.

"Can you do that? Just walk off and leave the controls?"

"Auto. It's clear of rocks in this stretch of water. I'm going below to freshen my drink. You sure you won't join me? I make the best Tequila Maria in Baja."

She shook her head for the tenth time. "How about some water instead?"

"Water?" His face showed disgust.

She wasn't sure if it was because she wouldn't drink with him, or the thought of actually drinking water.

"You know what fish do in water don't you? Come on. I hate to partake alone."

Isabelle doubted he'd have trouble drinking at any time of the day. She forced herself to smile. "I'll pass, but thanks for bringing me out. It's a beautiful boat." She'd gotten the tour earlier. The Bayliner had a full cabin below, complete with galley, Captain's quarters, and head.

"She cost a pretty penny." He turned to grin at her. "But she hasn't been christened yet. If you know what I mean?"

61

Isabelle knew exactly what he meant. She decided to play dumb. "I didn't know they christened smaller boats, just ocean liners."

He laughed. "You ever hear of the Mile-High Club?"

"Not a member. Are you?"

"They should have named it after me." He laughed again. "Hell, maybe they did. I've got me a new little club. I call it the Mile-Out Club. Don't really have a Baja chapter yet, but I'm working on it." He winked at her and then moved back to the control panel. He moved a stack of papers aside and picked up the bottle of *Conmemoritivo* tequila. "The best damn tequila they make and since you won't join me." He lifted it and took a long drink.

She stared at the bottle in surprise. My God, it was half empty. He must have mixed those drinks half and half. She looked from the beach, toward Isla Santa Maria. Was she going to have to swim for it? The island looked closer.

"You bring your suit?" He came toward her. His words were clear, but his eyes were glassy.

"Why don't you go below and change?"

"My suit's under my shorts and t-shirt."

"Well, get out of them. Let's get some sun. "

He pulled his tank top over his head. His chest was pale and freckled.

Sparse darker hair had made an attempt to sprout between his nipples. Unbidden, the image of Cristiano's tanned flesh popped into her mind. "I hope you have on some sunscreen."

"Never use the stuff. I have to get a good burn before I tan."

Stupid and drunk. "You know what, I just remembered I was supposed to meet Andres Fuentes this afternoon."

"The gay Mexican kid? What the hell you wasting time with him? He can't give you what you need."

Anger mixed with the unease in her stomach. "And what do I need?"

He laughed. "Relax, baby. You're all hot because you're over dressed. Let's get you stripped down to your suit."

Carl grabbed the shoulder of her t-shirt and she twisted away. "Back off," she snapped. "I've been undressing myself for years. When, and if, I want to strip, as you put it, I'll damn well do it myself."

"Come on, Belle. I know what you want. It's been six months you've gone without." He smiled and rubbed himself beneath his shorts.

"God, you're an ass."

His face filled with color. "Yeah? Well, you're a prick teaser. I know you're type. Take me for a boat ride, out to dinner, then when it's time to pay up, you don't."

He reached for her again and she backed up against the side of the boat. "You take me back, now, or I'll swim for it."

"You stupid bitch. You won't even drink with me. Have a damn drink with me." He thrust the bottle toward her and she slapped it away.

It sailed across the boat and over the side. "Well, shit. That's the only one I brought with me. I've a good mind to make you go get it."

"Better yet, why don't you go get it. Wait, you can't swim, that makes it even better."

His eyes narrowed. "You know what? I figure you owe me. For the gas, for the boat, and now for my tequila." He came toward her.

"Back off, Carl."

"What are you going to do? Scream. Who the hell would hear you?"

"Shit. You're a nasty drunk."

He took a deep breath and raked his fingers through his hair. "Oh, come on, Isabelle. Okay, things have gotten out of hand. Hey, I'm sorry. Let's go below. I'm sure I can find a beer or something." He lunged at her. She darted to the left and he came up hard against the side of the boat. Cursing, he whirled to face her.

Without another thought, Isabelle climbed up onto a bench seat and dove from the boat.

The chill April water of the gulf surrounded her. She kicked to the surface. Carl stood in the Bayliner. "You dumb bitch. I hope you freeze your fat ass off."

He turned and in a few seconds she heard the boat's motor change from a purr to a roar and he sped away.

Ah, shit, back in the water again. She looked around. *And no Cristiano in a panga to rescue me this time. It's just as well. Look what that led to.*

She looked toward Isla Santa Maria. It did not seem that far away. Isabelle began to swim.

She flowed with the water, enjoying its silken touch upon her skin.

Isabelle paused in her stroking, treaded water, and looked toward the island. It was getting closer. Just where will I be watching the sunset tonight? She was afraid she knew the answer. She hadn't been really alone in a long time, there had always been Sammi-Sue and Longfellow. A flutter of concern tightened her muscles. They'll be fine. They're both inside with water and food. More than I can say for myself.

She turned onto her back and watched the clouds float by overhead. Someone is always fishing around here.

Maybe Cristiano…nope not going there. She turned over and began swimming again.

Kick, stretch, pull water, and breathe.

Kick, stretch, pull water, and breathe.

It seemed to go on endlessly-and then she felt a swell lift and carry her forward into the shallows. With her next stroke her hand connected with the sandy bottom. She raised herself onto her hands and knees. Breathing deeply, she remained there for a moment.

Good God. I jumped from a boat. I must be losing my mind. Yes, I made it to the island, but with no food and no water.

She pushed herself onto her feet and stumbled forward onto dry sand. "But at least I'm still wearing my top."

She looked around. The small, narrow beach extended maybe one hundred yards in either direction. Thirty feet or so inland the sand became patterned with tall ocotillo and clumps of lupine. Beyond the purple lupine a few pale green creosote and saltbush had managed to grab hold. Up the slope there were palo verde and ironwood trees, enough to offer some protection from the sun.

Isabelle shaded her eyes and tilted her head back. The dark gray cone of the volcano jutted toward the sky. Just don't start your rumbling while I'm here, she thought, and then added, please.

She shifted her gaze to the mass of blue water-empty for as far as she could see, but it was still early in the day. A panga could cruise by.

She looked down at her tan shorts and white t-shirt. If anybody did look her way, she'd blend right into the sand. Isabelle pulled her t-shirt over her head. Her floral tankini top would be easily seen from a distance.

Her stomach grumbled and she licked her lips. Isabelle sat down, and pulled her knees to her chest. In moments, her skin heated. *I could get sunstroke. I should move up into the shade, but I wouldn't be seen there at all and if Carl-the-asshole tells someone what happened, they'll be looking for me here.*

She snorted a laugh and pushed her still damp hair back from her face. *Who am I kidding? He won't tell anybody. Attempted rape is not something you brag about. Okay. Just who knew I went with him? Not a damn soul.*

Isabelle felt a tiny kernel of panic form in her stomach. How long could she be here before rescue? A breeze blew across her damp skin and she shivered. She knew nothing about building a shelter. The nights had been mild, but she did not welcome the thought of spending one alone in the dark.

With a sigh, she got to her feet. *This is not getting me anywhere.*

Inland or follow the beach? She looked at a small spit of land that hadn't been there a few moments ago. The tide's going out. This is my best chance to see what's on the other side of that rock.

She put her t-shirt back on, unzipped her shorts, took them off and placed them on her head. She laughed when she saw her shadow. The short's legs stuck straight up and then bent over at the top like wilted lettuce. She looked like she had sprouted floppy ears. Taking a deep breath, she headed toward the dark patch of wet sand.

She welcomed the coolness on her bare feet. The current around the outcropping of rock didn't look too strong. Her adventure in the estuary popped into her mind. Isabelle thrust it away and waded out.

The waves lapped at her knees and tried to push her against the rough rock, but she braced herself with her right hand. Something brushed her calf and she gave a short scream, thinking of jellyfish, but a quick look showed only a length of kelp.

Then she was around the outcropping and her hopes and spirits sank. A rocky inlet stretched before her, ending at a small rise and then more creosote and saltbush. Damn.

At the top of the slope she turned and looked back. *Is the beach a better bet? Well, I'm here now.* She bent and picked up a small limb. It made a good walking stick. At the first set of bushes she came to she used it to beat at the grass between them.

Satisfied, she pulled the shorts off of her head and put them back on. She swallowed and licked her lips. *Okay, Izzy. Think about anything but water. This is an adventure. Something to regale the buddies about when you're back home.*

She cleared an area free of rocks, large enough to sit, then pulled her knees to her chest and laid her head upon them. Just as she'd settled, she caught sight of a scorpion scuttling to a new hiding place. With a shrill scream, she leapt to her feet and grabbed her walking stick.

Chapter Six

Cristiano's head jerked up and his fingers halted upon the keyboard of his laptop when he heard the scream. He looked across the camp, toward the beach beyond. It did not come again and he had almost convinced himself it was a gull's cry, before he gave up, logged off and got to his feet in disgust. It was probably nothing, but the other geologists had headed to town for the night and the fishermen would have all ready called it a day.

The sound came from the shoreline. It better not be some stupid gringo out of gas. If so they can sit on their ass until someone comes for them.

A figure sat slumped, head on its knees. He looked beyond. There was not a boat in sight. Just how the hell. . .? As he neared he saw it was a woman. A branch snapped beneath his boots and her head jerked up. Mierda, not her. What kind of trick is fate playing?

Isabelle stared in horror. Shit, not him. What was he doing here? She scrambled to her feet, her stick held before her like a sword.

True, Cristiano tromping toward her with a scowl on his face meant rescue, but she had almost rather not be rescued-almost. His first words weren't exactly promising.

"How the hell did you get here?"She was tempted to lie and would have, if she could have thought of one, but since nothing came to her she blurted the truth.

He frowned as she finished. "A boat ride. Alone. With a stranger."

Her face burned hotter. "He wasn't a stranger. I've known him for awhile."

He shook his head. "What? You've seen him on your jaunts to Baja. You don't know the man."

"I made a mistake, but I don't need a lecture. What I do need is a ride back to my beach. . .again," she added, looking away.

"Can't help you there."

She jerked her eyes back to his. "What do you mean?"

"I don't have a panga. . ."

"Well, how did you get here?"

"Not in a panga, and no one will be coming back until morning."

"No one. . .until morning?"

"If you don't plan to skewer me with your stick – sword how about lowering it?" He turned from her. "I've got a camp. You're welcome to share it with me. You look like you could use some water." He didn't wait for her answer, just turned and walked inland.

Isabelle lowered her walking stick and followed. Drinking with the devil was better than not drinking at all.

The camp was a large, clear circle, at the base of a wall of rising rock. Flattened grasses looked like they had been the victim of more than just one pair of feet. Was this a fishing camp? A quick glance around suggested otherwise. Cots, three tents, a propane stove and a metal table with an open laptop upon it. In the middle of the clearing was a well-used fire pit. Kindling lay in the center waiting for a match and more wood was piled nearby.

"Three cots?"

"There are usually three of us. The others went to San Felipe for some fresh food and water. They'll be back tomorrow."

"Then no boat until then?"

He nodded. "Just like I already told you." He crossed to a cooler and opened it. "Here." He tossed her a plastic bottle of water.

"Thanks." She opened it and took a long drink.

"You hungry?"

"No this is fine for now." She looked around the campsite again and back at him. "You're not a fisherman, are you?"

"I never said I was. You assumed it."

"You said you came from a long line of fishermen."

"I do. My father is a fisherman, as was his father and my great-grandfather. It's the family business."

"And your business is?"

"I am a scientist. I study volcanoes."

She felt her face heat. He had played her for a fool, let her give him money for gas. Damn him. "I see."

Seething and afraid to say more, she moved away and perched upon one of the camp stools with her back to him.

He had seen the anger in her eyes, the red cheeks and now her posture, stiff as the stick she had gripped earlier. Cristiano felt a flash of guilt and did not welcome it. It was she who jumped to the wrong conclusions. Gringas! He walked to the table and turned on his laptop again.

The silence stretched, broken only by the occasional cry of a gull. He caught her movement out of the corner of his eye and turned in time to see her touch the skin of her upper arm and wince.

"There is sunscreen if you would like."

She jerked her head toward him. He saw instant refusal on her face, but then nodded and said shortly. "Thank you."

He stood, walked to a knapsack and removed a plastic bottle. He crossed to her and held it out.

Cristiano noticed she took great pains to make sure their fingertips did not touch as she took it from him. "Smear some on your face, too. Your nose looks like Rudolph's."

"What?"

"You know. Santa's lead reindeer." He smiled at her.

She glared, before she turned away, but he had seen the corners of her lips start to curve, before she had remembered she was angry at him, and he sighed.

"Señora, wait. We must remain here this night. I suggest a truce. It will be easier for both of us."

Isabelle turned back. She hadn't worked a blob of sun screen in and it stood out whitely upon her left cheek. Without thought, he reached to smooth it in with his thumb. She went very still, her eyes staring into his. Then she stepped back and turned away.

While Cristiano had worked at his laptop, Isabelle had played over in her mind the times they had been together. Yes, she had made assumptions. The misunderstandings were not all her fault, but some of them were. They did have some hours alone here to get through. If he wanted a truce, then she was okay with it. Tomorrow, he would get her back to her beach and she would never have to lay eyes upon him again.

She turned to face him. "Okay, a truce. But first an apology." She watched his shoulders tighten. "Not from you, from me." Isabelle took a deep breath. "I did assume you were a local fisherman. I know how you feel about us. We've come into your home, and forced our dirty money into your wide open hands…"

"Señora, it's not the money. It's the attitude."

"Hey." And she pointed a finger at him. "I'm apologizing here and just for the record, maybe it's your age and all, what are you, twenty-five? But maybe you should find out a little more about a person before you jump to conclusions."

She watched color flood his face. "I'm thirty and my age has nothing to do with it. And I know who you are."

"No, you don't. You look around my house, see rich Americans, too many windows and you smirk at my stupidity and decide to make me feel an even bigger fool." She heard the anger in her voice and decided this apology wasn't taking the direction she'd planned. She abruptly stopped and took another deep breath.

"I knew more," Cristiano said. "I asked Andres about you."

Her eyes narrowed. "I see. Recent widow. So you thought I was ripe for…"

"Of course not. I don't desire women like you."

She stepped back from him. "Women like me? Gringa women? Older women?"

He raked his fingers through his hair. "You're not so old."

"Then it's because I'm not Latina. Now who's the bigot?"

His skin flushed. "It's not your heritage. It's your attitude.

"Yes, the Americana snobbery. But you never even gave me a chance before you decided I was egotistical and out to rub your nose in my money. So, who's the real snob?"

Cristiano stared. My God, she was beautiful. Her eyes flashing, the specks of gold sparking within the pools of amethyst. Her cheeks were flushed and her breasts, pressing against the thin fabric of her tee shirt, rose and fell with each angry breath. She radiated passion and fire and made the other women he knew seem pale in comparison. His blood rushed south and he felt himself harden. He wanted her naked beneath him. He wanted to smother those truths she spoke with his lips, until all she could do was moan his name.

"Did you hear me?" she demanded when he did not answer.

"I heard you." His voice was hoarse.

His husky words stopped her own and she looked into his face. Jeez. He was just staring at her and the heat in his eyes had her heartbeat going double-time. I'm not his type. I'm too pale. He said as much. I'm fifteen years older.

She was not sure who took the step, but the space between them vanished and his hands were on her hips. Cristiano pulled her closer against his hardness as his mouth descended. And then there was nothing but his smell, lime and leather, his skin hot beneath her hands, and wave after wave of sensations that started at her toes, sky-rocketed upward, and exploded out the top of her head.

Chapter Seven

With her eyes closed, Isabelle smiled. She felt wonderful…no, that wasn't the word for the contentment that made her want to purr. She hadn't felt this relaxed in….actually, she had never felt this good before.

Still half asleep, her mind floated. Now why was she so happy? Her thoughts played over yesterday's events. Carl. Her smile faded. The boat ride, her impromptu swim, the island, Cristiano. Her stomach did a roll. Oh my God. She became aware of a warm weight around her waist.

Isabelle opened her eyes. The campfire had burned down. She looked skyward. Stars dotted the blue-blackness. A full moon hung among them, spreading its white glow across the island's sand and shrubs.

The two of them lay like spoons, her naked back pressed against his chest. His arm circled her waist, held her close. She felt her body heat. My God. How had this happened? She smiled. Well, she knew how it had happened….slowly and with much expertise.

They lay on a spread sleeping bag. Cautiously, she lifted his arm and inched from him. Cristiano murmured a complaint, rolled onto his back. Her gaze went to his body. It was beautiful. Bronze skin with a mat of dark hair on chest and groin. Her hands ached for paper and pencil. She smiled again. No, she didn't need to sketch him. His form was burned forever upon her mind. She raised her gaze to his face. Those lips. Heat flared in her stomach. Kissing like that should be against the law.

Isabelle looked down at her own body, round breasts, not riding as high as they used too…thank you very much, dear gravity. Her waist was still trim, but she'd never had a flat stomach. She groaned. And she hadn't shaved her legs this morning.

In the darkness, she looked around for her clothes. She saw her tankini top on the sand. A little distance from it she spied her shorts and tankini bottom. She turned and glanced at Cristiano. His eyes were still closed. Please let him really be asleep.

"Why?" An irritating voice asked in her head. "It isn't as if he hasn't already seen you naked."

I just don't want him to. Okay?

"There's nothing wrong with your butt. It's a woman's butt."

It's too big…Donald always said….

"Donald was an ass."

She chuckled at her own sub-consciousness' choice of word. But still she darted another glance at Cristiano before she tightened everything up and sauntered toward her tankini bottom and shorts.

Isabelle stepped into the shorts and pulled them up, grimaced as sand scratched her tender nether regions. She didn't care what that old movie said, making love in the sand wasn't all that grand.

Tankini and shorts in place she glanced at Cristiano. He rolled onto his side. A slight frown creased his forehead. Is he missing me, or just a body next to him?

I need a bath, but a quick dunk in the ocean will do. Isabelle looked around for her stick. The beach wasn't far, but who knew what kind of critters could be night-roaming.

"Bella, where are you going?"

His words sent a shiver up her spine.

She turned. A wash of moonlight lit his body, but left his face in shadows. "I'm restless. I thought I'd take a walk."

Cristiano sat up. "I'll go with you."

"No, I'd rather go alone," she said in a rush.

"I see."

Judging by the chilly tone of his voice, he didn't. "I mean. I want to freshen up. I'll just need a minute."

"I understand."

She walked back to him. "Cristiano, what happened? We don't even like each other. You think I'm a snob. I think you're a close-minded Mexican bigot."

His eyebrows shot up at her words. "I am not a bigot. According to my family, I am too progressive in my thinking."

Isabelle raised her hand. "Let's don't go there again."

He shook his head. "I thought we'd gotten beyond that. I made assumptions. So did you. We both were wrong."

She sighed. "I guess this was bound to happen. It's been a long time since I've...and you did get me going."

In the moonlight, she saw his face flush.

"Did?" he said. She felt her own face heat. "It was great and I'm glad we did it, but that's it. It won't happen again..." He remained silent and she let her words trail away.

"You keep saying, 'it'," he said at last. "We had sex. Is it so hard to say?"

Isabelle looked away from him. She hadn't said sex, because part of her yearned for it to be more. Casual sex wasn't her style. "Of course I can say the word. Sex. Sex. Sex." She turned away from him.

"Yes, I can see you are truly a modern woman who knows how to get what she wants."

Her shoulders stiffened at his words. "In this world you have to learn to take care of yourself."

"Most Americanos are good at doing just that."

Isabelle looked into his eyes for a long moment. Angry denial pressed against her lips. Why bother? They were what they were, both of them. She turned and walked away in silence.

Cristiano winced at hearing his words and wished them instantly back. Why did this woman bring out his sharp tongue?

She wounded your male pride, said a voice in his head that sounded an awful lot like his Uncle Ramon. *When has it been that a woman has crept from your bed like a thief?* I am nothing to her. She needed an itch scratched.

Perhaps. But why does it bother you? Have you not sought out women to do some scratching yourself?

I am a man. He slammed shut that train of thought. A wry laugh came from him. *And perhaps not such a forward thinking one at that.*

Cristiano started to stand, then sat back. Maybe it was better this way. They had their one time together. Both had their curiosity satisfied. Yes. It was best to leave things as they were. They were adults. They could be civilized about what had occurred between them. If Isabelle wished to talk more about it, they would. If not, he lifted a shoulder in a shrug and lay down. Cradling his head with his hands he stared up into the dark sky and waited.

"Most Americanos are good at doing just that." Isabelle sing-songed the words with a clenched jaw. She kicked out at an innocent sea shell. What an arrogant ass. And fantastic lover or not, she sure as hell didn't want another man like him in her life.

Cold water lapped her feet and she danced back with a yelp. What the…? She turned and looked back up the slight rise, toward the campo, and then laughed. She'd been so pissed by Cristiano's words she'd tromped by the island's brush and rocks without giving one thought to snakes, or whatever.

Beneath the full moon, the island looked bleached out, like a faded black and white photo. It was beautiful in a stark, kind of scary way.

Isabelle turned and walked down the beach. How soon until

daybreak? She wanted off this island and away from him. *Maybe I should pack it up and go back to San Francisco.* She jerked her head up, turned and glared toward the campo. *No way. This is my time. No man's going to screw it up.*

Above the waterline she saw a flat rock, as good a place as any to wait for the dawn. A breeze lifted her hair and she shivered. It seemed to have gotten colder. Isn't that what they said…it was always colder right before dawn. Wait. No, it's always darker before dawn. She rubbed her bare arms. Dang, it had gotten colder.

She glimpsed movement out of the corner of her eye and turned toward it. Someone stood on the beach, stared across the water. Her stomach dipped. It had better not be Cristiano. She looked closer. No. Too slight a frame and whoever it was had long hair. But he said they were alone on the island. Anger warmed her. What else had he lied about?

Isabelle walked toward the person. "Hey."

The woman turned, stood silently as Isabelle neared. She had felt the moment the other stumbled onto her sand. She hadn't known exactly where on the island Isabelle was; only that she was upon it.

She felt the tidal wash of emotion as Isabelle and the man coupled and used it as a beacon. But their lust ended before she completed her hunt.

At the memory, jealousy and rage surged, quickly swallowed by a deep, hollow sadness. She ached for the connection to another, to feel heat and passion again.

Isabelle stopped in front of her, rubbed her bare arms. "Hey, are you okay? Have you been in an accident?"

An accident? Why does she ask such questions? She looked down at her body and for the first time realized she wore only a floral swimsuit. Why? Is this why I am so cold? No answers came to her and she turned to face the waves in silence.

"How did you get here? Do you have a boat?"

I am just here. She felt anger rise again. Why does she ask all of these stupid questions? It is not the way I wanted us to first meet. She turned toward Isabelle.

"My God. Your face. What happened?"

The woman touched her cheek. What is wrong with my face? Am I ugly? No. No. No. What will my love think when he comes for me?

"I'll get help." Isabelle whirled and ran down the beach.

My face. I must see my face. She watched the fleeing Isabelle. *It is not our time. We will meet later.* The woman stood and moved out over the placid waves.

"Cristiano, Help."

Her call had him on his feet. Naked, he ran toward the beach. What had happened? Had she stepped on a jellyfish? A rattlesnake? Questions didn't stop his headlong rush to the sand below. In the moonlight, he saw her running. His gaze went to the beach beyond. From what did she run?

She stumbled to a stop in front of him. He grabbed her shoulders.

"What? What is it? Are you hurt?" Cristiano swept his gaze over her. His heart pounded as he waited for her answer.

She swallowed, blurted. "You're naked."

"Yes, I am naked. Why did you scream?"

She stared at him in wide-eyed silence. Her tongue came out and licked her lips. And was that a small groan?

"What? Did you fall? Hit your head?" He reached to brush her hair from her forehead and felt a tremor move through her.

Isabelle stepped back. "No. No, I'm okay, but there's a girl. I think maybe she was in an accident. Her face… it's scraped and bruised, and she has a huge gash above her right eye. "

"A girl?"

"Yes, on the beach."

"Get the sleeping bag from the camp. I'll see to her." Cristiano turned away.

"Like that?" Isabelle said.

"If she has not seen a naked man before, then I will apologize."

He turned and jogged away.

Isabelle dashed to the camp and grabbed the sleeping bag.

Back on the beach, she saw that Cristiano walked toward her…alone. Oh God. What happened? Was the girl dead? She rushed toward him. "What's wrong? Where is she?"

"I saw no one. No footprints….nothing."

She dropped the sleeping bag. "We've got to find her."

"You are sure you saw someone?"

"Of course I did. I spoke to her."

Cristiano remained silent. She looked into his face and saw doubt there.

"Hey, she's there. Why the hell would I lie?"

"I saw no one and I hiked the island this morning."

"Well, then she showed up after your hike…like I did." Isabelle moved by him. "I'm going to find her. She needs help." She didn't look back to see if he followed.

Isabelle passed the rock where she had seen the girl. Moonlight filled an empty stretch of sand. Where could she have gone? She looked down the beach. The sand ended at black, jagged rocks jutting into the water. Could she have climbed…no, she wasn't wearing shoes, she'd rip her feet to shreds.

Isabelle walked to the razor-edged lava rocks. Waves splashed high against them. Did she wade around the point? That would be suicide.

She turned inland and looked up the rise. The girl must have gone up. It didn't look like it was too steep. She started toward the slope.

"Isabella, no. I will look."

She turned at his voice. "You're not dressed for exploring." She noted he did not carry the sleeping bag and she tightened her lips. "She has to be here someplace. I saw her. I spoke to her."

"You wait here. I will grab some pants and shoes. Then I will look. If there's a girl up there, I will find her."

If? She opened her mouth to say more, but then closed it. Just let him see for himself.

In less than five minutes Cristiano was back. He climbed the slight rise, then disappeared from sight.

The woman stared into the serene pool. Her reflection looked back, pale eyes, blonde hair and smooth alabaster skin. She touched her pink lips. There is nothing wrong with my face. Anger rose. Why had Isabelle frightened her? Is she jealous of me? She had seen that time and time again in her life. The envious glances when she and her love entered a restaurant. She'd known instantly the others had wanted her man. Was that it? Did Isabelle want her love? Is that why she is here?

The woman stood, paced. Isabelle knows he is coming for me. She does not want it to happen. It must be she who has kept him from me. She is why I have waited so long. No. She will not stop him. She has the other. She will not take mine from me.

Isabelle glanced again at the tall grass and trees. What is taking Cristiano so long? Should I go back for the sleeping bag? I'm counting to sixty, if he's not back by then....

He crested the rise and came toward her. "There is nothing up there. Just more rocks."

"She has to be here somewhere. You just didn't see her." She started by him.

He grabbed her arm. "And you will?"

"Let go of me."

He released her and stepped back. "Wait until daybreak. We will search again."

"Wait? But…"

Cristiano pointed to the horizon. "Dawn will be here soon. It is too dangerous now."

The sky had brightened in the past minutes and light would make their search easier. "Okay. But right here…not at your camp."

Cristiano walked toward a rock and sat down on it. "Fine, we will wait."

*****

Frustration knotted Isabelle's stomach. Her hands tightened into fists as she saw the beach and her house grow closer. She and Cristiano had searched and searched Isla Santa Maria, and when the other two scientists had arrived with the boat, they too joined in the search. But the girl was not to be found.

I saw her. I did not imagine it. What happened ? Did a rogue wave drag her into the sea?

It was just Isabelle and Cristiano in the runabout. The others had stayed; they'd promised to keep looking, but she'd seen their faces. As far as they were concerned, there was no girl.

Isabelle brushed hair from her forehead. I must look a sight. She scowled at Cristiano. How can he do that? Make those damn shorts and tee shirt look like an Armani suit.

He cut the motor and she felt a swell pick them up, rush them toward the beach. The boat touched bottom. He jumped into the sea and then dragged the runabout higher onto the sand.

"I'm fine from here," Isabelle said. "You don't have to go any farther."

"I know I don't have to." He reached up to help her from the boat.

Avoiding his eyes, Isabelle took his hand to steady her jump, but instead, Cristiano grabbed her by the waist, lifted her and carried her the short distance to the dry sand.

When he did not put her down, she felt her body stiffen. "This is fine."

He kept on walking.

"Cristiano."

"Relax, we are almost there."

And they were. She heard Sammi-Sue's excited barking. In the shade of the ramada he sat her on her feet . "Thank you." The words seemed silly, but she couldn't think of anything else to say.

"Isabelle, I will notify the authorities about the girl you saw."

She looked at him. "You will? I didn't think you believed me."

He shrugged. "I know of no missing girl, but there is no sense taking chances."

"I have a phone inside. You could call them from here."

"It will be better to report this in person. I have to go into San Felipe to check something at the office. I will do so then."

"Oh. Okay. Well, thank you." Sammi-Sue let out a plaintive howl of disapproval. "I've got to get inside. I've never left Sammi and Longie alone all night before."

"You are a weaver, yes? I would like to see some of your work. I try to paint...."

She stared at him. He looks like that, is a scientist, and now he paints? The gods aren't fair. "Now? Don't you have to go?"

"My jeep is at the Fuentes'. I would like to give them a few more minutes of sleep before I arrive."

She'd forgotten how early it still was. "I could fix some coffee. Are you hungry?"

He grinned. "I am always hungry. Just ask my mami."

Isabelle opened the door and Sammi-Sue charged out. The basset hound hopped up and down and warbled a welcome at the same time. "I know, baby, I know. But I didn't plan it. Besides you had plenty of food."

Sammi raced away, squatted and emptied her bladder.

"You go on in. Sammi's gonna need to do more than pee." She turned away, then looked back. "Would you see if Longfellow is still speaking to me?"

"I will find and explain. All will be fine." Cristiano walked into the house and closed the door behind him.

"Come on, Sammi, and make it quick."

The basset hound took care of her business in record time, then charged toward the house.

"What's with you?" Isabelle said. "It better not have anything to do with our guest."

She opened the door for the impatient basset hound. Without a backward glance, Sammi bounded inside.

"Traitor," Isabelle murmured, following, but at a much slower pace.

Cristiano wasn't in the kitchen. She heard his voice from the living room. "I'll start the coffee," she called.

"Thank you. Do you require help?"

"Not for coffee." She opened the refrigerator and looked inside. "Scrambled eggs with cheese and toast sound good?'

"That will be fine, señora."

She almost laughed at hearing the word, señora. Oh come on. They'd spent hours rolling around making love…no, having sex…and now he called her señora? What was next, Mrs. Donald Allen? She punched the On button of the coffee grinder with more force than required.

"Señora, I see there are weavings on the wall. They are yours?"

"Yes." The word came out stiffly. "And would you please call me Isabelle."

"But of course. Isabelle, may I look closer at them?"

"But of course," she repeated back at him. "The coffee's on."

"Beautiful, very beautiful." His soft words came to her and she felt her stomach clench. He'd whispered the same words to her on the beach. Heat rose into her face as she walked to the living room.

Cristiano stood in front of her weaving of a phoenix. The mythical bird had just been reborn. With wings outspread, she rose from a nest of fire, scarlet flames outlining her golden body.

Cristiano reached to touch the head of the phoenix. "Truly beautiful."

"Thank you. It was the first I designed after Donald's death."

"I see. A re-birth for yourself."

Isabelle shrugged as she looked away from his dark eyes. "Maybe. It just came to me and I had to do it."

He moved to another of her weaving, the sun rising over a desertscape, an ocotillo plant in the foreground bloomed orange, but she had woven in tiny flames of red around each branch of blooms. Cristiano leaned closer, looked at the plant. In silence he walked to the five others hanging upon the walls. The last, a seascape. A mermaid sat on a rock and held in her right hand, a small blue and orange flame. "Remarkable. The flame seems to move."

Isabelle's cheeks heated again. "Thank you."

"You have passion in your weavings."

"I try to evoke a response."

"No, I mean you weave passion…the flames, they are in all of these."

She smiled. "Some form of fire is in all of them…it just happens."

"Yes…passion."

Isabelle frowned. "I don't understand."

Cristiano turned to look at her. "The flame is a totemic symbol for passion. You did not know this?"

"Totemic?"

"Totems. Spirit guides."

She waved her hand. "I know what totems are, but I thought they were just animals."

"There are also forces of nature. How more elemental can it be than fire, water, air, and earth?"

She laughed. "Spoken like a true," Isabelle hesitated for a moment before adding, "scientist."

Cristiano smiled. "Ah, but then I study volcanoes, don't I?"

"Is fire your totem? God knows, you're no stranger to passion." Her face heated and she wished the words back.

He stared into her face for a moment. "I do not know what my totem is. I have never felt the urge to search for it. Maybe I should." He smiled. "Perhaps it would be water, and that is why we are so incompatible."

Fire and water. Well, she knew one thing when they'd had sex, things had sure been boiling-hot. She turned and walked toward the kitchen. "The coffee's ready. How do you take yours?"

"Black with sugar, and real sugar, no sugar substitutions for me."

Isabelle nodded. Of course, he would want the real thing. "Give me a second. I'll bring it to you."

"No. We will join you in the kitchen." He looked down at Sammi-Sue and Longfellow. "Is that not right?"

They all walked into the kitchen and it seemed to shrink in size. Don't be silly, Izzy. You, Sammi and Longie have been in this kitchen hundreds of times...one single man can't make such a difference. This kitchen's as big as some entire apartments in San Francisco.

Isabelle opened the cupboard and reached for the coffee mugs. Cristiano's thigh brushed her backside as he moved by her to look out the windows, and she almost dropped both coffee mugs onto the floor. With a gasp, she placed them on the counter and reached for the sugar bowl. "Lots of sweetener, you said, right?"

"Not sweetener, sugar." He moved toward her. "Here, I will see to it myself."

"A spoon. You'll need a spoon." She almost ran to the far drawer and jerked it open. The clink of silverware as she fumbled through it sounded startlingly loud to her ears. Get a grip, girl. You still have to scramble some eggs. Drops of sweat formed on her forehead. It looked as if they had another hot day ahead of them. And it could get even hotter, she mused.

Isabelle closed her eyes, recalling again their bodies beneath the full moon. Sex in the kitchen. She'd seen it more than once on television and it had always turned her on.

"How would you like it?" he said.

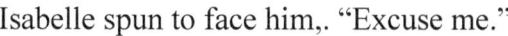

Isabelle spun to face him,. "Excuse me."

"Your coffee. How do you take it?"

"Oh, with milk only."

He reached to take the spoon from her. "Thank you."

Their fingertips touched and she felt the sizzle all the way to her toes. She backed away, turned and hurried to the refrigerator. "How many eggs would you like?"

"Three would be fine."

"And toast?"

"Two slices."

"With butter?"

"But of course, and jelly if you have some."

"Orange marmalade." She turned in time to see him wrinkle his nose.

"Then I will pass on the jelly."

She pulled out six eggs, cheese, milk, and butter. He stood right behind her as she turned.

"You seem to have your hands full. May I help?"

"No. No. I'm fine," she said as she stepped around him. "But you could start the toast. The bread's right in there." She pointed toward a wood bread box on top of the refrigerator.

"And the toaster?"

"Cupboard next to the dishwasher."

Her breath exited in a rush as Cristiano crossed the kitchen.

She piled everything on the counter. Let's just get this over with. Isabelle cracked eggs into a bowl, added milk and gave them a good stir. "Salt and pepper?"

"Much pepper. No salt."

She nodded.

"I saw you had orange juice. Do you also have champagne? We could enjoy mimosa with our breakfast."

"No, nothing chilled," she said. Thank God for that. A little alcohol added to the mix and she just might go up in flames. "And there's nothing worse than warm champagne."

"Agreed. Then it will be just milk for me."

The butter had melted, so she poured the egg mixture into the pan. The toast popped up and she jumped at the sound. "Glasses are right above your head."

It seemed forever, but at last they were seated at the table across from each other. Isabelle picked up her fork and played with her eggs.

Cristiano took a large bite, chewed, and swallowed. "This is wonderful. Perhaps some time you will let me cook for you?"

"You cook?"

He took a long drink of milk before answering. "I am known for my vegetable lasagna. I use much garlic."

"I love Italian food."

"Good, then soon I will make some for you." He glanced at her plate. "You are not eating. Please do not tell me you are one of those women who peck like birds if they but gain an ounce."

"Oh no, I'm not." She took a bite of the eggs. "But I suppose most women think they could lose a few pounds."

"No, Isabelle, you are perfect they way you are."

At his words, she stopped with the fork halfway to her mouth. "Well…oh…thank you."

"You are welcome." He suddenly pushed back from the table. " Dios. I must go. I'd forgotten that today is the morning Miguel goes in early to town."

Isabelle stood. "Well, thank you for offering to report the girl. I still can't figure out what happened to her."

"We shall find out if it is possible."

Sammi-Sue and Longie followed as Isabelle walked Cristiano to the door. As he opened it, he looked back at her. Their eyes met and for one long moment silence stretched between them. "I will call you to set up our dinner," Cristiano said at last. He bent to scratch between Sammi's ears first and then Longie's. "I would not be against them also coming."

"Really? Well, Sammi-Sue would love it. I don't know about Longie. He doesn't travel well."

"Then bring Señorita Sammi. I will prepare for her a special treat."

Isabelle smiled. "We'll both look forward to it." She held out her hand. "Have a great day."

He looked at her hand, then with a smile, picked it up and pressed a kiss into her palm. "You also."

Isabelle exhaled a deep breath as she watched him walk away. She looked down at Sammi and Longie. "Oh babies, this is not good. Not good, I say. What I need right now is a hot...no... make that a cold shower."

Chapter Eight

Cristiano frowned as he walked from Isabelle's casa. What had happened between them on the island? It all seemed to have been a dream - a delightful, hot and sexy dream - but still a dream. It defied logic. Isabelle did not like Mexican men. No, that wasn't fair. She didn't want to get involved with any man. And who could blame her after her late husband. What did she call him…Donald-the-ass? And that bastard Carl.

What about himself? He had sworn no more Americana women, not after Catherine. Cristiano turned and looked across the sea toward Isla Santa Maria. Isabelle's skin had been warm and soft. She'd smelled of honeysuckle and lemon. He sighed and moaned. He turned from the ocean and raked his fingers through his hair.

If I'd told her the truth from the start, would things have been different? She would have never offered me money for gas. I would have never been invited into her home. She would never have walked with me on the beach at the Fuentes' party.

Her eyes, they sparkle like amethyst when she is angry. They had done so on the island, right before they'd found themselves in each other's arms.

Cristiano shook his head. "We are too different. I must put it from my mind."

"What's that?"

The words came from behind him, he turned. Andres stood there. "Stop sneaking up on people."

"I didn't sneak. You weren't paying attention."

Cristiano shrugged. "You're up early."

"I'm heading to Izzy's. She hasn't answered her phone all night." He looked closer at Cristiano. "You wouldn't know anything about that would you?"

At the question, Cristiano felt an instant urge to protect Isabelle's good name. "Why would you ask such a thing of me?"

"Well, it's early for you too, and you're coming from the direction of her house."

"Yes, I was with her…"

"Damn it, Cristiano. I don't want to see Izzy hurt. You've…"

"It was nothing. She became marooned on Isla Santa Maria last night. I discovered her. She spent the night at my camp and I brought her home this morning."

"Marooned? How did that happen?"

"I will let her tell you herself."

Andres glanced toward Isabelle's house "Well, I am almost sad nothing did happen."

"How can you say that? You know we are all wrong for each other. There can never…"

"I saw how you looked at each other at Grandmother's party. There is heat between you."

"Isabelle is an Americana…"

"True, but she's not Catherine."

Cristiano held up his hand. "No Andres. Not even from you." He turned and began walking toward the Fuentes.

Andres kept pace beside him. "I will say this, Cristiano. You may knock me on my ass afterward, but I will say it."

Cristiano stopped and turned to glare at him.

"Glower all you want, but I will say it again. Isabelle is not Catherine. Why do you dwell upon her...you were young. You thought you loved her. Yes, yes, yes," he held up his hand to stop Cristiano's words. "Maybe you did love Catherine, but she did not love you. She wished for a Mexican boy to thumb her nose at her rich papa, and you were handy." Andres took a step back. "Now hit me if you wish."

"Don't be stupid. Catherine isn't worth it."

"No, she isn't," Andres said. "Now, you will forget her?"

"I don't know what you mean. I put it behind me years ago." Cristiano turned from him. "Now I must be going."

Andres watched him walk away. "Sure you have, amigo. I just wish your heart believed your mouth." He began to walk toward Isabelle's. It would be interesting to hear her version of the night on the island.

Stepping from the shower, Isabelle heard the ship's bell on the front ramada ring.

"Izzy, you in there?"

She recognized Andres Fuentes' voice.

"Andres. Come in. Just out of the shower and getting dressed." She stepped around Sammi-Sue again. "Go see Andres." The basset hound shot her a wounded look, then sauntered through the bedroom door.

Isabelle smoothed lotion on her sunburned skin, stepped into panties, then slipped on a soft cotton wrap dress and went out to Andres.

He sat perched on a stool at the kitchen island.

"Holy mother. What happened to you? You're as red as a tomato. You're going to blister and peel. Why didn't you wear your hat? And where have you been? I called three times last night. If you hadn't been here this morning…."

"It's a long story. Yes, I'm exhausted, and yes, I got too much sun, but I won't blister and peel. Let's sit over here, we'll be more comfortable." She walked to the sitting area, plopped on the sofa, and shifted the pillows around her.

"Well, tell, tell, Isabelle." He sang the words in a dramatic falsetto as he crossed to the rocker opposite from her, then leaned back with a look of exaggerated interest on his face.

She smiled at his display of flamboyance. "You can cut the crap. This is me. Remember? Not your momma. I don't shock easily."

"Touché," he said and then grinned. "Now tell me everything."

Isabelle narrated the events, becoming enraged all over again as she told of the action on Carl's boat, but only hinting at what had passed between herself and Cristiano. "And that's that."

"That's that?" Andres said. "You avoid rape, meet a girl with a battered face, who just disappears, and you say, that's that?"

She shrugged.

He held her gaze with his.

Oh, and one little thing more," she added.

He leaned forward. "Yes."

"Yesterday, I had a dream about the same girl. I'd forgotten until I was in the shower. The beach was different, but the girl was the same. At least I think she was." Isabelle frowned. "I wonder if I'm losing it. The last six months have been a wild ride, and now this." Isabelle stood and walked to the liquor cabinet.

"What are you doing?"

"I need a drink. How about a cuba libre?"

"A drink? It's a little early…."

"I know, but I'm having one anyway. You?"

"Well, okay."

"Get us some cinnamon pita chips. There in a bag above the fridge."

While Andres got the chips, she fixed the drinks and sat his on the coffee table.

Andres settled in the recliner across from her again. He glanced at her as he picked up his drink, looked as if he was going to say something, and then looked away.

"What?" She grabbed a pita chip and bit into it.

"Isabelle, there's something I think you need to know. It may be nothing, but… no, you are not losing it." He shifted in the chair. "You don't have any cigars in the house, do you?"

"Andres." Her voice held a warning. "What do you mean I'm not losing it?"

"Well, if I'm going to drink this early, I'd like a cigar, too."

"Yes, there are cigars. I don't know how long they stay fresh. They were Donald's thing, not mine."

She rose, crossed to the bookshelf near the guestroom door, picked up a walnut humidor, and brought it to him.

He opened the box, selected one, held to his nose, and then rolled it between his palms.

"They are fine." Andres avoided her eyes as he lit the cigar. He sent an elaborate stream of smoke toward the ceiling. "Fine cigar, fabulous really."

"Andres." Isabelle warned, then picked up another chip and bit it to it.

"All right. All right. Two or three years ago, there was a terrible thing that happened here. Some people from Rodrigo's camp came to their house for a family reunion. Everyone was there, aunties, cousins, granny and pa, the whole family, really. They were a large group, among them a man and his fiancé. One day the man, Brad something or other, his intended and his sister decided to go out to the islands. They prepared for only a short outing." He smirked at her. "For as you know, the islands are really not far."

She gave him a hard look. "Watch it, smart ass."

Andres smiled at her and then looked away to examine the cigar. He drew on it again, exhaled, and sat the cigar aside in the ashtray. He suddenly snapped his fingers. "Collins, Brad Collins, that was his name. His sister was Amy and his fiancé Patricia Mullins." He took a long drink of his cuba libre. "They rented a small, wooden boat from one of the locals." He shook his head. "The boat had not been in the water for years, the wood was dry. An old car seat had been put in the boat for extra seating, very heavy. Perhaps that was the problem. Anyway, the wind came up suddenly, and to get to the point, the small boat crashed against some hidden rocks, everyone was tossed into the sea. Life jackets were found amongst the wreckage, but apparently not anyone was wearing one.

Only Brad Collins survived. A Casamiro shrimper spotted him in the water clinging to a piece of the boat."

"Casamiro?"

"Yes, the boat belonged to Cristiano's father."

Andres relit his cigar, smoked in silence for a moment. "A rescue effort was mounted. Many people joined the search; the navy even came to investigate. The body of the sister was found days later near Isla San Francisco. His fiancé's body was never recovered."

"Oh, my God." Isabelle's hand covered her mouth for a moment. She stood, walked around the sofa, sat, and then stood again. "No, oh those poor people....it must be the same way the family is feeling about that girl I saw last night."

Andres straightened, stared across at her. "You do not think it's the same girl?"

She drew back. So this was it. He thought she'd seen a ghost. "Are you loco? I saw a girl. Not a ghost."

"Are you sure? She just disappeared."

"There are no such things as ghosts. Jeez, now you sound like my friend Sharlee. She's never seen or read a ghost story she didn't accept as fact."

"You don't believe spirits can be stuck on this plane?"

Isabelle smiled. "Well, I've never seen one."

"Haven't you?"

She lifted her hand to her eyes. "Whoa, that drink went right to my head. Can we talk about this later? I want to lie down."

He stared into her face for a long moment and then shrugged. "I see, of course. I'll stop by later and check on you."

Shaking his head, Andres walked from Isabelle's house. So that is how she ended up on the island. He glared down the beach. He had an urge to pay a call on that bastard Carl. He took three steps in the direction and then stopped.

Andres turned and looked back at her house. Does she really not believe it was a spirit, or is she just in a pattern of stubbornness, a leftover from endlessly defending herself to Donald-the-ass?

Yet why would a trapped spirit appear to her, a matter of fact lady and a pragmatist at heart, not the sort to invite a communication from beyond the grave. The lost woman, Patricia Mullins, she had been an artist of some kind. Not a painter, was it sculpture? No, pottery; she was a potter.

His cousin Rodrigo had one of her pots in his house; the family had given it as thanks for his help in the search after the accident. It was a beautiful piece, the way the colors bled into each other, red, violet, purple and yellow. It reminded him of the sunsets over the Sea of Cortez.

He sighed. Maybe it was nothing. The girl on the island could be another girl, not a ghost. Yet, it couldn't hurt to see what his Grandmother thought of the whole thing.

Chapter Nine

Andres arrived bearing horchata. He held out the pitcher "Grandmother, good afternoon.".

Magdalena eyed first him, then what he carried. "Now what is this?"

"Horchata. I thought we could share a drink together, perhaps some lunch and visit. We haven't had a chance to speak since you returned from the conference."

"Ah, the conference. Ciudad Obregon hasn't changed a bit, and the people who govern Durango state haven't either. Many of the conference attendees fell the same, they believe indigenous peoples should live in huts eating lizards and stones. They refuse to consider the larger picture, a way for the people to move into the modern world and preserve their culture at the same time."

"These are the old guard?"

"Yes, those who see the people as primitives, their religion and folkways as superstitious yearnings. Still, we more contemporary thinkers will outlive and out think them, enable the culture to adapt and evolve."

Magdalena smiled as she took the pitcher from Andres. She lifted the handkerchief covering the top and inhaled the sweet cinnamon aroma. "Well done, Andres. I think you may have mastered the recipe for horchata. Sit, make yourself comfortable."

After questions about one another's health, she grew quiet and regarded him over the rim of her glass.

"I believe Isabelle saw something on Isla Santa Maria; something having to do with the drowning of those women three years ago," Andres said.

"Why was Isabelle on my island?"

He frowned. "She went out on a boat with that bastard Carl, he made advances; she leapt from his boat and swam to the island. Cristiano was there. He brought her back to the beach this morning."

Magdalena lifted an eyebrow. "I see. Go on."

"Izzy says the girl was alive, but…."

Magdalena nodded, staring over his head. "Three is a number of balance, yet, for the girl to appear now…." She took another drink of horchata. "Andres, I must go to my place, to think, to understand, to seek the help of my guides. You bring water and the firewood, I will gather the rest."

"Of course." He glanced at his watch. "Grandmother, don't you usually wait until moon-rise?"

"I will require a fire that will start quickly and yet last through the night. And I must have the special wood for the morning."

"I will see to gathering the wood, perhaps some food as well?" he asked, but Magdalena was all ready moving into the hall toward her small bedroom.

"Return by sunset," she said. "We will discover who is on my island, and what she thinks she is doing."

Magdalena held first a small bundle of sage and then one of lavender toward the flickering candle on her nightstand. With one in each hand, she walked around the room, waving the smoke above her head.

With the room purified, she picked up her basket and walked to the locked cabinet. *I will need sage to turn negative energy away, sweet grass to attract positive influences, lavender to restore balance, and copal for strength.*

Magdalena frowned for a moment. Some of the plants had been harvested only a month ago. They should be fully dried, but, just in case, she added a pinch from the small black box in the very rear of the cabinet.

Four hours later, Andres found Magdalena sitting near the fireplace, stroking her Siamese cat, Mira.

"Are you ready, Grandmother?"

Magdalena nodded silently as she stood, then moved by him and out the door.

He grabbed her bag and carried it to his Jeep. Magdalena already sat inside the truck, so he placed the bag on the seat next to her.

The back of the Jeep held branches and small cuts of three different kinds of wood - piñon, roble, and madera de salvia - all stacked separately as Magdalena had ordered.

Andres climbed in, started the engine, and in moments they were on the beach, at the chosen place.

The sand stretched before them. Andres unfolded a chair and draped a down comforter over it. Magdalena climbed from the Jeep, seated herself, and arranged the corners of the comforter around her shoulders.

"I'll bring a few more rocks and have the fire started soon."

Magdalena, deep in her thoughts, didn't respond.

She remembered the sad day and those who had drowned. It was April, with a strong east wind, water temperature in the 50's. The search continued for days, but they never recovered Patricia Mullins' body.

"It's possible," she murmured as she watched her grandson feed the small fire. "Do you have the proper wood?" she called out to him. "I want the piñon to begin. It is most important."

"Yes, Grandmother. Then the roble, and the madera de salvia. I will be most careful. Do you wish a bite to eat?"

"Perhaps later. I believe I am ready. Thank you for the tea. Rest now, and stay near, tend our fire." She reached for her bag, passed the strap over her head and shoulder, then stood.

Magdalena stopped often to pick up small, sea-smoothed pebbles as she walked toward the top of the berm. Three times she brought thumbnail-sized pieces of the herbs from her bag, to her mouth. Time slowed, the pebbles in her pocket warmed as she reached outward, searching for her guides and the answering awareness of the Other.

Near the small fire, Andres watched his grandmother. He became entranced, forgetting for a moment everything but her measured steps. She was only the width of the beach away, but he knew where her soul journeyed he could not follow.

A log settled into the fire and he jumped. Andres released a shuddering breath, then stood and reached for a piece of wood on his right. He stirred the fire and carefully added the small cut.

Magdalena walked in a circle, creating a path in the sand. The spiral she traced led to the core of her heart, the place where she would rendezvous with those from the other side.

Every few paces she dropped a pebble. The first sounded a mere whisper, yet she knew by the time her pocket emptied, each would reverberate in her bones. A screech, an echoing boom, as grains of sand landed in new resting places. They scattered outward from the opaque glow of the mother stone, a spiral of echoes.

The tide crept in, bringing a salty resonance to the air. The breeze came alive as the spiral grew. When Magdalena reached the center, the last pebble thundered as it hit the sand.

Andres watched her arms rise from her sides to meet over her head, palm to palm. A glow traveled from the middle of her body, up her arms to her hands. The top of her head began to pulse with light.

A dulcet call filled his ears. He looked beyond his grandmother to the shallows. Bottle-nosed dolphins had gathered. He watched in astonishment as they swirled and leapt, circling and dancing on their tails.

Swaying, Magdalena faced the tumbling assembly. She sank to her knees. The dolphins calmed and began to rock in time with her. The glow moved from Magdalena's body, onto theirs, until it shrouded all.

Their vocalizations became less random. From the dolphins' minds and into hers the experiences of those on the small boat became known.

Tears running down her cheeks, Magdalena fell back onto the sand. As she watched, the dolphins rose from the water as one, then turned and headed out into the bay.

The wind roared, and Magdalena felt her spirit leave her body. She saw her small beach camp from the top of the island's volcanic crest. The wind increased, blew spray through her.

The wind and water cried, "Why hasn't he come for me?"

Then Magdalena was once more on her beach. She heard her own voice, pleading, "Why hasn't he come for me?"

"Grandmother, I have come. I am here."

Hands lifted her. She felt the warmth of the fire. Magdalena opened her eyes and looked into Andres' face for a moment.

"I think we must invite Isabelle to my house soon. There is much I would speak to her about."

Chapter Ten

As the sun sank behind the mountains, the sea reflected the orange and vermilion hues of the sky.

Andres walked around the front of the Jeep to open the door for Isabelle. "You look as if you're dreading this, Izzy. It's okay. Magdalena is looking forward to talking with you about the girl you saw on the island."

They walked toward the house.

Magdalena opened the door before Andres could knock. "Isabella. Come in, come in."

She led them into the cool interior, gestured toward a grouping of chairs near the fireplace. "May I offer you something to drink, a cool glass of horchata? Something stronger, perhaps?"

"Grandmother, here is your mail from town."

Magdalena glanced at the magazine on the top of pile, and then frowned. "Place it all by the fireplace. I will look at it later."

"Horchata would be delightful, thank you," Isabelle said.

As Magdalena left the room, Isabelle looked closer at the magazine laying on top of the mound of mail. "Is that your grandmother on the cover?"

"Yes. I thought of not bringing it to her, but…."

"Judging from Magdalena's reaction she might have liked that better."

Andres shrugged. "Grandmother wasn't what they expected."

"Go ahead, read it," came from behind them. Isabelle turned.

Magdalena held a tray with two tall glasses brimming with horchata. A cloth, embroidered with red and yellow bird of paradise blossoms, covered the tray. Her ankle length dress swayed as she walked, mirroring the tropical images of the cloth.

"Why don't you put on some music, Andres; something classical, and not too loud. I already know what the article says, rather, I know what I told the person who conducted the interview. Who knows what they printed."

Isabelle picked up the magazine. *Beyond,* in bold red letters against a background of black, marched across its front. "I'm not familiar with this*."*

"They started publication three years ago," Magdalena said. "They do interviews with psychics; investigate paranormal activity…that sort of thing. I'm surprised they'd put me on the cover. We disagreed on my key points."

On the cover photo Magdalena sat on her patio, Mira in her lap. She wore a turquoise t-shirt, tan slacks and leather sandals. Her auburn braid hung over one shoulder and rested against her breast. Next to her photo, a caption declared *A Modern Day Psychic. Page 39*.

The magazine also promised the latest information on paranormal investigations in Denver and New Orleans, and a checklist for researching and hiring your own investigator.

Isabelle flipped to page 39. A series of photographs of Magdalena were on page 40. The first pictured her dressed in a dark green skirt and blazer. She held a briefcase at her side.

"I don't know where they dug that up," Magdalena said. "Behind me is the library at the University of Arizona."

"Were you a student?"

Magdalena smiled. "No I taught cultural anthropology. My specialty was the pre-history of the people of the coasts of the Sea of Cortez."

"Grandmother has a doctorate in marine biology," Andres said with pride. "She is also a certified diver."

"Sometimes the treasures are beneath the water," Magdalena said and she shrugged.

"I had no idea," Isabelle said. She looked at the second photo. It showed an ancient woman dressed in Native American, ceremonial regalia.

"That angers me," Magdalena said. "I know Mae would never have given permission for the photo to be used. It had to be her grandson. He had no reverence for his heritage."

"Mae was a...."

"Pima shaman, and my teacher. I studied with her off and on from the time I was twelve years of age. She died last April."

The third photo showed Magdalena at a lectern. A man stood behind her. He had eyes only for her, his look of adoration plain to see.

"My grandfather," Andres said.

"Oh, I didn't know you were married."

Magdalena looked at Isabelle a moment before saying. "I have never been married."

Isabelle's face heated. "I…I'm so sorry…"

"Don't be. Rodolfo and I loved each other very much. But he was married and did not believe in divorce." Magdalena smiled. "His wife was understanding. We had our house in La Paz. Then when my father died, we inherited this home. Rodolfo would come to me whenever he could."

"Did you live in La Paz?"

"Some of the time; and in Tucson, when I was teaching. I traveled with my work, but spent my free time here at the beach with my father." She leaned toward Isabelle. "Our daughter, Roslyn, loved this place best of all."

"My parents live in Spain, have for years," Andres put in.

"The times Rodolfo, Roslyn and I spent here with father are what I have left of him now. My Rodolfo passed away not quite a year ago. See, Isabella, I too am a widow.

They exchanged a long look, and then Isabelle bent her head back over the magazine. "It says you are a seer. That a dolphin is your spirit guide."

"In that, they are almost correct. There are more than one. My dolphin sisters, they and the spiral will help us find the truth about the girl you saw on Isla Santa Maria." She held out her hand. "Now put the magazine away. I will bring you more horchata."

Isabelle gave her the magazine and her empty glass and Magdalena rose and walked toward the kitchen.

Isabelle looked at Andres. "Your grandmother…wow."

"She wasn't what the people from the magazine expected. I guess they thought a woman with her power should look quite different. Old, wrinkled and staring into a crystal ball or tea leaves." His cell phone rang. Glancing at it, he stood. "I'll take this outside."

Isabelle's gaze followed the flow of the stonework around the room and came to rest on an intricately woven rug covering the wall opposite the window. She got up and walked to it. It showed a woman wearing a crown of thorns, at her feet was a large red snake.

"Chantico," Magdalena said from behind her. "You know of her?

Isabelle shook her head.

"She is an Aztec goddess."

Isabelle stepped back. "It's beautiful work."

She turned and looked at the view. Beyond the large expanse of glass facing the beach, the sturdy timbers of the window framed the island. "Magdalena, I envy you the sunsets you must see reflected from the peak of the volcano."

"Ah, yes, very beautiful. The island is a grand place, the volcano part of every sunrise and sunset, but it also holds secrets."

"The girl I saw on the island? Do you have any idea who she is?"

Magdalena held out the re-filled glass and Isabelle took it. "I believe you have somehow come in contact with a spirit. Likely the young woman who was lost in the sea near here three years ago. A sad story, the Mullins family devastated by the boating accident. It happened between the beach and Isla Santa Maria."

Isabelle took a long, slow drink of the horchata, and then looked over the rim of the glass, at Magdalena. "Earlier, Andres told me about the accident. But I know the girl I saw was not Patricia Mullins."

"How is this?"

"Because I called her parents."

"Izzy. You did what?" Andres said, coming into the room. "How did you get their number?"

"The internet." Isabelle frowned. "Her father set me straight very fast. His daughter is dead."

She took another drink of horchata. "The girl I saw was alive. So it wasn't her."

"Si, Isabelle it was her, her spirit."

Isabelle shook her head. "I saw a girl…not a ghost."

"Are you so sure?" Magdalena went on when Isabelle did not answer. She stood and moved to the window. "There is a way for us to know; but you will have to return to the island. There is more to do."

"Return to the island." Isabelle felt her stomach muscles tighten, her breathing catch.

"We must know what the girl wants."

Isabelle rubbed at her right temple. "I just wish I knew what happened to her." She glanced at Andres. "You haven't heard from Cristiano have you? He said he was going to notify the local authorities."

"If he said so, then he will," Andres said.

Magdalena touched Isabelle's arm. "The girl is a spirit. Of this, I am sure. The dolphins have told me so."

"The dolphins spoke to you of someone else."

"If so, then we will help them both…the girl and the spirit. You have done all you can alone, now we must work together." Magdalena took Isabelle's hands. "And the first thing we must do is return to the island. We will go tonight."

"Tonight? Why not tomorrow?"

Magdalena shook her head. "We must go the beach where you saw your girl at the time the two of you first met."

Isabelle opened her mouth and then closed it.

"Andres will get us a boat."

"You don't wish me to go with you?"

Magdalena looked at him. " You think I am not able to make the run to my island?"

"No. No. Of course not. I'll bring the boat. What time?"

"Thirty minutes to the island, another hour to get to the site and make my preparations." She looked at Isabelle. "What time did you see your girl?"

"Around one o'clock in the morning, I would say."

"Then eleven-thirty will do, Andres."

"What do I bring?"

"Just yourself, Isabella." Magdalena turned away. "Now I suggest you rest. We will be seeing in the new day and set free a spirit to a new beginning."

Moonlight flooded through the window and cast a silver shroud across the bedroom. Isabelle glanced at the clock, again. Ten-thirty, one hour to go. She'd tried to nap, but her whirling thoughts had made it impossible. She shook her head. This whole ghost thing. It was crazy. The girl she'd seen on island was hurt, but real. Ghost don't have bodies, so how could she have seen the bruises, or did they keep the bruises they died with? A boat wreck would leave a lot of them. Sheesh. It was all crazy, but it couldn't hurt to humor Magdalena.

She punched her pillow and flopped onto her other side, receiving dirty looks from both Sammi-Sue and Longfellow.

"Hey, it's my bed, too," she grumbled.

But ghosts? She smiled wryly. I don't think so. Isabelle closed her eyes. Okay, one more time through it again. Maybe I've missed something.

She'd seen one girl on the island, the other in a dream. They'd resembled each other, both dripping wet with shadowed eyes and bruised faces. Were they wearing the same swimsuit? Isabelle frowned. Tropical prints. Okay, the swimsuits were similar and so what if they were alike. There had to be a hundred of them. She'd had one last year almost identical.

Could the girl she'd seen in her dream be Patricia Mullins? But why would she dream about someone she'd never met, or even seen? Maybe the girl on the island had come looking for….but why after three years? Why now?

"This is getting me nowhere." She kicked off the sheet, slipped out of bed and headed to the kitchen.

Isabelle checked Sammi and Longie's water bowls. Her stomach growled and she reached for a loaf of wheat bread. No sense going ghost-hunting on an empty stomach. She spread the bread with peanut butter, then topped it with sliced bananas. Her snack in hand, she walked to the bedroom. She took a bite out of the sandwich, then placed it on the nightstand.

"If I can't sleep, might as well get dressed." She put on jeans and a t-shirt, then placed a bandana, a pareo, and a windbreaker into her daypack, finishing her sandwich as she did so.

The telephone on the nightstand rang.

With any luck, that's Andres coming to his senses.

She picked it up. "Hello."

"Miss Isabelle Allen?" A male voice said.

She waited a heartbeat before answering. "Speaking."

"I know it's late, but I just found out, and I had to call."

"Uh, yes. Call about what?"

"Oh. I'm sorry. My name is Brad Collins."

Isabelle waited, but the speaker did not go on. The name sounded familiar, but she couldn't place the man. When it became clear he waited for her to say something, she did.

"Do I know you? Are you a friend of Donald's?"

"Patricia Mullins was my fiancé."

"Oh. I'm so sorry. I just heard about the tragedy."

"You called my father-in-law."

"I'm sorry. Mistake on my part. I thought maybe the girl I saw…but that was stupid."

"You really did see a girl on the island?"

"I did.

"We never found Patricia's body, just my sister's." There was silence for a long moment. "I'll be in San Felipe tomorrow I'd like to meet and talk with you."

"Why?"

"I just need to come back to the beach." He gave a short laugh. "My therapist says I have to, the dreams won't go away until I face my ghost."

Isabelle gasped. "What did you say?"

"I keep having dreams about Tricia. She's calling to me…waiting for me to come get her." His voice cracked. "My therapist insists I go back to the beach. Get some perspective. Her words not mine. I'd been thinking about it, then I got the call from Tricia's dad. It just seems to be the right time."

"You'll be here tomorrow?"

"I'll fly in. Sam and Phyllis Gustafson are family friends. They're expecting me."

"Then come by my place late in the afternoon. Just ask Phyllis which casa is mine."

"Thanks, Miss Allen. I need to put this all to rest. Then I can move on."

"I'll see you tomorrow." Isabelle hung up the phone, then stood and stared at it. It had given her a start when the man had used the word ghost. But he hadn't meant the same thing. She glanced at the clock. It was eleven-thirty.

As she turned away, the phone rang again. "What the…?" She picked up the phone. "Hello."

"Isabelle," Cristiano said. "I'm sorry this is so late. I just got in. I tried earlier, but the line was busy."

"That's okay. What did the policia say about the girl."

"They made out a report, talked long about being short-handed."

"They're not going to do anything, are they?"

"It may be a while."

"But the girl?"

"We searched the island. Alive or dead, she was not there. Perhaps a boat came for her, or…" His words trailed away.

"Don't you dare say she was a ghost," Isabelle snapped.

"I was thinking a wave could have pulled her out to sea."

"Sorry. It's been a long day."

"What's this about a ghost?"

"It's nothing. Something Andres said." She decided to change the subject. "I just had a weird phone call."

"Weird in what way? They did not upset you, did they?" The sharpness of his tone made the inside of her stomach flutter.

Isabelle laughed shakily. "It was Brad Collins…"

115

"The drowned girl's fiancée?"

"You know about her?"

"Patricia Mullins? Of course. Everyone in San Felipe knew. Mexico's Institute de Geologico helped with the search."

"He's coming here tomorrow. Says he needs closure."

"Understood. But, why call you?"

She told him about speaking with Patricia Mullins' father.

"Brad Collins doesn't think the girls are the same, does he?" Cristiano said.

"No. He just said it seemed the right time to come back to the island."

"But he wants to talk to you. Why?"

"I don't know. But I said I would. What can it hurt?" She glanced at the clock. She needed to be on her way to the meeting place on the beach. "Cristiano, it's late."

"I'm just about there, and hoped we could have a drink."

"You're coming here?"

"Not without an invitation," he said, and then chuckled softly. "I have a room always with the Hernandaz family waiting for me."

Her throat felt suddenly dry. They could have a drink…maybe more. She felt her face flush and the heat moved down her body. "I'm sorry. I can't tonight. What about tomorrow…wait Brad Collins will be here."

"I see." The chill in his voice came through loud and clear. "Please call me when you have some free time."

"Cristiano, I…" The line went dead. "Don't have your number," she finished into the phone. She sat it back in its cradle. "Men." She glanced at the clock. I've got to get moving. "Sammi, come."

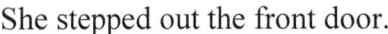

She stepped out the front door.

Isabelle looked at the sea, quiet and glowing in the moonlight, the islands beyond deeply shadowed, the tide resting at its height. Not the setting she'd picture for a ghost. But what did she know?

Sammi hopped onto the sand, ran a few steps, took care of her business, then trotted back toward her. Isabelle took another deep breath of the moist air, then turned back to the house.

Two minutes later she was ready. She heard her sneakers whisper in the sand as she strode toward the meeting place upon the beach.

Chapter Eleven

The full moon hung high in the black sky and washed the beach with its white glow. Isabelle heard the muffled voices before she saw them. Magdalena and Andres stood beside a boat the size of a nutshell. Yikes. Yes, the sea looked calm, but what if the wind picked up?

"Please, Grandmother," Isabelle heard Andres say. "I will wait in the boat. I won't even step onto the island."

"Isabelle and myself, no other. I've handled such a boat many times. It will be no problem."

"But you were younger then. When is the last time you took a boat out?"

Isabelle stopped beside Magdalena. The old woman glanced at her with a smug smile before saying. "Last week, grandson."

"What? Where did you go? Juan never said a thing to me. If there had been trouble…"

"There wasn't. Now put my bag inside. Isabelle and I must be there and prepared by one o'clock, and quit scowling," Magdalena said. "We'll be fine. It's just a quick run out to the beach, a little waiting time, then another run back."

Still muttering, Andres walked to the boat and heaved a burlap bag into it.

Magdalena followed.

118

"I have brought wood, matches, my smudging herbs, a battery-powered lantern, water and tea. That is all we will need," Magdalena said.

"Smudging?" Isabelle frowned.

"The area must be pure for when the girl arrives. We cannot take the chance of reaching something evil in her place."

"Oh. Of course. Wouldn't want that." Isabelle looked at the aluminum boat. "I'll be in the front, right? I don't know much about using an outboard motor."

"Yes, in the front. Andres will push the boat out. We will wade to it."

Andres worked the boat side to side to loosen it from the sand, then pushed as a wave receded. In moments, the small boat floated a good four feet from the beach.

Andres held onto it as it rose, then fell with the small swells.

Magdalena turned toward the waves.

"No wait," Andres called. "Izzy, you come first and hold the boat. I'll carry Grandmother out."

"Don't be silly. If I slip, I swim like a fish." Magdalena took a step into the sea.

"There's no sense you getting wetter than you need to," Andres said. "Please Grandmother. In this, at least listen to me."

Magdalena heaved a loud sigh. "Fine, Fine. Fine."

Magdalena sat in the rear of the small aluminum boat, her right hand upon the tiller. The sea was clear and quiet, the moonlight beautiful on the mountains behind the campo.

"Did you know, Isabelle, that you share a name with the mountain range you're gazing at now?"

"What?"

"Si, Santa Isabelle. They are named for the saint."

"No, I didn't know. Have you been there?"

"Andres takes me every fall. We harvest the piñon nuts; bring fallen wood for my special fires. It is very beautiful there, peaceful; perhaps you will make the trip one day."

"It would be a nice place to celebrate my birthday."

"It would be cool there in August, that's your birthday month, no? You are a fire-child."

"How did you know…?"

Magdalene shrugged. "Andres must have told me."

"I've never been here at that time of year. It's hot, isn't it?"

"August, like you fiery Leo children, can be so; but you would find the mountain cool and calming."

The boat slowed.

"To the right is the Laguna Piedres," Magdalena said. "Wonderful fishing here when the tide is right."

Isabelle saw tumbled rocks and pitted boulders of lava, dark with bands of silvery moonlight. Framed by looming lava spires, the narrow entrance to the lagoon turned then and opened into a small, protected cove.

"For tonight, we will pass by and go to the beach on the north side of the island."

"I can't believe how calm the water is," Isabelle said.

The woman, resting on the gray, pitted rock, jerked up and turned to face the open sea. "Isabelle comes to me." Her sunken eyes narrowed. "But she is not alone. And this other…I feel something from her. She means a change for me." Anger filled her, made her shiver. "The other has no right. She knows nothing about me, about my love. I cannot leave. I must wait. It is not for her to say."

She stood, moved to the water's edge. "Isabelle, yes. This other, no. She will not be allowed on my island."

The boat's bow suddenly dipped. With a scowl, Magdalena looked skyward. "I mean you no harm. We must talk."

"Who? Who are you talking to?" The boat lurched and with a sharp cry, Isabelle pitched forward. "What's going on? How can the sea change so quickly?"

"Hold, Isabelle. I will try to calm her."

"Calm who? Who in the hell are you talking to?"

Magdalena lifted her hand. "You want Isabelle, but not me. Is that so?"

To the left, Isabelle saw a spiral form in the water.

"Isabelle, say I am to be with you, that you will go no further without me."

"I don't…"

"Say so. She must know your heart."

"Magdalena…"

"Say it, child." Magdalena gripped the tiller with both hands.

"Fine. I want her with me. I won't come any nearer without her."

The boat rose, then fell into a trough. Cold water poured over the side, drenching their feet.

"Didn't seem to make much difference." Isabelle looked toward the island. *This is crazy. We shouldn't have come.*

The outboard motor sputtered, then stopped.

"Oh my God," Isabelle cried.

Magdalena held both hands aloft. "Help us, sisters."

"What are you doing? Magdalena, start the damn motor."

"It will do no good. We must trust now, Isabelle."

A wave lifted the stern of the boat, with a gasp Isabelle grabbed on to the sides. "Maybe we should try and swim it."

Magdalena shook her head. "I would not make it."

"But you said you swam like a fish."

"I could not make it back to our beach. Perhaps to another island…"

"Magdalena, the island isn't far. I'll help…"

"Help comes." Magdalena pointed toward the open water.

By the moonlight, Isabelle saw a fin cut through the water. "Sharks. It could be sharks."

"It is my sisters."

The boat whipped around in a circle and on her right Isabelle saw a jutting rock. "Magdalena."

"We will be fine. Trust, Isabelle."

*****

The woman watched the small boat wallow in the roughening waves. "Yes, Isabelle you may swim. The island welcomes you, but not the other."

"Patricia, you must not do this." The voices came into her head.

The woman whipped around, but saw no one. "Who are you? Where are you?"

"We are of the sea. We are Magdalena's sisters. You will not cause her soul to leave for the Beyond. It is not her time."

Her answer came, sullen. "She wishes me harm."

"Our sister harms none. She only desires to speak with you. She will call you with the spiral. Go to her, listen."

"If I do not?"

"You live with the results of your action."

Patricia stared out to sea, watched the churning waves. The choice was hers. She knew those of the sea would not stop her. She could send this Magdalena to the ocean's floor. But would her love, her Bradley, approve? Besides, a part of her needed to know what the old woman wanted to say. This visit gave her time for what she needed, to see what called to her from within Isabelle. She still remembered Isabelle's earlier words to her about her marred face, but had decided the words weren't lies, only that the moonlight and shadows had made her face seem so.

And if Isabelle proves to not be desired, then there was always their return trip by boat. "If your sister calls to me from the spiral with respect and honor, I may listen."

"Then calm the waves."

*****

"Yes sisters, yes," Magdalena said. She faced Isabelle. "We will be fine." Even as she spoke the words, the waves settled.

"I don't think so Magdalena. We should jump. Look." Isabelle pointed at the dark craggy rocks, almost close enough to brush with the end of her fingertips. Metal scraped against rock, sounding almost like a human shriek.

Isabelle stood.

"Sit down," Magdalena ordered. "My sisters will guide us to shore." She pointed to the ocean.

Clicking came from the darkness. Isabelle saw the bobbing heads of dolphins. The boat pulled away from the hungry rock.

"Maybe you should try the motor again?" Isabelle said in a quaking voice.

Magdalena shook her head. "We are almost there."

Isabelle looked toward Isla Santa Maria, and at the same time, the boat's bottom struck sand.

"Thank you, sisters," Magdalena said.

Isabelle stood, lowered herself into the water and tugged the boat higher up onto the sand. She wanted to keep going, get away from the water further yet, then drop to her knees and shake, but first things first.

They walked along the beach. The boat, pulled high upon the sand, waited behind them. The moon cast deep shadows, only the tops of the now serene waves reflected the light.

Magdalena looked at Isabelle. "What time is it?"

"It's 12:30."

"Let's rest here, sit for a moment, then we will gather rocks to shield our fire." They settled upon the sand.

"What happened out there? One minute everything's fine, then all hell broke loose."

"It is Patricia. She's upset that I've come to the island with you."

Isabelle dropped her head onto her raised knees. "I don't need this right now. I want to rest, then God help me, get in that dang boat, go back to our beach, and get in bed."

Magdalena shook her head. "Even more now, we need to release Patricia. She is confused, and now grows angry. She cannot stay on this plane."

"If she is a ghost, and I'm not saying she is, then she's made it damn clear she doesn't want anything from us." Isabelle stood.

"Isabelle, I must try."

"Fine. Then let's get this ridiculousness over with. I'll find the rocks for the fire ring." Isabelle looked down at the small bundle she'd carried from the boat. It hadn't been heavy. She didn't see how it could hold enough wood for any kind of substantial fire. "I just hope the wood didn't get too wet to burn."

"The wood and my herbs are fine." Magdalena patted the even smaller mound that rested beside her.

Isabelle glanced around. "There are plenty of rocks right here. It won't take but a few minutes to make a fire ring."

Magdalena created the spiral. The only sounds were her footsteps and the movement of the water climbing and receding from the shore. Behind her, Isabelle sat in the glow of the moon. It's light was enough, so they'd decided against using the lantern. "Only nature will provide for us on the island," Magdalena whispered.

The spiral complete, she faced the sea.

She raised her arms, pressed her palms together above her head, breathed deeply in, released the breath, in, out, the sand under her feet warmed, seemed to breathe with her.

She bowed toward the sea, turned, did the same toward the heart of the island, and lastly the volcanic peak.

Magdalena turned and began to walk slowly, following the trail of stones, toward the center of the spiral.

*****

Patricia watched the woman form the spiral. A scowl creased her face. She regretted now telling the ones of the sea she would speak to the meddler. But if she was called from the spiral...? She watched as the last two stones

Magdalena placed shifted away from each other. The woman did not notice and Patricia smiled.

*****

At the spiral's center, Magdalena brought a bag from her pocket, opened it and spread out matches and a small bunch of sage. She struck a match, put it to the leaves. As the flame grew, a fragrant aroma spread around them; Magdalena traced the infinity shape in the air with the sage bundle. The leaves flared. Letting out a long, slow breath, she lowered the flame to the wood. The small sticks lit and a shroud of light surrounded them. Magdalena tossed bits of sage from the bag onto the fire. She leaned forward and waved the smoke toward her. The sounds of the water seemed to quiet.

She hummed under her breath and felt a warmth grow along her spine. Hope washed ashore with the waves, burned in the fire and floated skyward in the fragrance of the sage. Magdalena settled onto the dry sand, crossed her legs. "Now I wait."

*****

Isabelle glanced across to where Magdalena sat, and then down at her watch. It was 1:25 A.M.

So where was this ghost?

She looked up into a sea of pale stars. The moon hung among them, a mother hen with a score of chicks.

I knew this was a waste of time. How much longer do we sit here?

*****

Patricia Mullins smiled. The woman's bones must be torturing her. How long will she wait? She stood. I've had enough of this. I need to speak with Isabelle.

126

*****

Beneath Isabelle the sand shoved upward. She sprang to her feet. "What the...?" She turned to stare across to where Magdalena still sat.

The stones of the spiral around her danced as if alive.

"What's going on," Isabelle shouted.

"El temblor."

Rocks slid down the face of the mountain, a rumble came from deep within. Wind lifted her hair and brought the smell of sulfur.

Magdalena stood. "Perhaps we should begin gathering our things, we may want to move toward our boat."

"May want..." The ground pushed against her feet. Isabelle bent and grabbed her backpack and a basket. The ground shook again.

"This way, Isabelle."

"How can you sound so calm?"

"It is only the mountain grumbling." Magdalena turned and started down the beach.

Isabelle followed at her heels. She had just spied the boat when she remembered. "Damn, I left my jacket. Well, it can stay there."

"Be calm, Isabelle, the mountain is finished speaking to us. I'll go to the boat. You go back for your jacket."

The ground had quit shaking, and that jacket had been the last gift she'd received from her mother.

Isabelle, now we meet.

*****

She saw her jacket on the sand and ran to it. She bent, scooped it up and turned to jog back down the beach.

"You do beautiful work. I am a potter. Do you know that?"

127

She whipped around. The girl stood there in the moonlight. Isabelle's arms erupted with goose bumps. "Where have you been? We've looked all over this island for you?"

The girl smiled. *"Do you know who I am?"*

Isabelle shook her head.

"Patricia Mullins."

Isabelle's legs began to shake. She'd heard it straight from the girl's mouth…she was a ghost.

"We were boating." The ghost looked across the waves. *"Something happened. I can't remember what. My Bradley somehow got me to this island…told me to stay until he returned for me."*

"Brad Collins," Isabelle whispered.

Patricia faced her. *"You know my love?"*

This isn't real. I'm not talking to a ghost. I'll wake up… "Uh, no, I don't know him. I know about the boat accident…"

"Why hasn't he come for me?" Patricia's voice rose with anger. *"I did as he said. I've waited."*

"I…"

"I've seen your studio, your weavings. I like the one of the Hawaiian volcano the best. The colors…I did a pot with those same colors. Bradley's mother has it."

The words startled Isabelle. "My studio? You can leave…."

Patricia Mullins waved a hand. *"I can occasionally. I can leave my body behind and go. But I always have to come back here."* She frowned. *"No, I really don't have to. That's wrong. I want to. I promised I'd wait here. So I will."*

"Isabelle." She turned to see Magdalena standing just beyond.

"No. I do not want her here."

"Santa Maria holds her. She must go onward to be with the other spirits."

Patricia moved around Isabelle and stalked toward Magdalena. *"I'm no spirit. I am alive."*

"No, child you drowned. Think about the boat. The cold water."

"I did not drown." Patricia's voice rose. *"Brad will come for me. He promised. Those were his last words."*

"Your love lives," Magdalena said. "You do not. You must accept this before you can go on."

"You crazy woman," the ghost screamed. *"I'm not dead, you hear me? I am not dead."*

Isabelle turned away from Patricia. "Uh, Magdalena, maybe we should stop with the being dead stuff, okay?"

"I created the spiral, called to you. Why didn't you come?"

"I will not talk to you. Never. Do you understand?"

"No, wait." Magdalena started forward. "I want to help."

"Get off my island." Patricia turned away and moved closer to Isabelle. *"We will talk again."* Then, as Isabelle watched, the woman faded. At first, she could see the beach, the sea through her, then she was gone.

She felt Magdalena's gaze, but she wasn't ready to meet her eyes. She shivered, put her jacket on, pulled it tight around her. Then she turned, walked a few steps down the beach and stared across the waves.

"Isabelle." Magdalena walked toward her. "We must go home. We can do no more this night. Look." Magdalena waved her hand toward the sea.

"What?"

"Fog. We must get back to our beach."

A gray line hovered. As she watched, it floated toward them, then began to swirl. What the…? Fog doesn't form tornadoes. Behind her came a rumble and she whipped around. Rocks bounced down the side of the hill, a sound like shattering glass echoed in the darkness. A gust of cold wind blew against her back. Isabelle turned. The fog, now a spiral, kicked up sand as it bounced toward them.

"Patricia is very angry with me," Magdalena said. "We should return to our boat. And quickly."

"Let's go."

The two of them raced along the beach. Suddenly Magdalena stopped.

"What is it?" Isabelle said.

"The boat is gone."

"What?" Isabelle looked around. The beach was empty. "Are you sure this is the spot"

"Yes. See, there are the drag marks. This is where we left the boat. " She pointed to the deep furrows above the tide line.

"Well then…?

"Por dios," Magdalena said. "Look." She pointed out toward the water.

Isabelle saw the bobbing boat. "But how? We dragged it high, onto the dry sand."

Magdalena sighed and looked back down the beach. "Patricia is angry. "

"Oh, come on. She couldn't do this by herself." Isabelle shook her head. "Maybe it was a little tsunami caused by the quake." She looked at the boat again. "Well, damn."

Chapter Twelve

Andres eyes snapped open. He looked at the hall clock, blinked, then rose from his chair and moved closer. Yes, three A.M. glowed. How could that be? He'd entered Magdalena's home, made a pot of coffee, and sat down near the fire with a book. Only an hour after their departure he'd looked at the clock, then back into his book. Now suddenly it was three A.M.

Worry moved up his spine. They should be back by now. His pulse increased the moment he admitted the fact to himself.

After the boat with his grandmother and Isabelle had disappeared from sight, he had walked slowly back to the house. The night was clear, the sea quiet. In his mind, he replayed the discussion, argument really, with Magdalena, and realized he'd allowed himself to be convinced.

He frowned and shook his head. No, they would be okay; his grandmother was capable of carrying out her plan, and she wasn't alone. Isabelle was with her.

Enough with the bullshit. Something had gone wrong. They should have been back by now. Oh, my God. Now what? Where can I get a boat? Cristiano. Yes, Cristiano. It will be all right, just call Cristiano. He'll know what to do.

*****

The phone's strident shrill jerked Cristiano from a confused dream, swirling with color.

He fumbled with the phone, almost dropping it twice. "Hello."

"We've got to help them, we've got to get out there. Something has happened, I know they're in trouble..."

It took him a moment to recognize Andres' voice. "What? What are you saying? Slow down, you're babbling."

"I wanted to go with them. Grandmother said no."

"Andres, calm down."

"They went out to Isla Santa Maria."

"In the middle of the night? I thought Isabelle said...never mind. We'll take the institute's boat. Be on the beach in twenty minutes, or I'll leave without you."

Cristiano recalled the last gas emission readings the team had taken on the island. They were not reassuring. He rushed out the door and climbed in his truck.

He and Andres both arrived at the same time.

Cristiano nodded as he turned to scan Mexico's Institute de Geologico's ancient boat.

"Let's go."

"Cristiano, they were...Grandmother said..."

"Don't talk. Move."

They jogged across the wet sand and splashed into the gulf's mild waters. Both were wet to their waist when they climbed the ladder.

Cristiano went immediately to the main cabin cockpit and fired up the twin inboard engines."Go out on deck and make sure all the navigation lights are working. I'll flash them once.

Andres ran from the cabin.

"I'm here. Flash them."

Cristiano did.

"Everything's fine."

"Bueno. Let loose the mooring line. I'm going to do an electronics check, then we're heading out."

The instrument panel blinked all systems operational. He eased the boat away from the mooring buoy, checked the GPS and compass headings, then aligned the bow toward Isla Santa Maria.

"Andres, get down here."

Cristiano stared out across the dark water as he waited.

" I'm here, Captain," Andres said.

"Get a life jacket from the locker under the starboard seat. I'm going to want you on deck watching when we get close. I'll come around the end of the island, then we'll cruise the shore. Take a spot light with you."

"What if they're not on the beach?" Andres said, fishing out the lifejacket.

"We have a half hour or so before we'll be in the area. Get a thermos of tea ready, they'll need it. Whose idea was this?" Cristiano asked.

"Well, Grandmother said she and Isabelle had to go to the island tonight to try and talk to the girl's spirit and she…"

"The girl Isabelle said she saw earlier on the island? Now the girl is a ghost?" He swore softly beneath his breath. "Get the tea going. If anything has happened to them, I'll skin you, Andres." Cristiano's gaze darted over the blue-lit instrument panel.

"You just calm down," Andres said, dropping the lifejacket. He found the kettle and placed it upon the front burner of the small propane stove. "There, tea in a moment. You know Magdalena and her beach camps. She's convinced the girl Isabelle saw was Patricia

Mullins' spirit, and that it must be sent on. Hasn't Isabelle said anything to you about this? Perhaps you haven't been engaging in conversation, eh?" At Cristiano's sharp look he hurried on. "So they went out to the island."

"And you let them go alone?"

"I didn't let them do anything, Grandmother insisted. I sent them with all they'd need for a two or three hour camp on the beach." He turned back to the stove and poured steaming water into the thermos, added tea bags, and turned to face Cristiano. "I'm sure the two of them are fine, they're just a little late and I thought…"

"Then why did you call me in hysterics?"

Andres put on a wounded expression. "I wasn't hysterical, just concerned and…" his words trailed away as he looked out the back of the cabin. "My God. Look at the fog. I've never seen it so thick."

"I'm slowing down. Don't know if a light is going to do much good, but get it ready anyway." Cristiano slowed the boat further, glanced at the instrument panel. "We're still a ways off the end of the island, but get out front with the light, and don't forget your life jacket."

Although the swell was less than two feet, the current running around the island kept Cristiano busy staying on course.

"I see the boat." Andres called from the bow.

"Put the light on it. I'll move closer."

Andres groaned. "Boat's empty. Slow, Cristiano. Hold us right here. I'll get the hook." There were a few moments of silence and then, "I've got it."

"Tie it off the stern." Cristiano frowned into the fog. "Where did they go for this midnight wonder?"

"The last time I was here with Magdalena she made her camp just the other side of the big slide."

"We should be about there. Shine the light up, I think the slide is ahead, port bow."

He watched Andres play the light on the tumbled boulders, work it side to side down to the beach then ahead, directly opposite the boat. "This damn fog is right down on the surface. I can't see anything. Wait. Do you hear that?"

A low rumble, then the sound of tumbling rock filled the quiet air. The powerful spot light revealed a gathering dust cloud as huge boulders, shifted, then moved lazily downward toward the beach, small chair-sized pieces bounced, almost merrily, to land on the very edge of the slide where it met the sea.

Gods, what next? Cristiano's eyes searched. He could see nothing but fog. If the volcano was starting up…"Keep that light moving along the shore. I'm going to take us out a bit until we get past the slide."

They made a small arc away from the hazardous bouncing rocks. Cristiano maneuvered the boat to a course paralleling the shore. He could see small waves curling inward.

"Cristiano, the fog is thinning… wait…over there," Andres shouted, moving the beam of the light to the two women standing close together on the beach. "Abuelita. Isabelle, we're here. Are you all right?"

"Not now," Cristiano snapped. "We've got to get anchored. Stand back, keep the light on them."

*****

From atop the rock where she stood, Patricia watched the two men on the boat. Their emotions poured over her; fear, excitement, anger, and with the emotion came an ember of heat. It glowed in her stomach. She gloried in its warmth.

First the man earlier in the panga, and now..?

Patricia felt the moment they saw Isabelle and the other, for the ember inside her cooled. "No," she cried. "No."

*****

Cristiano released the anchor. He shifted to reverse to hook it. A swell lifted the boat, gently at first, then with a rush of sound and water. "Hold on, Andres. Gods, what now? Keep the light on them. Get back Isabelle, get back."

The boat crested the swell and plunged into the trough. He watched the back of a ten-foot wall of water speed toward the beach.

"Look out," Andres shouted. "Here comes another one…" and the boat lifted again.

This wave broke on top of them.

Cristiano flung water away from his face and held the struggling boat. "See to the runabout. It's going to fill with water. Take a knife, we will have to cut it loose."

"But Grandmother and Isabelle," Andres protested.

"We'll have to try something else. Just do it…before another wave comes."

Holding onto to anything available, Andres made his way to the back of the boat. He looked down at the runabout. The small boat seats glistened with wetness, but there was no water inside. "Cristiano, the runabout is fine."

"What? How…?"

"I don't know, but it is," Andres called back. He caught movement out of the corner of his eye and turned. A dolphin leaped into the air. Then another. He saw more dorsal fins. Ah, he thought. Grandmother's friends.

Andres made his way back to Cristiano. "The runabout is fine."

"For now, but when…."

Andres watched Cristiano look over his shoulder to the open ocean. He turned, but all he saw was the gulf's seas, flat and quiet behind them once again. What the hell was that all about?

*****

A wave of weakness moved through Patricia and she swayed. Anger filled her. She pulled it close, fed it to the ember inside, but it did no good. The speck of warmth died.

Rest. I must rest. There will be more. I must have the heat…and now I know how to create it….

*****

"Andres, how you doing down there?"

"I'm soaked, that's how I'm doing."

"Get the light back on the girls, can you see them?"

"Yes. They've moved back from the shore."

Cristiano slowed the engines, stood and looked at the two women spotlighted on the beach. They seemed very small, holding on to one another. The flanks of the volcano rose abruptly behind them. "The anchor is holding," he said. "Let's get them. Do you want to go over with the runabout, or stay here?"

Andres appeared at his elbow. "I think you'd better go, you're a better boat handler. What do I have to do here? What were those giant waves about?"

"I don't know, but I hope there will be no more of them. There's really nothing to do here. I'm shutting down the engines, and the anchor is hooked. Keep the light on us, shouldn't take more than five minutes."

Cristiano called across to Isabelle and Magdalena, "I'm coming to get you."

He watched the two women gather their bags and move down to the shore.

As he neared with the runabout, he saw they were both soaking wet and trembling.

"Bueno, Cristiano, it's good to see you," Magdalena said as he pulled the boat up onto the sand.

"Magdalena, whatever was in your mind to…?"

"Cristiano, please," Isabelle said. "Not now. Just get us off this island. We're wet and cold."

"But of course. Excuse me for keeping you waiting," Cristiano said, pushing the small craft into the water. "Isabelle, come hold the boat. I will carry Magdalena out."

She did, then stood in silence, staring across the waves as he brought Magdalena to the boat and placed her inside.

He glanced at Isabelle. Something was wrong. What had happened here? "Do you require help?"

"No. I'm fine." She pushed up to raise chest high along the side of the boat before her arms quivered and she fell back in the water.

Without a word, he walked to her, and when she lunged again, he placed both of his palms against her backside and pushed. With a startled yelp, she fell head first into the boat.

Isabelle righted herself, turned to glare at him, before crawling to sit across from Magdalena.

Good. That was the Isabelle he knew.

Cristiano hoisted himself aboard, then brought the engine to life and headed toward the institute boat.

Andres met them. He helped Magdalena and Isabelle into the cockpit and handed them towels.

Cristiano moved by. "We'll find you some dry clothes and blankets. Then you perhaps can explain to me what you thought you were doing out here in the middle of the night."

Magdalena and Isabelle stepped down into the main cabin.

Cristiano led them to the forward stateroom. "In the drawers beneath the bunks there will be something for you to change into." He handed them more towels and backed out and slid the panel door closed.

Andres sat at the table, a steaming mug clenched in his hands. "Are they okay? I'm a nervous wreck. If I ever get back to my house I'm never coming out on a boat ever again in my life."

"Now, why do you say that? You are an exceptional first mate, you might want to think of this as a career."

"Cristiano," Andres glared up at him. "You've got a smart mouth on you. I'm taking tea to the girls."

Someone tapped on the door and Isabelle moved to answer it. Andres stood there holding two cups.

"Isabelle, Grandmother, are you two okay? Here, I brought tea."

In silence, she took the cups from him.

"I was so worried. We got here as soon as we could. My God ..."

"Andres," Magdalena said quietly. "Thank you for the tea. Let us dress now, please."

He nodded and closed the door.

Isabelle handed Magdalena a mug of tea. "Here, take a drink of this. I'll find us dry clothes."

T-shirts, trousers, socks and other items of clothing were jumbled together in the drawers beneath the bunks. She pulled out a sweatshirt and a pair of socks, tossed them on the bunk where Magdalena sat wrapped in a towel and sipped tea.

"Take off your wet things." Isabelle reached for the mug, placed it on the ledge above the bunk. "We've got to get you warm."

Magdalena pulled her wet and sandy dress over her head and let it fall to the floor.

"Do you need help?"

"No. I will manage." She tugged on a pair of sweat pants and sat on the edge of the bunk.

Isabelle watched Magdalena pull the sweatshirt over her head and then put the socks on. "Let me dry your hair while you finish your tea."

"Graciás."

She rubbed Magdalena's hair with a thick towel, then gently combed her fingers through the mass. "You're so quiet.

"I am concerned. Patricia is very stubborn and angry. Those huge waves... I fear we've..." She shook her head. "There is work yet to be done, Isabelle. Thank you for helping me dress, now I must rest. Until we have returned to our beach, I would like to lie here."

"Of course." Isabelle pulled clothes from the drawers for herself. "Whoa, what's this?" She stood and held out a purple filigree-lace teddy with red ribbons down one side. "I wonder if this was part of a scientific experiment?"

She and Magdalena exchanged knowing looks, then speculative smiles, but jealousy knotted Isabelle's stomach and the emotion angered her. Why do I care how many women he's had on this boat?

Magdalena smiled. "Graciás, Isabelle. I needed a diversion. Experiment, indeed. I've had some grand ones

in my time." She handed Isabelle the mug, pulled a blanket over her head, and with a slight chuckle lay down.

Isabelle grabbed a university sweatshirt three sizes too large for her. She slid it over her head and followed it with a pair of faded, threadbare shorts, so big they could easily fall to her ankles with a slight tug. She scooped up their wet clothes and stepped out into the main cabin.

Cristiano stood at the wheel. He glanced at Isabelle, his gaze traveling from her bare feet to her towel wrapped head. "Well, I can't say your midnight ramblings have done much for your style."

"Oh? Perhaps you would prefer I model the flaming lingerie I found in there?"

She gestured angrily with her chin toward the stateroom. "The purple silk number looked as if it had been involved in some vigorous experimentation."

She wanted the words back as soon as they were said.

"What are you talking about?" Cristiano's eyes darkened. "Is this your way to change the conversation? I can understand why. What were you thinking…wait you couldn't have been thinking at all."

"Now just a minute." Isabelle put the wet clothes and the tea mugs on the table beside her. She took two steps toward Cristiano. "Magdalena and I were fine. We would have gotten ourselves home without your help."

"How? Your boat, if you could even call that thing a boat, was floating away. By daylight, it would have been on the beach in front of your casa. Were you going to swim from Isla Santa Maria? We both know how well you do that. What did you think you were doing on that island in the middle of the night? Magdalena shouldn't be pulled out of bed at that hour."

"Lower your voice, she's resting. And furthermore, it was her idea. She believed the spirit of Patricia Mullins was trapped on the island. We went to free her."

"And did you indeed, free this spirit you're so obsessed with?" Cristiano said.

"I'm not obsessed with anything, except getting home to a hot shower, Sammi, Longie, rest, and maybe, someday, a little studio time." Her voice was harsh and ended with a sharp exhalation of frustration. She turned away from him, hands on hips, and glared out the passageway to where Andres sat in the cockpit looking worried, his hands clutched tightly between his knees.

"Did you even see this so-called ghost?" Cristiano said.

"Don't you dare take that mocking tone with me."

"Andres," Cristiano snapped over his shoulder, "go forward and keep a lookout. It's getting close to sunrise, pangas will be heading out to fish soon."

Andres stood quickly, moved toward the bow as if he had been waiting for an excuse to escape.

Isabelle frowned. "Just because you can't admit the possibility of a world that's not included in your narrow vision, that doesn't give you the right to…"

"Isabella, Isabella. You don't know me well enough to know what I do or do not believe."

"Don't call me Isabella. I've had it with you and your stiff-necked, narrow minded, opinionated view of the world." She unwrapped the towel from her hair, balled it up and threw it at him.

It hit him directly in the middle of his back. He turned. A red flush climbed into his face. Their gazes locked.

She didn't know who took the first step, but somehow she was in his arms. His hot mouth pressed against hers, his hands rested on her hips, then slid inside the short's loose waistband and pulled her closer yet. His palms were like brands against her still-chilled skin. She felt his arousal. A moan escaped her lips. Her hands rose, she ran fingers through his fog-damp hair. Why does he affect me like this?

Cristiano broke the kiss and she groaned in protest, then his lips trailed scalding nibbles down the side of her neck. Her knees turned to water, and only his hands pressing her hard against his length kept her from falling.

"Cristiano. Izzy. I've been thinking. This thing between you has to..." Andres voice came from behind them.

Isabelle twisted away from Cristiano. What was she doing? She was angry with him. Wasn't she?

"Oh, I'm sorry," Andres said. "I thought...I didn't want the two of you to upset Grandmother. I see...well, that doesn't seem to be a problem any longer..."

Isabelle kept her head down as she fled by the two men. "I'll check on Magdalena."

Chapter Thirteen

"Andres, the tide is full in. We'll use the runabout." Isabelle heard Cristiano call to Andres as she and Magdalena came from below. She watched him secure the big cruiser to the marker buoy. Magdalena was asleep when Isabelle entered the cabin. She had taken some time to pull herself together and calm her raging emotions.

Isabelle frowned. That little scene between her and Cristiano, it had to be because of everything that had happened. They'd been in danger, then the ghost, and the boat had floated away. She'd just been so happy to see Andres and Cristiano.

Yeah, you wanted to rip off his clothes and have sex with him right there because you were so filled with gratitude.

She pushed the thought away. *I can't deal with this right now.*

Andres lowered the small boat into the water.

"Grandmother. Isabelle, I am ready for you."

The sun had just begun to rise from the sea as the four of them headed toward shore.

Isabelle thought it was the most beautiful sunrise she'd ever seen, glorious pinks and reds reflected off the quiet water.

Andres jumped from the boat and guided it up on the sand. He lifted Magdalena from her seat and headed to the top of the berm. "I'll take you home now, Abualita. You need your bed and your cat."

"Yes, Mira will be missing me."

Andres put Magdalena on her feet at the top of the beach. She turned toward the sunrise and raised her arms, her palms met over her head. She held the pose for a moment, then turned toward her house.

Cristiano secured the small outboard motor and climbed from the boat. He coiled the rope, then dropped it into the bow. "My truck is here, Isabelle, may I drive you to your house?"

Their gazes locked. There was more than a ride being offered, but so much had happened. She needed time to think. "No. I'll walk it."

"As you wish."

His uncaring tone made her wonder if her thoughts had been right. Maybe he wasn't offering her anything more than a ride. She was careful to avoid his eyes as she walked away.

Chapter Fourteen

Sammi-Sue met her at the door, a wiggling body of joy. Beyond the basset hound she saw Longfellow. He looked at her, turned and with a twitch of his tail, stalked away, his message clear. Two nights in a row? You had me neutered for less.

Isabelle knelt and gathered Sammi-Sue into her arms. "I know, baby. I know. Come on, let's go potty."

It didn't take the basset hound long and the time Sammi did spend on the sand she kept looking back to make sure Isabelle still stood within her sight. With each reassuring glance, Isabelle felt more guilt.

Back inside, she headed to the kitchen to make sure Sammi and Longie both had food. Their bowls were still full. They hadn't eaten a bite. She felt another stab of guilt as she emptied both and refilled them with fresh food.

Her simple actions seemed to take forever, it was as if she moved in slow motion. "Food. Bath and sleep. That's what I need."

With a towel wrapped around her Isabelle stumbled, nearly comatose toward the bed. The shrill ring of the phone halted her. "No," she moaned. "Somebody better be dying." She picked up the receiver. "Hello."

"Miss Allen?"

She almost said, she isn't here. May I take a message? Her automatic response to telemarketers at home, but this wasn't San Francisco. "Yes."

"It's Brad Collins. I'm making sure our meeting for this afternoon is still on."

"Mr. Collins, of course. You're here already?"

"I arrived last night."

"How about five this afternoon?"

"Great. I'm looking forward to our talk."

Isabelle yawned before she answered. "Five o'clock then. Good night."

There was a pause before he responded. "Uh, okay. Good night."

She smiled as she put down the receiver. "He must think I'm a real head case." Still smiling, she stumbled toward bed.

*****

Isabelle took another sip of herbal tea and glanced at the clock. Brad Collins would be here soon. She really wanted an espresso, but knew the caffeine would put a hitch in her plans for dropping into bed early that night.

When she'd awakened after her six-hour nap, Sammi had been snuggled beside her and Longfellow had been at her feet, an unusual experience, for both normally preferred their own crates and blankets. Longie had greeted her with a small meow before jumping down.

"Forgiven, huh?"

Both pet bowls were empty.

She and Sammi had taken a long walk on the beach and found some blue and green sea glass to add to her collection.

Isabelle took another sip of tea.

The only jarring moment of the beach walk had been seeing Asshole-Carl in the distance. They'd both turned away. Something would have to be done about him, but she'd take her time. Revenge was best served cold, or something like that. Whatever she did, her actions would fit the crime and she looked forward to it.

Sammi-Sue scrambled to her feet before Isabelle even heard the knock. She followed the barking basset hound to the front door. "Quiet."

Brad Collins was six feet or more, with closely clipped, dark blonde hair and brown eyes. A mustache sat above full lips. The khaki shorts and blue golf shirt he wore fit his lean body well. "Miss Allen?"

She opened the door wider. "Please, come in. And it's Isabelle." Sammi whined. "This is Sammi-Sue."

He held out a hand to the basset hound. "How do you do."

Sammi sniffed, then wagged her tail.

"Would you prefer to talk in the kitchen or living room?"

"The kitchen's fine with me."

Isabelle led the way. "Something to drink? Iced tea, wine, or maybe a beer?"

"Iced tea would be great."

"It all ready has lemon and sugar."

"Terrific."

Brad stood by the kitchen table and talked softly to Sammi as Isabelle got a glass and poured the tea.

Sammi likes him. He's closer to my age, and he's not going to have any Americano hang-ups. Her hand froze in mid-pour. God, what am I thinking? She put the iced-tea back in the refrigerator. I'm not man shopping. I refuse to be one of those women who aren't happy without some guy in her life. Look what things were like with Donald.

Longfellow came into the kitchen and spotted Brad. Isabelle thought he would turn away, but instead he sauntered up to him.

And Longie gives him his seal of approval, too.

"Who is this?" Brad said.

"Longfellow. The cat that owns me."

Brad laughed. "Isn't that the way of things? I have a chocolate lab and three cats."

She handed him the glass of tea. "What are their names?"

"The lab's Hershey." He lifted his empty hand. "I know, don't laugh. It seemed cute at the time. We call him Hirsch. The cats are Larry, Moe and Curly. And yes, I'm a Three Stooges fan."

Isabelle smiled. Dogs. Cats. Good-looking and American. What more do I need? That is if I were looking. The image of Cristiano slipped into her mind and she shoved it away. "Which movie's your favorite?"

"I like *The Three Stooges Meet Hercules.*"

"A good one. But I'm more into Abbot and Costello."

"They're good, too, but lack comic timing in my opinion."

"It seems they've had everything chasing them, even a ghost..." Isabelle stopped, the word hung between them. "The girl on the island..." Her words trailed away. How was she going to handle this?

"I have a better photo of her." Brad reached into his shirt pocket, pulled out a picture and held it toward her. "It was taken the morning we went out on the boat."

The photo showed a smiling young woman with blue eyes, long braided blonde hair and a thin pretty face. She wore thigh-length white shorts over a one piece tropical-print swim suit.

"Is this who you saw? She wouldn't be dressed the same, but…"

Isabelle looked into his face. "She wasn't wearing the shorts, but it's her."

Brad swayed and she grabbed his arm.

"Sit down."

He let her guide him to a chair, then dropped into it. He shook his head. "How can she still be alive? It's been three years…where has she been? Why hasn't she called me?"

Isabelle stared into his stunned face. How was she going to drop this news on him? If she hadn't seen the woman…watched her disappear right in front of her.. There wasn't any right way. "Brad, she isn't alive."

He lifted his head, looked into her face. "What do you mean? You said you saw her."

"I did. I spoke to her."

"Then what are you saying?"

"Think about it. You looked for her, right? The police did, too." Isabelle stood and picked up his glass. "The girl I saw is the girl in this photo. She wore this bathing suit. Her hair was long and blonde, her face bruised." Isabelle turned toward him. Just say it. "Patricia is dead. But she's still waiting for you to come get her."

Chapter Fifteen

Magdalena lay curled on her bed, a pillow hugged to her chest. Mira snuggled against her. She opened her eyes slowly. *I wonder if it will work…*

"Andres, " she called, "bring me tea, will you? Not the manzanillo. I've rested enough, some of the black tea I think."

He walked into her room with a book in his hand. "How are you feeling, dear? You've only slept a couple of hours."

"Well enough, well enough. Please bring three piñon logs in, will you?"

"Certainly, Grandmother."

A breeze brought sounds of the sea into the room, a brush of air with a salty breath. He turned in the doorway, "I'll fix the tea first, then get the wood." He paused, then added, "You only use the piñon for, uh, special times. Is this one of those?"

"Si, I believe this will be a very special time tonight," she said.

"But Abuelita, so soon after the island?"

"It must be soon. Please bring the tea, then the wood."

With a troubled frown, Andres turned away.

Magdalena sat up, whispered to Mira, then rose from the bed and walked across the room. She opened the cabinet where she kept her herbs, reached in the very back and brought out a small blue jar.

Magdalena shook her head. *Patricia must move on. She grows stronger with her anger. How am I to get her to do so? What will it take? I must find out.* She opened the jar, pinched a bit of the contents between thumb and forefinger and placed it under her tongue. The herb's warmth and bitter strength twined through her and she shuddered.

Andres knocked twice and came in with a tray.

"Ah, graciás. Will you be able to stay the night, to tend the fire for me?"

He moved across the room and sat the tray next to the basket. "But of course, Grandmother. Are you feeling well enough…?"

"I am quite well, perhaps a little chilled."

"Well, if you must do this tonight…I'll make a call after I bring the piñon in. Maybe I'll fix a little caldo for us later."

Andres turned away with a deep sigh. "I'll get the wood."

Magdalena walked into the living room. A sudden need to connect with those of her blood, both living and the ones who'd gone ahead, moved through her, and she turned to face the family pictures.

Their faces, both laughing and serene, filled a wall, the oldest at the top of the pyramid. The current generation of children began at waist level. *How many more will be added before it is my turn to go beyond?*

Andres returned with an armful of wood and placed it into the firebox.

"A little more kindling, please," Magdalena said as he walked into the living room. She arranged a blanket on the floor beside her basket. In front of the fireplace, candles and incense sat on the hearth. She lit the candles as Andres returned. "Do not worry. All will be well."

He crossed the room and put the wood next to the tub. He sat on the hearth and leaned toward her, his forearms on his thighs.

"I want you to remain in the sewing room," Magdalena said. "Take a book with you; keep an eye on the fire. Do not come to me. Do not speak, no matter what you hear."

"Grandmother, are you sure…?"

"Andres, you're not arguing with me, are you?" She turned to him, her hands on her hips. "Now, I must bathe. You fix your caldo. By sundown, I must be prepared. Vamanos. Go on now and stop your fussing."

Magdalena sat on the edge of the steaming tub. She unbraided her hair, tossed in a handful of dried lavender, then lowered herself into the fragrant water.

She floated in silence, her hair streaming around her.

The blue hues of the bathroom split and coalesced, wavered in the steam and candlelight until the room resembled a grotto. She smiled at the faint clicks and trills of the dolphins that surrounded her.

Magdalena's body became light and seemed to dissolve into the water.

She rolled, flipped her dolphin tail; saw a small boat with three people in it, Isla Santa Maria in the background. She recognized the light haired woman as Patricia Mullins, the man was Brad Collins, and the smaller dark-haired woman his sister.

The gray sky and sea were one. The wind blurred the line between water and air. Swirling spray coated the faces of the three in the small boat as it tossed and spun upon the violent sea. A towering wave swamped them and they took on water.

In the middle of the boat, Brad's sister suddenly stood and moved toward him where he struggled with the tiller. He yelled, motioned for her to sit down.

The boat turned parallel to the waves, and the next one flipped it.

None of the three wore a life vest.

Magdalena watched them fight the sea.

Brad yelled and waved at the women.

Patricia swam strongly toward him, grabbed onto a piece of the hull.

"Hold on, Patricia, hold on. I've got to help Amy."

A wind-whipped wave flooded over his floundering sister and with her white face frozen in a rictus of terror, she sank into the ocean.

"Hold on." Magdalena heard him scream to Patricia. "Stay with the boat." And he struck out to where Amy disappeared.

Magdalena and her dolphin sisters watched as Brad dove time and again calling and searching.

Patricia clung to the wreckage, white faced and struggling in the chill water.

Magdalena's sisters' trills alerted her to an approaching shrimp boat. She felt Brad's hopes rise when he spotted the shrimper.

"Hold on Patricia," he screamed. "Help is coming. Hold on."

The boat angled away.

"No. No," he screamed. "I have to get closer to them. Wait for me. Wait for me. I'll come back for you. I'll come back."

The currents moved him toward the shrimper. *No. I'll never make it...*

A sleek gray form leapt from the water in front of him. Shark, his mind screamed, and he kicked out. The form jumped, trilled at him. No, not shark. Dolphin. He grabbed for the dorsal fin and held on as the dolphin towed him toward the shrimper.

More dolphins danced on their tails as men's voices cried out. A life-ring landed near him and he grabbed it.

Magdalena's heart beat with joy as the pescaderos stole Brad from the hungry sea, and then chilled with pain as she watched the bowline from the shattered boat entangle Patricia's legs and pull her down in a death spiral. The dolphins leapt and cried out their distress.

Chapter Sixteen

Brad stared at Isabelle as if she'd sprouted green scales and a pointed tail. "Excuse me? She's dead? But she's waiting for me?" His gaze shifted to the door.

He's looking for an escape route from the ghost-spouting whacko, Isabelle thought with a small smile. I can't blame him for that. "I know. I didn't believe it either. I saw her, talked to her and she faded to nothing right in front of me."

"Miss Allen…"

Uh oh, we're back to being formal.

"Brad, can you keep an open mind?"

He shook his head and stood.

Okay. Time to use a different tactic. "Can you walk away without knowing for sure? Maybe I'm not crazy. Maybe I'm right? And the woman you love is a spirit, trapped here? What if you are the only one who can help her find peace? Can it hurt to see i? Hey, I'm not going to kill you and drop your body overboard."

Brad did smile at hearing those words. "Isabelle, I don't believe in ghosts."

Well, good at least we're back to first names. "I didn't either. I'm not from Missouri, but this was one time I had to be shown…"

"And you were?" His tone was skeptical, but she heard something else, a resonance of hope and curiosity.

"I was."

"What do you want me to do?"

That stumped her. She didn't have the slightest idea. Would they have to go to Isla Santa Maria, or could they draw Patricia to this beach? And, dang, did it have to be at night again? She hoped not. "Magdalena will know." Isabelle said the words with more confidence than she felt.

"When?" Brad said.

She glanced at the clock. It was six o'clock. They could go to Magdalena. Isabelle cringed at the thought. She didn't want another dose of ghost-encountering. Isabelle knew she was making excuses, but.... "Tomorrow some time. I'll call you."

"Okay." He stood. "What about tonight? Do you have plans?"

She shook her head.

"Would you like to go into San Felipe with me?"

Isabelle shuddered at the thought of the bone-jarring three-hour ride. "I should stay with Sammi and Longie."

"We'd take my helicopter. Sixty minutes in, some dinner and then back. A couple hours at the most. I could use the company and you can tell me more about seeing Patricia."

A helicopter. She had never been in one and she had always wanted to see what it was like.

"I should be prepared, don't you think?" Brad said. "After all...a ghost..."

"Okay. I'll go. What did you have in mind? Fancy or local color?"

"A carnitas burrito and a fantastic margarita. That's what I want."

Isabelle smiled. "I know just the spot, Casa de la Playa. It's a jeans and t-shirt place and you can't beat the food."

Brad stood. "Great. Then you won't need to change. How about we leave in twenty minutes or so? I'll head back. Tell the Gustafsons our plans. You okay with meeting me at the helicopter? It's behind their place."

"Sure. That's fine."

He scratched behind Longie's ears, patted Sammi's head and turned toward the door. "Twenty minutes. I'll see you then."

Isabelle nodded as he walked to the door.

She liked this Brad Collins. She liked him a lot.

Brad came around the corner of the Gustafson's house.

"Isabelle. Right on time. Come on, I'm all ready for you." He held out his hand and she grasped it.

The helicopter sat some yards from the Gustafsons' back door. It was small, all red and chrome. "Wow. She's beautiful." Isabelle looked at Brad. "Do you call helicopters *she* like you do boats?"

"I don't know." He walked to the helicopter and opened the door. In the back was a long, white leather bench seat. Two more seats were in the front. The seat on the left faced a dashboard full of gauges. There wasn't a steering wheel instead there was a curved bar like an arcade game's joy-stick. In front of the seat were two foot pedals.

"Watch your head," Brad said as she climbed aboard.

Isabelle settled down into the right seat and strapped herself in.

Brad climbed into the pilot's seat and reached for a headset. "There's one beside you. Put it on or we won't be able to talk."

Isabelle did and heard his voice, a little tinny now, coming into her ears.

"She trembles a little when we first go up, but then she'll smooth out."

She nodded, then realized he couldn't see her and said. "Got yah."

"Why don't we take a swing out over Isla Santa Maria. You can show me the beach where you first saw Patricia."

Was he starting to come around, or was he humoring her? "Sure."

Isabelle felt the helicopter come to life. It hummed beneath her, vibrations going up her spine.

"Okay, we're going up."

The ground fell away. Her heart pounded. They rose higher, and Isabelle felt her stomach drop to her toes, then everything smoothed out and she looked through the window. Her mouth dropped open in awe. With all the glass, it was as if they were floating in a bubble. This must be what Glenda-the-Good-Witch felt like when she dropped in to visit the munchkins.

The scenery below changed; first sand, then the expanse of ocean. The Sea of Cortez flowed different shades of blue, some dark, some light. The pangas looked like colorful pea pods. As the sun set, the sky lit up in breathtaking rays and arcs of color. A true vermilion twilight.

Chapter Seventeen

Magdalena stretched in her bath and opened her eyes. The lavender scent grounded her, welcomed her back home. She rose from the tub, reached for the towel and wrapped it around her.

The sight of Patricia, ensnared by the rope and being pulled down made her heart ache. The sound of the dolphins, clicking and vocalizing their distress as they circled the down spiraling woman, still buzzed in her ears. She shuddered and lit a small candle and sent up a prayer for the lost ones.

Andres stood as she walked into the front room. She shook her head in warning and continued to the west-facing patio.

As the sunset flared over Pico San Miguel, Magdalena lit a stalk of sage. The smoke circled and she chanted softly in the vermilion light.

Time pulsed and she was once again in the grotto.

Ascending trills and clicks swirled. She floated, moved with the churn of the sea, her senses tuned to the watery cave and the ones nearby. She rolled and stretched toward the surface. Her dolphin sisters surrounded her, their words came into her mind.

Magdalena, blessed daughter. You are, as we, only messengers. The Lost One's love must find and release her.

She swam with her sisters to the small beach at the back of the cave. The spell deepened. She felt her body begin to change. Human once more, she rose to her hands and knees, then stood.

Magdalena walked toward the rear of the small cave, the dark sand warm beneath her feet. The lava tuff formed deep striations and curved overhead to form a domed ceiling. She turned and faced the sea. The dolphins swam in slow circles before her in the deep green water.

Their voices rang in her mind.

The Lost One's anger feeds upon itself. She is frustrated, is becoming more powerful. The girl does not accept her death. Your power threatens her, for messengers do not always deliver welcome news.

Magdalena nodded.

And Sister..there must be five. For the Lost One to leave this world, not three, but five.

Why five?

Five, the number required for change and freedom.

Then five. Si, but, who are the other two?

They are the Fire-Child's other hearts.

I don't understand... .

The air in the small cave shimmered in waves and Magdalena felt the temperature increase. At the same moment, sand fell from overhead and she heard a deep groaning. Small pieces of pumice bounced off her shoulders and as the temperature grew the smell of sulfur reached her nose.

The dolphins circled faster, crying out their alarm.

The cave began to shake and grind as Magdalena ran to the shore and dove into the water.

Chapter Eighteen

You okay?" Brad's words came into Isabelle's ears through the headset.

"I love this. How hard is it to learn to fly?"

Brad laughed. "You're hooked, huh?" The helicopter angled left. "Is that Isla Santa Maria?"

"Yes. That's the one."

*****

Patricia stood on the beach, letting the waves flow over, then recede from her bare feet. Her arms quivered with a sudden chill. Would she ever feel warm again? She heard the low, whomp, whomp, whomp, of a helicopter and glanced upward. Who was it? Could she make them fear, provide her the warmth she craved?

Her body went still as she absorbed the flow of energy from the two above. Then she laughed.

"It's Isabelle…and…what is this? It's my love, my Bradley. She has brought him to me!" Patricia ran to stand in the middle of the beach. "I'm here. I'm here. I stayed. I waited as I promised." She lifted her hands out to her sides and spun in a circle. "He's here. He's here."

She felt for them again. "No." Patricia let her hands drop. "He does not think of me." She narrowed her eyes. "He thinks of her. And she…Isabelle…thinks of him."

Patricia curled her hands into fists. "They are going to San Felipe, to eat, to drink margaritas."

The sand beneath her feet shifted. "They will be warm. He wants to touch her." In the sea, water rose, formed a whirling spout.

"Isabelle, you have betrayed me again. First the old woman.... No. You will not have him!"

*****

Suddenly the helicopter dropped, rose, then dropped again.

Isabelle watched Brad struggle with the controls. "What's happening?"

"Rough air." Brad's strained voice came to her ears. "It came out of nowhere. Tighten your seatbelt."

Her stomach dove and rose, matching the roller-coaster ride they were on bump for bump.

She looked down. They were directly over Isla Santa Maria. A sudden wave of hate made her gasp and her vision wavered. "Get us away from the island."

"I'm taking us higher."

"Get us away from her."

"Her? What are you talking about?"

Isabelle's stomach sank into her shoes again. "Get us away from the island."

"Okay. Okay."

Isla Santa Maria grew smaller beneath them. The helicopter angled to the left and the island disappeared from sight.

Their ride smoothed out.

"What the hell?" Brad said.

Isabelle shook her head. "What was I thinking? I've made everything worse."

"I don't know what you're talking about," Brad said and she heard the exasperation in his voice.

"Patricia was the jealous type, right? Of course we pissed her off, us together. She probably thought...."

Brad turned his head, glanced at her, then faced front again. "She was a little possessive, but...wait I get it...you're back to the ghost bit."

"Over the island, that was her...."

"No. It wasn't." He spoke slow, emphasized each word. "It was some rough air. Didn't you say there was a volcanic vent there?"

"Yes, but...."

"The hot air caused turbulence, not some angry spirit." He looked at her again, grinned. "Now what makes the most sense? I'm the pilot, remember? I know rough air when I feel it."

It could have been the volcano. But what about the blast of hate? Did she imagine it? No matter, Brad wasn't ready yet to believe in Patricia as a spirit. Like her, he would have to be shown. But that could wait until tomorrow. Tonight she was going to relax and have some fun.

Outside the front entrance of the airport, Brad waved a taxi toward them.

On the six-mile ride into San Felipe he chatted about the airport facilities. Isabelle smiled, made appropriate comments and brooded.

How strong is Patricia if she messed with us in the air?

*****

As the light on the sea began to fade the taxi from the airport dropped them in front of Casa de la Playa.

165

"Here we are. I've got pesos." She paid the driver, then turned to Brad. "What do you think of the mural?"

Christmas lights over the arched door of the restaurant highlighted a playful scene; whimsical piggies with pointed hats and chickens in shorts with suspenders played guitars and flutes and danced alongside pink giraffes and purple hippos.

They stood a moment and watched the scene along the street. Children ran and couples strolled. Lovers leaned into one another as they sat on the sea wall next to the sidewalk. Cars moved along the one-way street with windows down.

On the beach side of the sea wall, pangas rested on the sand. The fishermen would be in Casa de la Playa having a cerveza or two before heading home. Musicians serenaded the crowd, their words floating above the sea's own rhythmic beat.

"You ready to go in?" Isabelle said.

Brad nodded.

Casa de la Playa was standing room only. The buzz of conversation flowed over them. Isabelle tugged on Brad's arm. He lowered his ear to her lips. "There's a patio out back. Follow me."

Isabelle wound a path through the tables and bodies.

Dark eyes, flashing white teeth and greetings of, "Hola," followed them.

She saw a waitress and angled toward her. "We're heading to the patio."

The waitress smiled her acknowledgment and Isabelle and Brad continued toward the arched rear door.

A sea breeze greeted them as they walked onto the patio. Patrons moved among the tables and plants. A beehive fireplace with a griddle and wide hearth provided warmth. A woman made fresh tortillas and waiters carried full baskets of them to tables.

A couple stood, left an empty table close to the low stone wall at the edge of the sand patio. Isabelle tugged on Brad's hand, pointed toward it. He nodded and took the lead, plowing the way.

They settled into their seats. White lights wound around potted cactus and a million stars were the only illumination. Above the voices and laughter Isabelle heard the ocean's bass voice. "Look," she said and pointed. Lights bobbed on the dark waves like hovering fireflies. "Yachts. San Felipe is becoming less of a secret each year."

A man sauntered by wearing cut-offs, t-shirt and purple flip-flops.

A frazzled looking, but still smiling, waitress appeared at Isabelle's shoulder.

"Two carnitas burritos with guacamole, and two margaritas on the rocks, no salt," Brad ordered.

"Bueno," she said, and hurried away.

Brad took a deep breath. "I love the smell of the sea. Maybe we can take a walk later."

"Sure. Here or back on our beach?"

He reached across the table, took her hand. "Why not both?"

She smiled without answering and twined her fingers with his.

The waitress returned with their drinks, a basket of still warm tortilla chips and a bowl of salsa.

"Graciás," Brad said, releasing Isabelle's hand.

The margaritas were icy. Isabelle plucked lime from the rim of her glass, gave it a squeeze, then took a drink.

Brad grabbed a chip, dipped it into the salsa. She watched his eyes water as he chewed. " Perfecto."

Isabelle shook her head. The fiery local salsa was not for her.

Brad took a drink of his margarita. "This is my one and only. But you have as many as you like."

"What? Just one," she teased. Her stomach felt warm and her head light.

"Darn right. One's my limit when I'm flying."

"Smart man." Isabelle smeared the top of her burrito with guacamole and dug in.

Halfway through their dinner, the waitress appeared again.

Brad asked for the check. As soon as the waitress departed, Isabelle pushed her chair back. "I need the rest room."

He nodded.

Inside the doorway she stood for a moment getting her bearings. She swept her eyes over a couple in an intimate corner, then jerked her head back. No. Her heart cried in pained shock. She was wrong. It couldn't be. It was the play of light. But her eyes didn't lie.

Cristiano leaned toward a beautiful young woman. He touched her hand; she ran her fingers along his cheek. Isabelle's stomach rolled. She spun around, walked back to their table.

Brad looked up. "What is it?"

"Long line. How about that walk on the beach?"

"Sure." He laid pesos atop their bill and stood.

At the end of the patio, three steps led down to the sand. Isabelle kicked off her shoes, bent to pick them up. The sand felt warm on her bare feet, but inside she felt like ice.

"You're shivering and stupid me didn't bring a jacket."

"No. I'm fine." Isabelle knew a sub-arctic parka wouldn't ease the chill she felt. She grabbed his hand. "Let's walk."

Casa de la Playa was behind them and the sea kissing her toes before she could take a pain-free breath.

It's for the best. There isn't any future for Cristiano and me. I'll be going back to my life in San Francisco. I have friends there, a house.

Isabelle stared across the dark sea to the bobbing lights and blinked back tears. She just seemed unlucky where love was involved.

Love? Who'd said anything about love? I don't love Cristiano. We've just met.

Her thoughts made her stumble and Brad pulled her closer against his side. "You okay? You've been quiet since we left the restaurant."

"It's been a long day."

"You want to head back?"

"Yes, I think I do.

*****

Isabelle opened the door and let Sammi out. Brad reached to pat her head and the basset hound wiggled with joy. "Let me check Longie, grab the leash, and a potty bag."

Inside she took a moment to draw in two, deep, ragged breaths. Why does it hurt so much? I've only known Cristiano for three days.

Longie jumped from his spot on the window sill and wound around her legs. "Yeah, I'm home. I'm giving Sammi a quick walk." She picked up the leash and a plastic bag and headed to the door. Isabelle clipped

Sammi's leash on. The moon shone bright, casting a sliver glow upon sand and water.

"I enjoyed tonight," Brad said.

"Yes, Casa de la Playa has never disappointed me." *Not until tonight. I don't know if I'll ever be able to go there again.* Sammi stopped to sniff a shell.

Brad faced the sea. "Is that Isla Santa Maria?" He pointed.

"That's it."

He looked like he was going to say more, then stopped and stared at the dark island.

What's he thinking? She noticed he gave the island a wide berth on their return flight. She felt a wave of exhaustion and stumbled.

Brad reached for her arm, steadied her with a grin. "Whoa, too many margaritas?"

Too much of something, she thought, before saying, "The last couple of days have been a challenge."

He looked into her eyes for a moment and then yawned. "Yeah, I could use some shut-eye too."

Isabelle glanced at Sammi who had finally decided to take care of business. "Why don't you head on to the Gustafsons. I've got to clean up after Sammi, then I'm to bed."

Brad took both of her hands into his. "I enjoyed our dinner. I'd like to get to know you better."

Know me better? But it had been three years since Patricia's death.

Saying good-bye at the front door. It never ceased to be awkward. She hadn't really expected it tonight though. Hadn't thought of this as being a date. *Brad's letting me make the choice. Do we kiss or not?* There hadn't been a

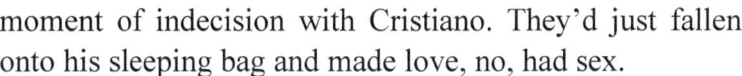

moment of indecision with Cristiano. They'd just fallen onto his sleeping bag and made love, no, had sex.

She pushed the thoughts away. Cristiano wasn't a part of her future.

"I think I'd like to get to know you better also."

She didn't resist when Brad pulled her close. She shut her eyes as his head lowered toward her. His lips were warm. Isabelle dropped Sammi's leash, reached around Brad's waist and pulled him closer. Their kiss deepened. She felt his hands settle on her hips. Warm pleasure moved from her toes upward. Isabelle felt his arousal against her stomach. It would be so easy to let her body react, maybe blot out the image of Cristiano and the woman in the dark corner of the cantina. No. She wasn't being fair to Brad. She stepped back, ended the kiss.

"Can I call you tomorrow?" she asked. "After I talk with Magdalena."

Brad looked puzzled and her face warmed. Isabelle understood. She'd gone from sizzle to let's shake hands and be friends in less than a minute, but damn, using him wasn't right.

"Sure you can," he said. "Well, goodnight."

"Goodnight, Brad. Thanks for the helicopter ride."

He smiled. "Anytime. I'll see you in the morning. Maybe next time we can have breakfast together?"

Isabelle knew what he was asking. "Maybe."

He turned, walked away.

Sammi had taken advantage of the dropped leash and wandered down the beach. Isabelle whistled and slapped her leg. The basset hound looked up, dropped her nose to the sand.

"Sammi, I'm not in the mood...." She swallowed, blinked and let the tears come.

The off shore island, the stars, and the moon, blurred. Just get it, him, out of your system. It's not the first time you've trusted and been cut off at the knees.

She wiped tears from her cheeks. No. Not the first time, but it will be the last.

She heard a soft whine and looked down. Sammi-Sue, beside her, stared up, her brown eyes concerned. "It's okay, princess. Come on, it's bed time."

The phone rang as the two of them came into the house.

"Hello."

"Izzy, I've been missing you terribly."

Her friend's words made the tears start again. She choked out, "Sharlee?"

"What is it? Did someone die?"

"It's so good to hear your voice."

"No one died? Then who is he? And what did he do to you?"

She heard instant protectiveness in Sharlee's voice "How's everything with you?"

"I'm in San Felipe.

"Sharlee, I'm here for some alone time."

"I'll be there in the morning.

"Sharlee."

But the phone clicked, and all she heard was dial tone.

Chapter Nineteen

Magdalena opened her eyes. "Andres?" She lay in his arms in front of the fireplace.

"Grandmother, you are back."

"What in the world are you talking about?" She sat up, then wiped perspiration from her upper lip.

"You've been asleep for a long while. Are you all right?"

"I'm fine. What time is it?"

"It's morning, nearly nine thirty."

"Then the caldo must be ready." She let him help her up.

Mira stretched and rearranged her tail, her eyes on Magdalena.

"It is ready, Grandmother. May I prepare a tray for you?"

"You may, and some tortillas as well. Then you will go to Isabelle and bring her to me. We must talk."

"Of course, at once," Andres said, as he moved toward the kitchen.

Sammi-Sue's bark jerked Isabelle from sleep. "What? What is it?" She sat up and glared at the hopping basset hound. Someone pounded on the door. She glanced at the bedside clock. It was nine forty-five. She'd been asleep all of six hours. Oblivion was hard to come by when your damn mind wouldn't shut off.

"Okay. Okay, I'm coming," she muttered as she kicked the comforter aside.

Isabelle grabbed her robe as she passed the chair, slipped her arms into it as she stumbled to the front door. "Who is it?"

"I brought sticky buns," Sharlee's voice answered.

Isabelle opened the door. Sharlee stood there looking fresh as spring in green walking shorts and a flower-print camp shirt. Her short-cropped auburn hair clung to her forehead and cheeks. Isabelle felt her eyebrows rise at sight of the spiral-craved, abalone pendant around Sharlee's neck. It wasn't a new piece, Sharlee wore it alot, but with everything that had happened with Magdalena....

"You got an early start this morning." Isabelle said while, between them, Sammi-Sue squirmed in joy.

"First things first." Sharlee thrust a grease splotched bag at Isabelle, then squatted to basset hound eye level. "Yeah, princess, it's great to see you, too. Where's Longie?"

As if her words had conjured him, Longfellow bounded from the kitchen in a very un-cat-like style and stopped before Sharlee.

"Well, there's our Longie. How are you, baby?" The cat rubbed against Sharlee's bare ankles.

"Get in here," Isabelle said. "I've been out voted, even if I had planned to shut the door in your face."

"Got coffee?"

"I will have." She led the way to the kitchen.

Isabelle started the coffee while Sharlee scratched behind first Longie and then Sammi's ears.

"So what's new?" Isabelle said.

Sharlee glanced at her. "You haven't been gone that long."

Isabelle sighed. "It seems like weeks, instead of days." She removed two plates from the cupboard and placed one sticky bun on each.

"They're not warm now," Sharlee said. "But the first one I had was and it was to die for."

She looked at her friend's trim figure. She never could figure out how Sharlee indulged her sweet tooth and never gained an ounce.

She poured two cups of coffee and carried them to the table.

"Okay Sugar, now tell me why y'all were cry'n last night." Her tone was casual, but Sharlee's southern drawl had kicked in, a sure sign her friend was upset.

Isabelle bit into a sticky bun, chewed, played for time, then washed it down with coffee. "These are great. Did you get them at Chala's?"

Sharlee nodded. Waited. Her eyes on Isabelle's face.

"It's complicated."

Her friend laughed. "How complicated can it be? You've only been here four days."

"You tell me."

She gave Sharlee an abridged accounting of everything that had occurred. Her disastrous swim - well, the first one - meeting Cristiano, Magdalena's birthday party, Carl, another swim, the island, Cristiano again, sex, the girl, another trip to the island, Patricia the ghost.

Sharlee stopped her.

"Say what? The girl you saw on the island after whoopee is a ghost?"

175

"Yes, a ghost. Patricia Mullins, killed in a boat accident three years ago. Brad Collins was her fiancé. I went into San Felipe with him last night."

That was her friend. Everything else became milquetoast at the mere mention of a ghost. Sharlee's easy acceptance of the supernatural was a balm to Isabelle's bruised spirit.

"A ghost? You spoke to a ghost. What's it like? Did she look real? Well, of course, she did. You thought she was alive when you saw her. Do you think you'll see her again?"

"Slow down. She tried to make Brad's helicopter crash…"

Sharlee's eyebrows shot up. "Excuse me? You left that part out."

"I was getting to it." Isabelle told her the rest of the story, about Cristiano and the woman at Casa de la Playa.

"Well, that Cristiano's a real bastard." Sharlee pushed the plate with half of her sticky bun still on it toward Isabelle. "You have this, hon."

Isabelle shook her head. She wouldn't have been able to get the roll past the lump in her throat. She stood, grabbed her still half-full cup and moved to the coffee pot, stood for a moment blinking back tears, then swallowed and said. "Need a warm-up?"

"No. I'm fine. But you're not, huh?

Isabelle turned, forced a smile. "I will be. It's all been…not what I planned on."

Sharlee laughed. "Well that's for sure. Have you done any weaving?"

"I haven't even completed the sketch."

Someone knocked on the front door and both women turned.

"Could that be Cristiano?" Sharlee said. "You want me to answer it?"

"God, no. It's a little early for bloodshed." Against her will, hope rose. Maybe it is Cristiano. Maybe he had an explanation... . No. She wasn't going there. She'd had one cheater in her life. There wouldn't be another.

She walked to the door. "Yes," she said without opening it.

"Izzy, it's Andres. Grandmother wants you and Brad Collins right away at her casa."

Chapter Twenty

Magdalena sat on her patio with Mira and her morning coffee. The sun bathed her face in welcome.

She and her father had built the patio before they began the house. They camped there often while construction went on. The east, north and west walls were low and allowed views to the sea and mountains. Stucco covered the adobe brick in subdued desert colors and the walls flowed, formed benches, niches, and small planters. Three cordon cactus anchored the northwest corner and a large palo verde tree, the northeast. A fountain resembled the Aztec pyramids; a fire pit with grill space balanced fire and water elements.

Shortly, Andres would bring Isabelle here, they would talk.

"Ah, Mira," she said, "these are tiring days, no?" The cat twitched an ear in Magdalena's direction. "I thought the players were all in place; myself, the spirit discovered by our fire-child, Isabelle. But the sea-sisters say there are two more. Five hearts altogether. The number signifies evolution, Mira. Appropriate, yes? Cristiano is the third, Isabelle's second heart, even though he does not know it yet. But who are the fourth and fifth?"

Magdalena stood and stretched, walked to the canterra stone dolphin statue and ran her hand along the curved form.

She turned, saluted the sun and hummed her morning gratitudes.

She looked again at Mira, picked up her cup of tea. "Yes, we'll go to the island once more, unless our island decides to come and visit us, eh? You feel it too, don't you? The ocean is warmer; the desert floor ripples like the sea at times. Ah, well...."

Magdalena set her cup on a small tile table. "Of course we could talk with Cristiano, see what his scientific mind can tell us about the volcano. But these days he seems more involved with his heart than the volcano."

She reached to stroke Mira, and at that moment felt and heard again, the same grinding, disorienting movement, she had experienced in the grotto.

Magdalena swayed, as Mira, ears flat against her skull, crouched and growled. A pot decorated with spirals fell from the table, scattering soil and leaves across the patio tiles. A gust of wind brought a sulfur breath.

"Calm, Patricia. Our concern is for you."

A spiral, thick with the acrid smell and gritty with sand and shards of the broken pot, formed above the patio tiles.

Magdalena shielded her eyes with her hands and put her head down as the whirlwind advanced. She lurched toward the palo verde tree that grew near the wall of the patio, but before she could reach its safety, the wind gusted and changed the tree into a sharp-edged menace.

Her knees gave out and she dropped to the tiles.

Mira growled a challenge as she sprang forward, crouched in front of Magdalena. The cat slashed at the air with her claws.

"Dios, Patricia. I don't understand, where does your anger come from?"

A gust of wind tipped the carved canterra stone dolphin from its base. It crashed to the tile, narrowly missed the furious cat. As quick as it arrived, the wind disappeared. Sand drifted onto the tile and the patio became quiet.

Magdalena stood and on legs that shook moved to the bench near the fountain and sat. She touched her cheeks where the whirling sand had struck, dipped her hands into the water and splashed it upon her face. The patio wavered and she took deep calming breaths.

Her faintness slowly subsided.

Magdalena stared toward Isla Santa Maria. "I understand. For now it is yours, but this is my home. You will not come here again. My sisters and I will see to it."

She heard Andres' Jeep arrive. Magdalena stood, smoothed her dress. She walked into the house, to the front door and opened it. "Come in, come in."

Isabelle stood next to a young woman. "Magdalena, this is my best friend in all of the world, Sharlee."

"Si. I understand. Isabelle's third heart. Four are here, yet there must be five."

"What?" Isabelle said.

Magdalena smiled."Welcome, señorita."

"I'd have been here earlier if I'd known about Patricia," Sharlee said.

Isabelle looked from Magdalena's face to her friend's and back again. "Say what?"

180

Magdalena took Sharlee's hands. "You are no stranger to the other side. I feel it."

"I inherited some physic ability from my father's mother."

Isabelle stared at her in surprise. "I didn't know that."

"The three become four." Magdalena nodded.

Magdalena watched a man approach. She knew him at once - Patricia's lost love and the fifth that was needed. The circle was complete. "Señor Collins. It has been a long time. I did not know you had returned to our beach. Welcome to my casa."

"Graciás, señora." Brad took Magdalena's hand. "It's good to see you again, too. Isabelle's caught me up on everything that's happened. It's quite a story."

"Come, let us sit here near the fire." Magdalena gestured Andres to her side. "Will you bring a tray, perhaps coffee and some of the old brandy?"

When they were settled, Magdalena came straight to the point. "Señor, not just a tale. It is the spirit of Señorita Mullins we have encountered. There are many things under the sun which we do not understand but must still accept. Si?"

"With respect, Señora, I'm not sure I'm buying it. Even if—and I repeat if—the ghost, or spirit, or energy of Patricia is near this area, why has she waited until now? Why not last year or the year before?"

Magdalena shook her head. "I am not sure, but I believe it's because of her interest in Isabelle."

"Me? What does all of this have to do with me?"

"We must ask Patricia that question," Magdalena said.

Brad shook his head.

"I know it sounds crazy," Isabelle said. "I wasn't about to accept a ghost either, not until I saw Patricia fade away in front of my eyes. And after what happened as we flew over the island, I'm..." she broke off as Andres approached with the tray.

"What? What over the island?" Andres insisted as he handed out mugs of coffee and began to pour brandy.

"It was a little low pressure area over the island, pushed us around a bit, that's all." Brad took his coffee from Andres and leaned back into the sofa.

Andres and Magdalena exchanged glances over the tray.

"Tell us what happened," Andres said.

"It was no big deal, just a little rough air, I tell you."

"Brad, there's more to it." Isabelle turned to Magdalena. "I felt the same thing on the island the night our boat disappeared into the fog. Andres, what about the huge waves and the landslide when you and Cristiano came out? Didn't you feel it? A kind of heaviness to the air, time slowing, and a blast of hate. " Isabelle stopped and looked away."Yes, that's it all right," Sharlee said. "You've been in the midst of psychic energy, but the animosity you felt concerns me."

Brad glanced at her and smiled. "So you've seen ghosts also?"Magdalena watched the young woman bristle, but Sharlee's tone remained calm as she answered. "I've not been so honored, but maybe this time..."

Brad shook his head

Magdalena put her hand on Isabelle's shoulder. "I know in my soul, Señor, the girl who was never found is here, on this beach, as well as on the Isla Santa Maria." Magdalena sipped brandy, then turned to glance at the patio. "Her essence does not accept the death of the body. Patricia's frustration and anger grows."

The five sat in silence for a long moment.

Andres spoke. "Grandmother, you're not saying we're in danger here in the campo, are you?"

"When I last visited the island with my dolphin sisters, I felt a presence. Then the mountain began to move."

"Now, wait a minute," Brad put his coffee mug on the table. "You can't tell me a spirit or ghost or whatever, can manipulate a volcano. That's too much."

"Señor, there are things I can tell you, many things that will challenge your imagination and your sense of reality. But it would be far better for you to see and know for yourself."

"Brad," Isabelle said. "Instead of fighting these ideas it would be best to simply let go of what you think you know, and accept. Not easy to do. I know it sure as hell wasn't easy for me, but it's worth a try." A frown formed upon her forehead. "Magdalena, you said earlier there must be five. What did you mean? I thought it was you, Patricia and myself."

"My dolphin sisters have shown me." She looked down at her hands. "It was never the three of us. I was arrogant. On Isla Santa Maria when I formed the spiral the stones shifted, left space for three more… Señor Collins, Cristiano and this one." She nodded toward Sharlee. "The final stones of the spiral must be placed by all of us, not just myself."

Isabelle surged to her feet. "Then I guess Patricia won't ever be free," she said. "Cristiano won't agree to any of this. He was furious about our last trip to the island."

"It will not be at the island. It will be here. We are going to a small cove just beyond the next point."Why not here on our beach?" Isabelle said.

Andres reached toward Magdalena. "What has happened, Grandmother?"

She told them what occurred on the patio.

Absolute quiet followed her words. Magdalena faced Brad. "Señor, earlier you asked what it means if the spirit of Señorita Mullins is still here. She is trapped. Her spirit will never go on."

Brad stared for a long time into Magdalena's face. "Well, then I guess we better do what you think needs to be done. It can't hurt one way or the other. How do we begin?"

"We will walk the spiral. The cove is safe, but I will make it safer."

"Does it have to be at one in the morning, like last time," Isabelle asked.

"We will do it today…in the sunlight."

Sharlee stood and Magdalena felt a calm force move through the young woman, a cool touch, a silent call, and she turned to look at her.

Sharlee's face wavered and another with silver skin looked into Magdalena's eyes.

Magdalena glanced at the others. From their expressions it was clear no one else saw Sharlee's transformation.

Sister of the Earth.

The words came into her mind.

Who are you? Magdalena felt no fear of the face that floated over Sharlee's features, only an instant rush of love.

Do you not recognize me? It is I, Marita.

Marita? Her dolphin guide? *Sea-Sister, I am honored. You've never…*

Beware the cove.

Magdalena frowned. *Am I to choose another place?*

No, the cove it must be, but beware.

Sharlee's face wavered again and Marita's features were gone.

"Grandmother? Grandmother, are you okay?"

Magdalena blinked, then faced Andres. "I'm fine."

"But, for a moment…"

She waved a hand at him. "I said I am fine." She turned toward her bedroom. "I will get what is required. Then we will go." She glanced at Isabelle. "Someone must call Cristiano; tell him he is needed."

Andres stood. "I will."

"No, you must get your Jeep."

They all looked at Isabelle. God. She didn't want to be the one. But she heard herself say. "I'll do it. But you realize it will take him hours to get here from San Felipe."

"It will not be hours." Magdalena walked away.

Isabelle watched her retreating form. The call would be a waste of time…no way would he agree to take part in a—a—well, she wasn't quite sure what to call it.

"Use the phone in kitchen," Andres said. "There's a notebook next to it. Cristiano's number is in there."

Isabelle stood, turned toward the kitchen.

"I'll come with you," Sharlee said.

In the kitchen, Isabelle looked down at the small notebook. It lay open to Cristiano's number.

Sharlee picked up the phone. "I'll do it."

Isabelle shook her head. "No, I said I'd do it and I will."

"You sure, Izzy? After last night…"

"I'm sure."

Sharlee handed her the phone.

Isabelle wrapped herself in yards of uncaring. She'd grown used to doing it married to Donald. The ease with which it happened made her slightly queasy. She punched in the number.

Cristiano answered on the third ring. "Hello."

"Good morning. It's Isabelle. I hate to bother you so early but...."

"Isabella. It is so wonderful to hear your voice. I thought of you last night."

His words ripped through her layers of protection. Her legs shook and she collapsed onto the stool next to the phone. Like hell he's been thinking of me. "I'm sure you were," she managed to get out. "I'm at Magdalena's."

In the background she heard a giggle. Then a woman's voice called. "Cristiano, I need your help."

Her stomach churned and she swallowed.

"One moment. Isabella, what is going on?"

"Who is she?" Her words came out a hoarse whisper.

"What?"

"The woman. Who is she?"

"My sister."

Without another word, Isabelle turned, thrust the phone at Sharlee. "I can't..."

"I will speak to him." Magdalena stood in the doorway.

Isabelle handed her the phone, turned and walked blindly toward the back door. She jerked it open, stumbled outside. She fought tears as she gulped air. Isabelle felt a hand on her arm and knew without turning it was Sharlee. "She was there with him," she choked out. "That woman spent the night. His sister...he said she was his sister."

"Maybe she is."

Isabelle laughed. "A sister doesn't touch her brother like I saw her do."

"Sugar, all families aren't like yours. Some parents even hug their children."

Isabelle wiped at her eyes. "It doesn't change anything. It's over...." She laughed again. "Well, it never started so I guess it can't be over."

"Cristiano has agreed do his part," Magdalena said from the kitchen doorway.

Her heart beat faster. "He's coming here?"

"No. There is not time. He will take part from where he is."

"How did you talk him into it? He said…"

"Like Señor Collins, he does not fully believe, but figures it cannot hurt. We must hurry. Andres and I will take his Jeep. You three will follow. No," Magdalena said. "It's just a short walk from where we park to the sand. What you wear is fine. Now we must go."

Sharlee didn't have to be told again. "I call front seat."

"Hey?"

"You know I get car sick in the back. There's bound to be curves."

Chapter Twenty-One

Brad drove his SUV slowly on the sand-scoured road. Isabelle sat in the rear. She held on to the back of Sharlee's seat with a white-knuckled grip. "God, how much farther?"

"I don't know. I'm just following," Brad said.

Ten feet in front of them Andres and Magdalena led the way in his Jeep.

In a cloudless blue sky the sun highlighted palo verde trees, ocotillo, and a constant cloud of dust from the truck in front of them. Even with the windows up Isabelle's skin felt sweaty and gritty.

The SUV skidded to a stop at the edge of a shallow arroyo. The road dropped three feet, then continued across a gravel bottom.

They hit another rut and her teeth clicked together, hard. "Damn, this so-called road is getting worse."

Sharlee glanced back. "Magdalena did say the place was isolated."

The SUV crested a hill and Isabelle groaned when all she saw at its bottom was the start of another steep grade.

Brad shifted into low and they began their trip down.

"Look," he said.

Ahead of them Andres had slowed.

"They're turning."

At the spot where Andres disappeared, Isabelle could see two worn ruts. "Not much of a road, even by Baja standards.

Brad made the turn. Tall grass and brush grazed the sides of the truck. "Hope it doesn't get any narrower."

A half mile later the two ruts became packed sand that ended at the back of a cove shaped like a bowl tipped on its side. A small beach spread before them.

Isabelle noted the scattered wood, seashells and lumps of pumice along the high-tide line. With the tide full in the beach would be covered. She hoped Magdalena had taken that into consideration.

The narrow road left no room to turn around so Brad parked behind Andres' Jeep.

All three climbed from the SUV and walked to Magdalena and Andres.

"Reverse Beach," Andres said, then grinned. "That's what the locals call it. Because you have to back out until you reach the main road. And for sure you don't venture off the path, or you won't be going anywhere."

"Your attention please," Magdalena said. "I will collect most of the stones, but Brad and Sharlee you must find your own. Andres, Cristiano waits for your phone call, si?"

Andres nodded and patted his jeans pocket. "I'll call when you tell me to."

"Ah, what size rock do I need?" Brad said.

Magdalena looked at him. "You will know it when you see it."

"I'm not exactly dressed for beachcombing," he said, motioning toward his khaki slacks and high-topped running shoes. "I still say I should've stopped and changed."

"No time," Magdalena said.

Sharlee smiled. "You're fine. Just take off your shoes and roll up your pant legs." The two turned away; walked toward the point on the right.

"Well, I guess I'll just go this way—all by myself," Isabelle said, feeling a little miffed.

"Some forces you must flow with, Isabelle," Magdalena said. "It only tires you to go against them."

"What?" She glanced at the woman.

Magdalena smiled. "From you, I do not require a stone. From you I need a golden olive shell."

Isabelle looked around the small beach. "But there isn't one golden olive shell in sight."

"Bring it to me and do it quickly please. The tide will change in thirty minutes."

"Sure. Shell. Quickly," Isabelle muttered as she turned to walk the opposite way Sharlee and Brad had. But she couldn't resist glancing toward the two. Her friend stumbled. Brad reached for Sharlee's hand and didn't let it go.

Isabelle walked to where the waves broke. "Golden olive shell. Just one. How hard can it be?" She looked for a trail as a wave receded. "If Magdalena had told me we needed one, I could have grabbed one from the house." She saw a moon snail and started to pick it up, then stopped. "Nope. Not here to add to my collection."

A girlish laugh broke the silence and Isabelle glanced down the beach. Sharlee, sandals dangling from her left hand, danced back from an incoming wave.

"Oh, come on. It's like you've never gotten your toes wet before," Isabelle murmured, then frowned down at the sand. She hated the sound of her own petulant voice. *It's not as if I really wanted him. All I wanted was a* distraction from, a wave of pain poured over her and she wrapped her arms around her stomach. *Who am I kidding? All the Brads in the world wouldn't equal Cristiano.*

I'm taking care of this ghost thing, then I am so outta here. Back home things will settle down. I'll bury myself in my weaving and in time this will all be nothing but a memory.

Sharlee laughed again and Isabelle looked at her friend. *That's not her flirting laugh. She sounds happy. Well, more power to her.*

Isabelle turned to look at the water and caught a glint of gold out of the corner of her eye. She bent, scooped up the golden olive shell just before a wave claimed it. "Got you."

She rinsed sand from the shell and walked toward Magdalena. Sharlee and Brad were coming back, too. She watched him pick up his shoes. The three arrived in front of Magdalena at the same time. Sharlee's cheeks were pink and her eyes sparkled. Isabelle noticed Brad had lost some of the tenseness at the corner of his eyes and around his mouth. *They're good for each other.*

Brad sat down on a rock, brushed sand from his feet and put on his socks and shoes. "These broken shells and rocks are damned hard on city boy feet."

"Got my stone," Sharlee said. "It washed up right at my toes. So did Brad's." She extended her hand, palm up, but with fingers curled. "Show me yours and I'll show you mine."

"I had a different assignment," Isabelle said. She held out the golden olive shell.

Sharlee smiled. "That's perfect to represent you. You love those. You must have a hundred of them back home."

"I'm not too crazy about this being me." A flat, black stone lay in the palm of Brad's hand. "But Sharlee insists it is."

"It shows you are well-rounded, but haven't found what you need to add sparkle to your world." Sharlee's voice had changed tone. She sounded like she spoke from far away.

"And yours?" Magdalena said. "What does it say about you?"

Sharlee opened her hand. She held a pale piece of quartz with threads of black twining through. "I'm still following my paths, seeking."

"But look, child," Magdalena said. "Turn the stone over."

Sharlee did.

In the middle of the rock another black line had joined the first. The two came together, separated, twined again. The lines ended at the edge of the stone.

"There soon will be another joining your search," Magdalena said.

Isabelle looked from Sharlee to Brad. Could he...could they...?

"Let's begin. The tide is changing. Sharlee, will you walk with me," Magdalena said. "The rest remain here, please."

"Of course."

The two of them moved toward the lapping waves. They stepped over several snake tracks in the process. Magdalena felt the calmness flow once more from Sharlee and knew before she turned whose face she would see.

Marita's almond-eyed gaze looked into her eyes. They walked side by side, stepped over another snake track.

It surprises me to see so many of our Sisters-of-the-Sand here, Marita said.

Magdalena nodded. *Yet, I welcome them as teachers. To aid our growth, and...perhaps our change.*

Yes, they are to be respected—even feared. Do not let them draw your eyes from the true threat.

I will see that all stay vigilant.

Marita nodded and then Sharlee's face appeared again.

Magdalena patted the woman's hand. "Now it is time." She turned, waved the others forward. When they stood beside her, she began to walk the spiral. Every few steps she dropped a stone. At times she picked up a bit of shell, a piece of driftwood and placed them in her pocket.

As Magdalena completed the first circuit, three rattlers appeared from the shadow of a large rock and crawled to her.

"Grandmother. Rattlesnakes," Andres said softly from where he stood near the mouth of the spiral.She spoke without turning her head. "Si, grandson. They are not to be feared, but are here to help. I believe it is time for you to call Cristiano,"

He lifted his cell phone. "He's waiting."

"Good. We will enter the spiral now. Once you are inside the Sisters-of-the-Sand will close it."

Isabelle stared at the three snakes. "I don't know if I can do this."

"They are here to help. My dolphin sisters have told me this. Do you doubt?"

"No. I believe you, but...."

"The spiral Isabelle. Walk behind me."

Isabelle gave the rattlesnakes a wide berth and entered the spiral. Magdalena began to walk. Isabelle followed with Sharlee behind her. Brad and Andres entered last and the three snakes placed themselves across the spiral's mouth.

Sister-of-the-Land, I feel power growing and not all of it favors us.

Marita, our sisters have sealed the spiral. We are safe within.

"Brad, Sharlee," Magdalena said. "Are you warming your offerings with your heart? And Isabelle, the shell?"

"Uh, I guess so," Brad whispered. "I'm as ready as I can be, considering the company we have with us."

"Listen. Our Sisters-of-the-Sand sing now." Magdalena continued to pace and blended her song with the minor key tones of the snakes. She reached the center of the spiral.

Isabelle, Sharlee, Brad, and Andres watched her in silence. She stopped; pulled the bits she'd collected from her pockets, then bent, and arranged them at her feet.

"Each of you, place your stones carefully on the ground. Señor Collins, reach your heart to Patricia. Speak to your beloved; tell her of your sorrow, of your hopes for her peace. Isabelle, feel Patricia's anguish and incinerate what binds her to this plane. All of you, send your love…Andres?"

"Yes, Cristiano heard you and is doing so." Andres listened for a moment. "Cristiano has placed his offering." He frowned. "I'm losing the signal."

"His part is finished. Thank him for me. Now it is up to Patricia to accept."

"Cristiano, Grandmother says thank you." He paused, listened. "Yes, everything is fine…hello…hello." Andres looked at Magdalena. "I lost him." He flipped the phone shut.

Magdalena faced the sea. "Patricia, all are here. We appeal to you. We want to help."

The tide, nearing its fullness, seemed to still momentarily. Magdalena felt a breeze touch her face. The sun pulsed and even the sea birds stopped their quarrels. The three rattlers at the entrance of the spiral rose coiled into their striking position.

The ground shifted, tilted and the walls of the cove behind them began to crack and crumble into the arroyo.

Magdalena glanced at Sharlee, relieved to again see the face of Marita.

Magdalena, stand firm. The Lost One rages. She rejects your intentions, and has found allies in the scorpion clan.

Marita, how can we reach her?

I am not sure you can.

Dust rose from the walls of the cove and boulders piled between the beach and the trucks.

"Grandmother," Andres said, pointed toward the ocean.

She turned, could see dolphins as they leapt. They, trilled and clicked as one, their bodies halfway out of the water.

A voice shouted, rose from a low roar to a scream. "No. You will not. I will not." The sound echoed, split the air and ended in a metallic screech.

Magdalena. Patricia is here. You must leave.

But Marita, it is not over.

No more can you do here. Go safely, sister.

The dolphins fled.

"Grandmother, we've got to get out of here now," Andres yelled.

Magdalena turned toward Sharlee who shook her head, blinked and for a moment looked as if she didn't know where she was. "We must leave. Go slowly, step carefully. Andres, go first. Softly now."

He stepped from the spiral, a slow clicking, rattle started and the three snakes moved ahead of him toward the now, four-foot high, rubble-barrier that blocked the road.

"Brad, follow Andres," Magdalena said.

Another small temblor shivered the sand and Sharlee pitched forward. Brad turned quickly to catch her and the snake nearest him struck.

"God. No, " Sharlee screamed.

"I'm okay. I'm okay, it got my shoe."

"Andres, Señor Brad is unhurt?" Magdalena said.

"Si, grandmother. Serpiente got his shoe. The temblor has agitated them."

"The Sisters-of-the-Sand say the scorpions come also."

"Is it Patricia or the earthquake?" Isabelle said.

Before Magdalena could answer another scream pushed across the beach.

"Okay, here's what we're going to do," Andres said. "The snakes are calming, but I don't know for how long. Start moving toward the trucks."

"From the looks of the wall we're going to have to do some climbing. Unless we can go around it," Brad said.

"No we will climb," Andres answered. "I will go up first, then you hand the girls up to me.

Brad turned."How's everyone doing back there?"

"The tide is almost in," Sharlee said."And the spiral's nearly erased."

"Come along now. Before it is gone, move toward the wall."

Sharlee stepped from the center of the spiral.

"No. No, stay in the path for as long as you can," Magdalena said. "The less distance to travel upon the unprotected sand, the better."

Slowly the three women retraced the spiral.

A wave rushed across the stones in front of Sharlee. She looked back at Magdalena in doubt.

"Can you jump to where it begins again," Magdalena asked.

"Yes," Sharlee said.

"Then do it. Keep walking, we will follow." Magdalena touched the middle of Isabelle's back. "Hurry, Patricia takes away our protection."

Sister, el scorpions... Marita's voice warned.

Isabelle leapt across the erased portion of the spiral, turned to look at Magdalena. "Can you make it?"

"I will make it." Magdalena jumped and landed with ease beside Isabelle. "Now walk and when we reach the end of the spiral—run." She looked toward Brad and Andres. "Be ready," she called. "We must get out of here quickly."

"I'm ready, " Andres said, "But watch yourself. A scorpion just ran into that crevice halfway up."

"Scorpions. That's all we need," Isabelle muttered.

"They'll leave us alone, as long as we leave them alone," Andres said.

Magdalena said nothing.

Brad balanced on a rock amidst the rubble. Isabelle arrived below him first and reached up. Their fingers touched. The scream came again and a chill traced the back of her neck. "God, I wish she'd shut up."

Brad gave her a strange look.

"What? You still think it's not Patricia?"

"I don't know what the hell you're talking about."

He pulled on her arm and she scrambled to stand next to him.

"The screams, don't you hear them?"

"I hear the ocean, the damn rocks crashing, now give Andres your hand. Steady. Put your foot there." Brad pointed at a flat rock to the right.

She pushed off with one foot, lifted the other and placed it on the rock...the roar became a shriek, and the rock tipped. She yelped in surprise and her hand jerked from Brad's. Isabelle scrambled for a hold and her left hand slid into a dark hole. Something skittered across her wrist and fiery pain flared. "Something bit me." She jerked her hand from the hole. Just above her wrist, a red blotch bloomed, swelled before her eyes. "God, it hurts." An angry scorpion scuttled from the hole.

"A scorpion," Sharlee cried, an edge of panic in her voice.

"Stay calm, "Andres called down. "It's not fatal. It's a Striped Tailed scorpion, but you should get some ice on it."

"There's a first aid kit and ice compresses in the SUV," Brad said.

Andres climbed down the slope to Isabelle. "Can you lift your arm?"

"The right one." She reached toward him, gasped as Andres pulled her to the top of the wall.

"In the back, behind the driver's seat," Brad called. "That's where the first aid kit is."

With tight lips she nodded, held her wrist with her right hand, as she disappeared from sight.

"Grandmother is next."

Brad reached for her.

Magdalena stepped back. "No, Sharlee first. I still sing with the sand-sisters." She heard their hum in her mind, their rattle grew louder.

"Fine." Frustration rang in Andres' voice.

Brad grabbed Sharlee's hand, pulled her up beside him. Andres reached down and pulled her to the top of the wall.

"I'm checking on Isabelle," Sharlee called.

Isabelle sat in the SUV's back seat and held ice to her wrist. "How're you doing," Sharlee asked. "Good gawd, your knee's bleeding, too." She rummaged in the first aid kit, found an antiseptic wipe and ripped it open. "This is gonna hurt."

Isabelle looked up at her with a pale face. "I don't think it could hurt more."

"Did you take anything?"

"Dry swallowed a couple of extra strength Tylenol."

Sharlee watched a shudder move through her friend.

"What's happening on the beach," Isabelle asked.

"What beach? There's about three feet left of it. Magdalena's coming up now."

Magdalena glanced back toward the sea. A wave washed over the place where the spiral had been. Fear made her hand tremble as she reached for Brad. He pulled her up. Her body swayed and she leaned against him.

"Can you make it?" Brad said.

"I…"

"Andres, come down to us. Magdalena needs a hand."

Andres arrived beside them in a slide of rocks and sand.

"Careful," Brad warned. "I felt the wall shift again."

Andres took a moment to look into Magdalena's eyes. Then he picked her up. "I've got you. Sharlee," he called. "Come reach for Grandmother."

In seconds, Sharlee appeared.

"Up you go."

Andres lifted.

Magdalena grabbed Sharlee's hands and was pulled to the top of the wall. "How is Isabelle?" she said.

"I'm okay," Isabelle said. She came to stand beside Sharlee. "It's gone numb. Are you all right?"

"Patricia is having a magnifico temper tantrum." Magdalena turned, looked down at the beach. "Come now. We must get out of here."

"You go, Brad," Andres said. "The SUV has to back out first."

"Right."

Brad climbed to the top of the wall.

He called down to Andres. "Okay, now you."

Andres was halfway up the slide when Magdalena saw his foot slip. His fall seemed to happen in slow motion. He tumbled, rolled and landed in a heap at the bottom.

He sat up, screamed, grabbed for his right leg

Magdalena shouted, "Leave him alone."

Patricia's laugh filled her head.

Brad slid down the wall, stopped next to Andres.

"He's snapped his leg. Looks like a compound fracture. Search around up there, see if you can find something for a splint. There should be some Ace bandages in the first aid kit, and Tylenol, get me some Tylenol and a bottle of water."

They all jumped to follow his commands.

Sharlee scrambled down with the first aid kit, opened it and took out the packet of Tylenol. Brad tore it open and handed Andres two, along with the water.

With a shaky hand, Andres popped the pills into his mouth and washed them down.

"I'd like to give them a minute to kick in," Brad said. "But I can't."

"Understood."

"How are we going to get him up here," Sharlee asked. "He can't climb."

"My cell phone's in the SUV. Try it. See if we can get a signal."

Isabelle disappeared from site. She appeared again a minute later with his cell phone "I've got one. It's weak though."

"Call Sam Gustafson. His number's in the memory. Tell him to get here with the helicopter."

A wave played out inches from Andre's boots. "And tell him to hurry, please," Magdalena said.

Sister, the waves rise. The Sisters-of-the-Sand leave.
I understand.

She watched as the rattlesnakes made their way across the beach, soon to be lost among the rocks.

Brad grabbed the stick beside him. "Give me one of the Ace bandages."

Sharlee did.

He looked at Andres. "This is gonna hurt like hell."

"Do it."

"Gustafson's coming," Isabelle called down. "He should be here in twenty minutes or less. "

"That's good," Brad said without glancing up. "Sharlee, I need your help."

"What do you want me to do?"

"I've got to immobilize his leg. Try to keep him steady." Brad placed the stick beside Andres' leg. He worked the bandage beneath the ankle, wrapped three times around the stick and tied it off.

"The other one," he said. Sharlee handed him a second bandage. He moved up toward the knee and wrapped it the same way.

From atop the wall, Magdalena stared down at them.

Sister, Patricia will seek to strike at your heart.

What? She laid her hand against her left breast.

No. Andres. She feels your love for him. There will be more to come.

"Sharlee, gather rocks," Magdalena called. "Large ones, but do not get them from the wall. Take some to Brad."

"What's going on?" Isabelle said. "What aren't you telling us?"

Magdalena watched Sharlee pick up a large rock, carry it to Brad and put it on the sand beside him. He smiled, reached to brush her cheek with his fingertips—and a wail of pain, tinged with rage, vibrated in her head.

"My God," Isabelle cried. "Not again."

Goose bumps erupted on Magdalena's arms. She shifted her gaze to the bottom of the wall of rocks. First one, two, then five scorpions came from the shadows. "Sharlee. Brad. Look out." She pointed toward the scorpions who marched toward them.

Sharlee picked up the rock beside Brad. "I've only got this one."

The first scorpion arrived. Brad kicked out, connected, and it soared toward the water. At the same time Sharlee dropped the rock on another.

Three—four—five—Brad sent them flying after the first one. "Get more rocks," he shouted.

Sharlee turned, ran, grabbed a rock in each hand and dashed back. She saw a scorpion at Brad's left heel and dropped one of the rocks on top of it. "Got you, suckah."

Ten more scorpions came from the wall of rubble. Magdalena watched Brad and Sharlee share a look of horror. Then Brad turned, looked toward the sea and screamed. "Patricia, what are you thinking? The woman I loved would never do anything like this."

A sudden stillness came. It was if the world held its breath. The scorpions stopped their forward march. They scuttled back and forth, slammed into each other, turned and then scampered toward the shadow of the rocks.

The faint whomp, whomp, whomp, of a helicopter came to Magdalena.

"He's coming," Isabelle cried and pointed.

The red and chrome helicopter dropped from a cloud.

"Shield your eyes," Brad shouted.

In minutes it was on the ground. He ran to it, jerked open the door.

"What the hell happened?"Gustafson said.

"Andres broke his leg. Quake caused a land slide. We've got to get him to San Felipe."

"I'll help." Gustafson started to unfasten his seat harness.

"No, you stay there. Sharlee and I can get him in quicker." He turned, waved toward Magdalena and Isabelle. "I'm going with them. Sam's a little new to this helicopter flying. There's room for one more."

Before Isabelle could say a word, Magdalena slid down the wall, ran toward Andres. "How are you?"

He looked up at her. Face pale, lips pressed together. "Hurts."

"Soon we will fix that. But first there will be more pain."

"Understood."

"Sharlee, Magdalena, grab his shoulders. I'll take his legs," Brad said. A cold wave flowed around them and Andres shuddered. "We've got to get him out of here before he goes into shock." Brad frowned at Andres. "I'm sorry. Ready?"

They lifted.

Andres screamed, went limp.

They carried him to the helicopter, maneuvered him inside, onto the back bench and strapped him securely. Magdalena climbed in, covered him with a blanket. She lifted Andres' head and placed it on her lap. Brad settled in the co-pilot's seat. "Okay, take her up." He turned, looked at Sharlee. "I'll be back as soon as possible."

"We'll be at Isabelle's."

Brad frowned. "Will she be able to drive?"

"She'll have to."

"You'd better get back up there with her. It's going to get nasty here."

Sharlee's eyebrows rose as she stepped back. "You think it can get nastier?"

Brad smiled and slammed the helicopter's door.

Sharlee turned and ran for the wall as the blades began to rotate. Even then she felt the sting of flung sand along the back of her legs and neck.

Chapter Twenty-Two

"Shar, don't fuss. I can drive."

"Never mind the 'Shar, don't fuss.' I haven't been around to fuss and look what's happened."

"All right, forget I said anything. Let's get back to the house. Can you drive the Jeep? I can't manage a stick shift with this." She held up her arm.

"The ice seems to be helping. I see a little swelling but not much. Sure, I can drive the Jeep. Remember, I'm a country girl. I learned to drive on daddy's ol' tractor. We'll take it slow and be back at the house in no time."

"Okay. Do we have all our stuff? Have we left anything on the beach?"

"Honey, has that itty-bitty bite gone to your head? I think the only thing we've left on this beach is a lot of misery. Let's git."

Sharlee swung her legs out of the Jeep, slammed the door and jogged back to where Isabelle sat in the SUV, forehead on the steering wheel. "C'mon sugar, let's get you into the house. We'll play with Sammi and Longie, take a little break before we shower. I think we've earned it."

Sammi-Sue greeted them. She warbled, hopped, a tail whipping tri-colored welcome committee. They laughed as they shed bags and scarves beside the door.

Isabelle looked around. Of course, nothing had changed, they hadn't been gone more than three hours, but she felt as if she'd been far away for a long time.

Longfellow unwound from his nest among the sofa cushions, stretched and greeted them with a wave of his tail and a chirp of welcome.

"I'm going to take Sammi-Sue for a walk, Shar. Will you put the tea-kettle on? We'll take our time, so don't rush. Come, Sammi."

Isabelle looked toward the island. In spite of the clear sky, fog obscured her view. She unsnapped the leash and set the basset hound free.

Patricia's screams and howls seemed to have bothered her more than the rest of them. They'd gone on and on— and echoed through her even now. Against her will, her mind began a review of the last several hours. "No," she murmured. She didn't want to think any more. But her damn head wouldn't obey her. "Okay. Enough."

Sammi-Sue whipped around, her ears swirling with the abrupt movement. She ran to Isabelle and looked up with a soft whine.

"It's okay, baby. Go ahead. It's only your crazed mom." She patted the top of the basset hound's head. Sammi-Sue licked her hand and ambled away, along the beach, nose busy.

Isabelle turned toward the island. "What is it? What do you want? Damn. You hurt Andres, and you could have killed me with the scorpion. I don't...." Isabelle hands trembled. She took three deep breaths.

What's taking Brad so long? Did something happen on the way in to San Felipe? She looked back at the house. Sharlee stood on the front ramada.

I feel like I'm going to explode. God. I've got to do something. Isabelle sprinted to the shore and bounded into the water. Her momentum carried her another few steps, she dove into the clear, shallow water. Isabelle heard Sammi-Sue's frantic barking. She stood and wiped water from her face. The basset hound ran along the beach, barking as the small waves reached her toes. She bugled, turned and raced a few steps along the sand. Isabelle waded to the basset hound "Come on Sammi, let's go up."

"Quite a performance there, Izzy." Sharlee held out a towel. "Dry off and come in. The tea's ready. Feel better now, Sugar?"

"Yes, I do. Guess I should have jumped in sooner; I always feel better after a dip in the gulf. Ordinarily I have my suit on though."

"Why don't you take a shower; get those wet things off and warm up. I'll bring the tea in to you."

"Thanks, Shar. I think I will."

"Brad and the others should be back anytime. How's your wrist?"

"It's okay, still not swelling, kind of numb and tingly, but nothing like poor Andres' leg. He seemed in so much pain. My God, Sharlee, what happened out there?"

"You tell me. I felt like someone else was speaking through me.

"And Patricia's screaming." Isabelle said. "It made my skin crawl."

"What screaming?"

Isabelle looked at her. "You didn't hear it?"

"I heard the wind blowin', the rocks crashin', but nope, no screamin'."

"How could you not hear it?"

"A lot was going on....Sugar, get in the shower. Forget about it for now, I'll bring your tea."

Isabelle shivered. Sharlee hadn't heard Patricia. Had Brad or Andres? She knew Magdalena had. "I'm so glad you're here, Shar. I'd hug you but...." she looked down at her clothes.

"I'll pass on the hug."

Isabelle blew her friend a kiss and turned toward the bathroom.

When she came out of the shower in her sweats, Sharlee sat at the table, stared out the window, chin in hand.

"Go ahead, Shar, your turn, I left hot water for you. I feel better. I'm going to sit here with my handsome kitty-boy and rest."

Isabelle sat on the sofa with Longfellow and began to braid her damp hair. When she finished she rearranged the pillows, curled around the cat and fell asleep.

The sound of whomp, whomp, whomp jerked Isabelle awake. What the…?

Across from her, Sharlee sprang from a chair. A magazine fell from her lap. She ran to the door, looked out, and a smile lit her face. "Brad's back."

Isabelle scrambled to her feet. "Anyone else? Can you tell?"

"I see him and Mister Gustafson. I can't…"

A moment later Brad rushed in and they all began to speak at once.

"Magdalena went to her house…"

"What about Andres? What does the doctor say?"

"Brad, you've got blood all over you." Sharlee said.

"Andres is okay. How's the scorpion sting, Isabelle?"

"It's better."

"Good to hear. Look. Give me a few minutes to change my clothes over at Gus' and then I'll give you a detailed account. Be back in about ten minutes."

Sharlee stood for a moment and watched Brad walk away. "Izzy, I'm going to the bathroom to freshen up."

"How fresh can you get? You just got out of the shower." Isabelle frowned. "About this thing with you and Brad…."

"I know. It's strange for me too. It just seems as if I've known him for years." Sharlee shook her head. "But the timing sucks."

"Does it really make any difference?" Isabelle said.

"Yes, honey, it does, but I don't want to get into any of it right now. It's not the time. I'll be right back."

Sharlee joined Isabelle in the kitchen. She had changed into a black skirt with tropical flowers. Her spiral abalone pendant rested just above the curved neckline of a bronze tank top.

You look great. I'm going to open a bottle of the good wine. Would you like a glass?"Isabelle said.

"Just a thimbleful. Where did you get those pants, raw silk, aren't they? So pretty, blue is your color, Sugar; there must be ten different blues in that fabric, beautiful. All we've got for shopping at home is Sears and Penny's. I wish we had just one of your bay area boutiques."

Isabelle selected a bottle of cabernet from the case under the kitchen island. "Maybe, but you didn't find that skirt in a catalogue. Hand me the glasses will you?"

"Sure. I picked this up last time I was in Hawaii. I love the colors. And when I'm feelin' sassy I wear my cowboy boots with it."

Brad called from the patio.

"C'mon in, we're just fixing a tray. What'll you have?" Isabelle said.

"Can you pour me an Arnold Palmer?"

"What's that?" she said.

"Half ice tea and half lemonade."

"I got that."

"You guys go in the living room and sit right down," Sharlee said, as she added a bowl of crackers and napkins to the tray.

When they were all settled and after Brad had greeted Longie and Sammi, he leaned back on the sofa, took a long drink and said, "Well there's good news and there's better news."

"First Andres," Isabelle said. "And Magdalena, she's at her place?"

"Yes, Gustafson drove her home. Said she wanted a bath. Andres will be fine." Brad put his glass on the table. "He'll be in the hospital for awhile, needs surgery."

"Surgery?" Isabelle said.

"Why surgery?" Sharlee said.

"Two doctors examined Andres, they said he has a straightforward compound fracture of the tibia. They're sure they can fix him up, but they've got to wait until they take more x-rays."

"Oh, Andres," Isabelle said.

"He's quite a guy," Brad went on. "The first thing he asked is would he be able to dance again. Apparently he's got a second career with a flamenco group. One of the doctors knows Andres and asked him if he was still performing with 'that ratty old group' and Andres screamed at him."

"Here, try some of these." Sharlee handed the bowl to Brad.

Isabelle saw their fingertips touch and linger. "I'll bet he did scream. He's a great dancer, and the group isn't ratty."

"Just before I left, the doctor said 'Andres, I repair soccer injuries like this all the time, don't worry,' and Andres went out like a light."

"Thanks to you, he's being taken care of, you got him into town. Now, about that better news?" Sharlee said.

"Gustafson said the mariachi groups are in town for their annual meeting; lots of music and good times. Don't know about you, but I could use some good times and music. What do you say, ladies? Would you be my guests?"

Without giving Isabelle time to answer, Sharlee said, "We'll be delighted."

"Just for the record, I accept also." Isabelle stood. "I'll walk over and see how Magdalena's doing. Maybe she would like to come along."

Chapter Twenty-Three

Isabelle examined the bite on her wrist as she walked. *Guess I'll live.* She lifted her eyes to the island and stopped short. Shadows played on the mantle of fog covering the island and the light shifted. Laughter mocked, echoed.

It's all in my mind. But she walked faster toward Magdalena's house.

"Magdalena, it's Isabelle," she called from the patio.

"Pasa, Isabelle. Welcome. Don't you look beautiful," Magdalena said from the doorway. "Blue is your color." She crossed the room and touched Isabelle's arm. "Are you all right?"

"I've had all I can take for one day. I'm tired and I can't get her damn voice out of my head."

"Come and sit with me. Don't give in to Patricia; forget her for a while. Brad said he'd take us into town. We'll have a meal and listen to the mariachi music and forget our troubles. Now, tell me about this wonderful garment you wear."

"The jacket? It's a project I began a long time ago. I found the silk yarn and couldn't resist. I wasn't sure what exactly I was going to do, but when it was finished a friend made this little jacket."

212

"I've never seen anything like it, the flames around the bottom shimmer in the light. You will be striking on the dance floor."

"Magdalena. Isabelle," Brad called from the patio.

"Come in, come in. I'm ready," Magdalena said.

Isabelle stood, smoothed the shoulders of the short, swirling jacket.

Brad winked at Magdalena."Lucky me, three beautiful ladies."

Isabelle glanced at him. He appeared relaxed and happy.

They walked out to the truck. Sharlee waved from the front seat. "I am so ready for this."

Five minutes later, they were in the helicopter, ready for take-off.

"Okay ladies, here we go. Next stop San Felipe and an evening of good food, good music, and happy faces, agreed?"

Chapter Twenty-Four

Cristiano glanced at his watch, then at Angelina who haggled with a street vendor over the price of a woven bag. He swallowed an exasperated sigh; his youngest sister's photo should be next to the word stubborn in the dictionary. Yet the fault lay with him, for he'd indulged her from the time she could flash her dimples.

"We've got to hurry," he said again.

Angelina threw him an irritated look, then turned to aim her smile at the wrinkled man behind the mound of bags. It didn't work. He still shook his head.

"Perhaps if he were thirty years younger?" Cristiano suggested.

"Fifty pesos. It's my final offer."

The man turned his back on her and began arranging the bags. With a shrug, his sister stepped back from the stand, but he saw her yearning glance at the colorfully woven bag.

"It would have been great to carry my books in."

"Señorita."

Angelina beamed in triumph, but changed her expression to polite interest before she turned. "Si?"

"Fifty-one pesos. Not one less."

She frowned. Looked at the bag, then back at the man. "You're robbing me, but…si. Fifty-one."

Cristiano looked away so neither could see his smile. It had taken twenty minutes of haggling, but both his

sister and the vendor were satisfied, he could tell by their body language.

Cristiano turned, stared across the street and out into the sea. He didn't want to be here. He wanted to be with Isabelle, Magdalena, and the rest of them. What had happened? Andres had said everything had gone as planned, but the call had broken off. He'd tried to reach them…and nothing.

The small quakes began and he'd expected a call from the institute. So far nothing. If a call from work, he could bow out of the upcoming festivities, anything less and his mama would never forgive him. He checked his phone again. Maybe he should call his office.

The bargaining over, Angelina and the man chatted. Cristiano hit the speed dial button for his office.

"Institute de' Geologico," Mariel, his secretary said.

"Checking in. Do they need me?"

"Señor Casamiro. No, the seismic activity is small. The largest a 3.2 and there have been no more since," he heard her shuffle papers, "a 2.5 twenty minutes ago."

"Is it Isla Santa Maria's volcano?"

"According to Jorge they haven't located the epicenter."

"Call me if there is more news."

"I will, sir."

He snapped his phone shut.

Angelina came to stand beside him. "I would have to pay twice that much in Los Angeles."

He forced himself to push his worry aside. Everything was fine with Magdalena and the rest of them. He'd heard if it wasn't. Andres wouldn't leave him in the dark. He smiled down at his little sister. "That's great, now, no more shopping until after Mama's party. Si?"

She grinned at him. "I only have until tomorrow, then it's back to the grind of school."

"Bah. Save it for Papa. You love being there."

"Yes, I do, but I miss all of this." She motioned with her hand. "And you, of course."

"In three more years you will be home, with a degree in engineering. Who would have thought so?"

Her face became serious. "You big brother, you. You never doubted me. And for this, I thank you."

He felt his face heat. "You're welcome, little one. "

They walked by a display of lace mantillas and Angelina's face lit up.

"No. No."

"But Mama will love the ivory one. It'll only take a minute."

Cristiano groaned as she flashed him a smile, sauntered toward the young man behind the cart. At his sister's approach, the young man came to avid attention. Ah-ha, maybe it would only take a few minutes.

Turning to stare again across the azure sea, Cristiano thought back over the pleasant evening he'd spent with Angelina. How good it was to spend time with a beautiful woman who didn't challenge his every word and action, like the maddening Isabelle. His sister was intelligent and focused on her career. She had her own opinions, but tended to think long and speak little, unlike a certain other woman.

What was it about Isabelle? Why did his loins tighten at the thought of her? He'd known more beautiful women. But something within her called to him. When she looked into his eyes he felt she saw his soul, and more surprising, he did not feel the urge to protect it from her. Yet, she was so damn prickly, like the pear cactus, but its red fruit was sweet once you peeled away the hard shell, just like his Isabella.

He frowned. Her call this morning. The question about Angelina and Isabelle's abrupt ending of their conversation. What was that all about? There was more to it, he knew.

He thought of last night, his glimpse of the couple on the patio at Casa de la Playa. He had looked toward the yacht harbor and watched a couple step onto the sand, hands entwined. The woman had kicked her sandals off, bent to pick them up and there was something about her movements that struck a chord. It couldn't have been Isabelle. If she'd been there and seen him, she would have come over. But the phone call, did one have something to do with the other?

Cristiano raked his fingers through his hair. And this—this other, his part in the release of a trapped soul. It wasn't that he did not believe, he did, but why did it involve Isabelle? First the island, and now…Magdalena did not deny the danger. What had happened? If it wasn't for his mother's birthday celebration, he would already be there at Isabelle's door. Cristiano frowned. He would leave as soon as it was polite to do so.

*****

Sharlee, Brad, Magdalena and Isabelle, stood at the archway of Casa de la Playa.

"I love this doorway," Sharlee said. She traced the head of the painted purple hippo with a fingernail, but her cheerfulness sounded forced.

"Yeah, it's great," Isabelle said. She glanced at her watch that sat above the bruise left by the scorpion sting. "Shouldn't we have heard something from the hospital by now?"

217

"They'll call when Andres regains consciousness," Brad said. "Let's stop in for a cerveza. I'm dry as sand."

Isabelle frowned. "It's been a while."

Magdalena patted Isabelle's arm. "My grandson will be fine. I feel it here." She touched her heart. "Yes, it's been too long since I last visited."

An ancient man came from inside the cantina. He shuffled to an overstuffed chair, settled into it. When he turned and spotted them, a wide smile curved his mouth. "Buenos dias, Magdalena," he called and motioned with his hand.

"Esteban," Magdalena said, and returned his smile. "It has been many months since we've spoken."

"Come speak with me now."

He turned called into the doorway. "Bring another seat." A burly young man came from inside. He carried a chair.

Magdalena moved to settle beside Esteban.

Brad stepped back and gestured with his hand. "Ladies, after you."

Isabelle shook her head. She had been afraid they would end up here. No way was she going into Casa de la Playa."I'll wait out here for you."

Sharlee looked at her.

"You go on. You've got to see inside. You'll love it." She saw the indecision in her friend's eyes. "I'll be right here soaking up some sun and quiet." She turned and smiled at Brad. "God knows, we all need it, but just one beer, you hear. I've no intention of spending the night in town."

He laughed, bent and kissed her on the cheek. "Yes little mamacita." He stepped back, grinned at Sharlee. "Shall we?"

Isabelle watched them disappear inside. She walked to the low sea wall and leaned her stomach against its warmth. Children screamed and laughed as waves flooded over knees and toes.

It was all nice, but she so wanted to see this place in her rearview mirror. She'd thought today would be the end of Patricia's stubbornness, the spirit would have traveled on, and she and Sharlee would be on the way to San Francisco in the morning.

She shook her head. It seemed like the beach mess had happened days ago, instead of hours. They hadn't helped things. If anything they'd made them worse. What now? They couldn't turn their backs on a pissed off ghost, but even Magdalena seemed depressed and unsure of what to do.

She pushed the thoughts away. They had promised themselves a night off. No thinking about dear Patricia. She was going to do it, even if it killed her. She frowned. Maybe that wasn't the best choice of words.

"Fun. I'm going to have some fun."A woman with three young children glanced at her and Isabelle forced herself to smile.

*****

"Finished, brother, I promise," Angelina said from beside him. She held a wrapped package beneath her arm.

"Good. We must hurry now. Casa de la Playa is close." They picked up their pace. As they crossed the street he saw Isabelle turn to lean against the sea wall next to the cantina and his heart beat quickened.

"Isabelle?"

She recognized Cristiano's voice and her shoulders tightened. *Damn. Damn. Damn.* She took a deep breath and turned. He stood there, the woman from the night before beside him. Oh God. Could this get any worse? "Cristiano. What a surprise."

"So, this is Isabelle?" The woman said and looked her over from head to toes. "I love that little sweater. Silk isn't it? Did you weave the fabric yourself? I've heard about your affinity for fire."

"I did."

"Isabelle, this less than courteous thing, is my little sister, Angelina. She has just returned home from Los Angeles where she attends U.S.C."

Emotions ripped through her; surprise, embarrassment, then a wild explosion of joy. It was if the sun shone brighter. She really is his sister. He isn't another Donald. Smiling, Isabelle held out her hand. "I am so pleased to meet you."

Angelina grasped it. "Cristiano speaks much about you, which is a big surprise."

"Why?" She instantly felt defensive and hated the emotion. Damn you, Donald, look what I've let you do to me. I can't even accept a compliment without questioning it.

Angelina released her hand and stepped back. Her eyebrows rose in question and she glanced at Cristiano. "It's just…you're the first woman my brother has spoken of in some time. We'd begun to lose hope."

Isabelle's face heated. "Well, it was nice meeting you." She turned away.

"Where are you going?" Cristiano sounded confused.

"I'm with Sharlee, Magdalena and Brad. They're inside Casa de la Playa. I just stepped out to get some air."

"You did not mention Andres. He is not with you?"

Isabelle frowned. God, hadn't anyone called Cristiano? By his puzzled look of sudden concern, no one had. "Andres is in the hospital…."

"What? What happened?"

"He fell and broke his leg, but he's going to be fine. Sleeping right now. They'll call when he wakes up. I don't want to be rude, but I should get back inside." She turned to walk to the cantina.

"Wait." Cristiano grabbed her left wrist and she gasped. "What is this?" He turned her hand over. His lips tightened. "Scorpion sting. Isabelle what happened at the cove?"

A tremble moved through her. "Patricia's being difficult."

"The spirit is still on the island?"

Isabelle watched Angelina's eyes widen. "Uh, brother, what's going on? Broken legs, scorpion stings, and spirits?"

Cristiano frowned. "We will join you inside, then we both will be brought up to date." He stared at Isabelle. His look dared her to object.

Isabelle stood in the entrance of Casa de la Playa and let her eyes adjust to the dim light.

"Over there," Cristiano said and nodded toward the same table in the corner where she had seen him last night with his sister.

They moved to join the others. Seeing Cristiano, dismay clouded Magdalena's face. She stood, reached toward him. "I am so sorry. Please forgive me. I did not call and tell you of Andres." She shook her head.

"What happened, Magdalena? "

She sighed and settled into the chair. "It is not good. I have made things much worse."

"Not you," Isabelle said. "It's her. Patricia. You did nothing wrong." She rubbed her wrist, saw that Cristiano watched and flushed.

Angelina arrived beside Magdalena."Señora Hernandez."

"Angelina, Look at you. How is college-life?"

"Oh, I grow smarter every day."

"Smarter-mouthed," Cristiano said. "Now sit." He looked at Magdalena. "Tell me what happened."

Isabelle sat in silence as first Magdalena, Sharlee, and Brad, filled Cristiano in on the happenings at the cove. His jaw tightened when he heard of the scorpion encounter, and his face paled at the mention of Andres' broken leg.

Brad took a drink of his beer. "Magdalena and I went with him in the helicopter."

"It is not over then?" Cristiano said.

Magdalena sighed. "For today it is."

"Damn straight," Brad agreed. "We need a break from ghost-hunting."

"A party," Angelina said. "You need a party. I know where there is one and you will all be welcome."

Cristiano threw her a quick glance, nodded.

"Our mother is having a birthday celebration. It begins…" Angelina looked at her watch. "Actually it's already started and we are in much trouble." She looked at her brother, smiled. "Can you get us out of this one?"

He shrugged.

"Mama can never stay angry with Cristiano."

He pushed his chair back and stood. "Even with me, she has her limits."

Angelina looked around the table. "You will all come?"

"Well if Brad says yes," Sharlee said. "He's our ride."

Brad's cell phone rang. "Just a minute." He flipped it open. "Hello." He listened. Smiled. "Thank you." He flipped the phone shut. "Andres is awake and arguing with the doctors. He's going to be fine. About the party, it sounds like fun."

Cristiano touched Magdalena's hand. "I would consider it an honor to have you attend. She would have been at yours if she had not been picking Angelina up in San Diego."

Magdalena covered Cristiano's hand with her. "No, it honors me. I will happily attend."

"Then it's settled." Sharlee stood. "I need to freshen up. Ladies?"

"I'm fine," Magdalena said.

Isabelle pushed her chair back. "Where's the…?"

"I'll show you," Angelina said. "And then go on ahead and assure Momma."

Isabelle pushed the door open. The bathroom's tile floor gleamed. A granite counter, with two sinks and a mirror ran the length of the room. "Do you think this is a good idea," she asked stepping inside.

"She's his sister, like he said." Sharlee closed the door behind them, locked it.

"It doesn't change the other thing." Isabelle sighed.

"What? He's Mexican?"

She glared at Sharlee. "You know better than that. He's fifteen years younger."

"He's also sexy as hell, and hung-up on you."

"Sexy, yes." She smiled. "Hung-up on me, no."

"Whatever you say."

"Well, we came in here to freshen up. So let's freshen." Isabelle smoothed her braided hair.

"You call that getting party ready?"

"There isn't much else for me to do."

Sharlee groaned. "Turn around, Sugar."

"What?"

"Turn around."

Isabelle did and she felt Sharlee remove the band around her braid. "What…?"

Sharlee undid the plaiting, ran her fingers through the waves. "Bend over and give your head a good shake."

"Sharlee…."

"Just do it."

"Fine." Isabelle bent over, shook her head, ran her fingers through her hair. She straightened, looked at her friend. "Well?"

"You've got such beautiful hair. Just look at it."

Isabelle faced the mirror. Her blonde hair fell around her shoulders in soft waves. What would Cristiano think? He'd never seen her hair unbraided.

"Now, off with the jacket."

Beneath it Isabelle wore a pale-blue silk tank top.

Sharlee nodded. "Now you're party dressed."

"What about you?"

"Me?" She took off the camp shirt she wore over her bronze tank. Right below her shoulder a tattoo of a golden peach gleamed.

"Hey, when did you get that?"

"Three weeks ago. You like?"

"It's cool, sort of like a totem. Maybe I should get a flame."

"It didn't hurt much." Sharlee removed the belt from her full skirt, placed it over the tank and tightened it. She opened a small compact "A little lip gloss and we're outta here."

Isabelle frowned. "I still don't know about this party. Cristiano's family will be there."

"Don't sweat it. It's not like he asked you home to meet his mother. Now is it?"

"No."

"Then relax. We can use a little fun." Sharlee turned to the door. "Now let's go."

The rest of their group waited for them at the entrance to the cantina. Cristiano's eyes widened and Brad let out a slow whistle.

"Worth the wait wouldn't you say, Cristiano?"

Sharlee laughed.

Brad looked at Sharlee's small tattoo. "I bet there's a story behind that. You'll have to tell me some time." He turned to Isabelle. "Do you have any tattoos?"

"No, she doesn't," Cristiano said.

Isabelle's face heated and she wanted to drop through the floor.

There was an awkward silence.

Magdalena exited through the open door. "Come, we've a party to attend."

Chapter Twenty-Five

Although it was a short walk, Isabelle wished for an even shorter one before they arrived. Strappy heels might look sexy as hell, but they weren't made for hiking across uneven cobblestone. She'd tripped twice and would have landed on her butt each time, if Cristiano hadn't grabbed her arm. After the second time, he had put his arm around her waist and pulled her close against his side.

Cristiano stopped. "We are here." He led them down a short alleyway, halted before a brick wall covered with red bougainvillea. A pale wooden gate stood open, from within music and laughter flowed out to the street.

An older man came through the gate, stopped in surprise and then a wide smile curved his lips. "Cristo, it is about time. Elena is cutting the walls apart with her eyes even as her lips smile."

"Tio." Cristiano hugged the man. He stepped back. "This is Uncle Ramon. My mother's twin brother."

"Oh, it's your birthday also," Sharlee said.

He waved his hand in a broad flourish. "I no longer recognize birthdays. I stopped when I celebrated my sixty-fifth."

Sharlee laughed. "That sounds good. I think I'm going to do that also."

226

"Ah, Cristo, who are these beautiful young women?" He reached for Magdalena's hand and brought it to his lips.

"Ramon, you are so loco," Magdalena said. "I was at your wedding."

"Si, and you stood beside me when I returned my love to heaven."

He and Magdalena shared a sad smile, then he grinned. "It has been so long since we have spoken. I have forgotten your name."

"Bah," Magdalena said. "Take me to your sister."

Ramon offered his arm and Magdalena placed her hand inside it.

 Brad stepped forward. "Brad Collins. Glad to meet you."

Cristiano's uncle smiled. "Si. Welcome Señor Collins."

The uneven cobblestone of the alley became orange Saltillo tile as they entered the courtyard. Isabelle smelled grilled steak and smoky peppers. From a dim corner, strains of Frank Sinatra's *New York New York* drifted. It made her smile. Old Blue Eyes knew no age or cultural boundary.

Pink and lavender streamers, strung side by side, decorated the width and length of the courtyard. A playful breeze made them sway in time with the music.

Paper lanterns dangled from the streamers, while potted palo verde and Brazilian Pepper trees provided islands of green upon the sea of earth-colored tile. Wound around the tree trunks, and up into their leaves, tiny white lights mimicked miniscule stars.

"It's breathtaking," Sharlee said and Isabelle nodded.

227

A group of older adults gathered around a grill where three men flipped strips of steak. Bowls of every size and shape covered a long narrow table, except for an obvious empty space in the center.

For the birthday cake, Isabelle thought. She watched a woman come from the house carrying a platter of tortillas.

"Something to drink," Uncle Ramon asked. "We have beer, sangria, or Coca-Cola."

"Coke." Isabelle, Sharlee, and Brad all answered in unison.

Uncle Ramon gestured to a small boy who ran to them. "Coca-colas for our guests."

The boy grinned, turned and ran to a large, metal tub full of ice. He dug in, fished around and returned.

"Gracias," Ramon said and took the three Cokes from him.

"You are most welcome, Abuelo," the boy said and raced away.

"Tomás, my youngest grandson," Ramon said with pride.

Behind them the music changed to Gloria Gaynor's *I Will Survive*. A group of teen agers moved into the middle of the courtyard. Isabelle watched others urge a woman to join them.

"Oh, this will be good," Ramon said.

The woman laughed, threw her hands into the air and joined the group. They began to dance, and Isabelle realized they were doing the Electric Slide.

Sharlee touched Isabelle's arm. "Hey, we know that one."

"By all means, let us join them," Cristiano said. He grinned at Isabelle. "Unless, of course, you are too much of an adult…"

With at toss of her hair, she moved to the end of a line and began the dance steps. A moment later when she turned, she could see Cristiano beside her. She smiled as she stepped to the side, dipped, and pivoted.

Thoughts of their other dance together flowed through her mind, how their bodies had touched, swayed. It had been like making love with their clothes on. Heat moved through her and she swallowed. She glanced at him again and their eyes locked. She missed a step, bumped into the person next to her.

She tore her gaze from Cristiano, turned to see the woman they had been coaxing out to dance. "I'm so sorry."

"It's fine, señorita. He is a magnifico young man, si? Enough to muddle any woman's head."

Isabelle's face burned. "Yes, he is," she murmured. The song stopped and she hurried back to her Coke and took a long, cold drink .

"Whoo-eee, now that was fun," Sharlee said.

Cristiano and the woman came toward them. A wave of panic moved through Isabelle and with stomach churning certainty, she knew what Cristiano would say before he did.

"Let me introduce the birthday girl."

The woman beamed up at him, even as she slapped his arm.

"This is my mother, Elena Casamiro. Madre, this is Sharlee, Brad, and Isabelle."

"Happy birthday," Sharlee said, holding out her hand.

Elena Casamiro clasped it with both of hers. "Thank you, señorita."

"This is one great party," Brad said.

"I am a lucky woman to have so many to love."

Cristiano bent to kiss her cheek. "No, we are the lucky ones Mami."

"Is-a-belle." Elena drew the name out. "Your name means *devoted to God*. Did you know this?"

"My mother told me."

"Enjoy yourself. Cristiano, will you help me with something in the house?" She turned away.

"Of course," he said and followed.

Isabelle suddenly needed to sit. She walked stiffly toward a wooden chair and then collapsed into it.

"Izzy, what is it? You're looking sick." Sharlee hovered over her.

"She doesn't like me."

"Cristiano's mom? She just met you. How can you know?" She glanced at Brad. "Get her something to eat. It's probably low blood sugar."

He walked toward the food-laden table.

"Did you see how she took him away from me? I'm not what she wants for her son." Isabelle felt tears clog her throat and she swallowed.

"I think Cristiano can make up his own mind, don't you?"

Isabelle looked up into Sharlee's eyes. "Family is very important in Mexico."

"Family is important anywhere." Isabelle saw a quick flash of pain in her friend's face. "Here comes Brad with a snack."

He handed her a still warm tortilla stuffed with beans and rice. Isabelle smiled and shook her head. "Food's not gonna fix this."

Brad shrugged and bit into the burrito.

Isabelle watched Cristiano help his mother hang a piñata. He leaned and placed a kiss upon her head and with a huge smile she swatted at him.

From behind Sharlee came a chorus of hellos. Isabelle turned. A young man and woman entered the courtyard. The man rushed forward. The woman remained where she stood, highlighted by the flowered-covered wall. Her wrap dress, striped with springtime colors, ended demurely at her knees, but the soft fabric hugged each curve upward from there. Three men left the food table and rushed toward her.

She draws men like a flower attracts bees, Isabelle thought.

They buzzed around the young woman who smiled and toyed with her lavender scarf. She tilted her head, laughed and sunlight glinted off diamond stud earrings.

"Wow," Brad said.

"She sure knows how to make an entrance," Sharlee said. "I love that dress."

"It's nice, but the guys are attracted to what's in it," Isabelle said.

"Meow," Brad said. "The claws coming out?"

Her face warmed. "Maybe."

Angelina came to them.

"Who are the new arrivals?" Brad asked.

"Stephano Macario and his sister Cordelia. Their family and ours have lived next to each other since we were babies," Angelina said.

The young man walked to Cristiano. They grabbed each other's shoulders in greeting. Stephano turned, leaned forward and kissed Señora Casimiro's cheek. Cristiano's mother glanced at Isabelle, then waved Cordelia forward.

The woman swayed her way across the courtyard, five men in tow. Cordelia took both of Señora Casamiro's hands in hers. "Felicidades." They heard her say.

"I am so glad you and Stephano could come. I know your jobs keep you busy in Mexico City."

"I would never miss anything as important as this. I am between trials." She lifted her shoulders in a shrug.

"She's also a lawyer," Sharlee said.

"Man, have I been missing out." Brad grinned. "I've never had a lawyer that looked like either of you."

Angelina laughed. "Come, I will introduce you."

She led them forward.

Stephano turned from Cristiano. His gaze swept over all of them, jerked back to Angelina. "Angel, I didn't know you were home." He clutched his heart. "I am sorely wounded. You have not called. Did you not swear to forever love me?"

The girl blushed. "I was nine, you silly fool. I'm surprised you still remember those words."

"Ah, but you are nine no longer."

"But you are still as foolish." Angelina turned to the woman who had remained standing at her mother's side. "Cordelia, this is Sharlee, Brad, and Isabelle. Friends of Cristiano's."

"Americanos? Cristo, you are branching out. Your Papa must be very proud of your new found tolerance."

A moment of stunned silence followed.

"I've always been proud of my son." The words came from behind them. A man came to stand beside Señora Casamiro. Looking at him, Isabelle could see how Cristiano would mature. The same leanness, chocolate-brown eyes and deep dimples.

"Papa," Angelina said. "This is...."

"I heard, daughter." He held out his hand. "I am happy to meet you."

"Señor Casamiro," Brad said. "We met once. You were aboard the boat which rescued me. I never got the chance to thank you in person."

"Oh. So you are he. I am sorry you never found your fiancé. The currents around that island are deadly."

"No talk of death," Señora Casamiro said. "This is a party." Lively salsa music began to play. "Cristiano dance with Cordelia. It has been sometime since we have seen the two of you perform."

"Perform?" Brad said.

"Yes, they have won many dance contests," Angelina answered.

Cordelia shook her head. "We were children,"

"What?" Her brother chided. "You are too old?"

"I think not." She smiled at Cristiano and swayed her hips. "You?"

He held out his hand. "It would be my pleasure. But this time, I will lead."

She punched his arm, let him guide her out to the dance floor.

Their bodies moved in perfect rhythm. Hips thrust, mouths laughed. Soon the two were alone on the floor. Loud applause sounded as the music ended.

When the two joined them, Stephano offered a beer to Cristiano.

"Nothing for me?" Cordelia said.

"Perhaps some sangria," Angelina asked.

"No. I'll have some of his." She took the beer from Cristiano, drank from the bottle and held it out to him.

With a slight smile, he took it.

Señora Casamiro looked shocked, but Cristiano's father grinned. "Do not frown, Elena. Big city girls have big city manners."

"Come Mami, it is time to eat," Cristiano said.

"I'll find Magdalena," Isabelle offered.

"No. no, she is with Uncle," Angelina said. "They will be fine. "Come sit here with me. I want to know all about San Francisco. I have not made it there yet."

Isabelle found herself sitting between Angelina and Stephano Macario. Cristiano's father sat at one end of the long, narrow table and his mother at the other.

"Cerveza, sangria, or soda?" a voice asked at her elbow.

She turned. It was Ramon's grandson. "Sangria, please."

With a wide grin, he turned and darted away. "The señorita will have sangria," he yelled.

"Tomás," a young woman scolded.

Isabelle's eyes went to Cristiano. He'd been seated to the right of his mother and Cordelia placed next to him. Both women seemed to be engaging him in conversation. His head kept turning first one way, then the other. He glanced at her and smiled. Isabelle looked at Elena Casamiro and caught a frown on her face.

"So Isabelle, tell me more of San Francisco," Angelina said.

"I enjoy Golden Gate Park, Fisherman's Wharf...."

"No. No. No. I don't want to know about the tourist stuff. Tell me the about the real city."

Isabelle smiled. "Okay, if you really want to see San Francisco, ride a city bus."

"What?"

"You'll see men and women on the way to work, teens skipping school, and if you're real lucky, a transient will sit next to you and lay his filthy head on your shoulder for a nap."

She watched the girl take in her words. "I'm more interested in the museums."

"The De'Young in the Golden Gate Park is excellent. World class."

"I will make it a point to visit." Angelina took a bite from her burrito. "And the night life?"

On Isabelle's left Stephano laughed. "That's what she really wants to know. The clubbing scene, and shopping of course."

She watched Angelina lean forward and give the man a pitying look. "Too bad some of us still have yet to mature." She settled back and smiled at Isabelle. "But since it has been brought up, what is the nightlife like?"

"I'm sorry to disappoint you, but I don't know."

Cristiano's sister looked shocked. "You don't know?"

"Not if you are asking about clubbing. We never explored that scene. Donald and I went to plays, ballets, and operas. If not them, then we were attending charity events."

Angelina sighed. "How terribly boring."

"What a thing to say," Stephano said. "If your mother had heard…"

The girl's face flushed. "I'm sorry, that was…."

"Your sangria." Tomás stood at Isabelle's elbow again.

"About time," Angelina said. "I thought maybe you've forgotten all about her."

The little boy's lower lip came out.

Isabelle hurried to take the glass of wine-punch from him. "Thank you so much."

Tomás threw a glare at Angelina before he turned and charged away.

"Niños," Angelina said with shake of her head.

"Yes, children can be trying," Stephano added and Angelina scowled.

Isabelle looked down to hide a smile. "Tell me about your classes in Los Angeles."

"Oh, they keep me very busy," Angelina said.

The rest of the dinner time was filled with descriptions of Angelina's classes, and her fielding of Stephano's barbs.

Cristiano's father stood and all voices hushed in anticipation. He held up a glass of sangria. "To my darling wife, who grows younger and more beautiful each year."

Isabelle watched Elena Casamiro's face color with pleasure. Cristiano leaned forward to kiss his mother's cheek. On Elena's other side Cordelia did the same.

I can't see myself ever doing that, or her even letting me. Isabelle pushed her chair back. "Which way to the bathroom?" she said to Angelina.

"I'll show you."

"No, your mother's getting ready to cut her cake. I can find it."

"Through the patio doors, across the living room and down the hallway. It's the second on the right."

"Thank you. I'll be right back."

As she walked across the patio, a spot between Isabelle's shoulder blades itched, as if someone watched her. She glanced back, expecting it to be Cristiano, but locked gazes with Cordelia. The woman smiled and laid her hand across Cristiano's. The message was quite clear.

Isabelle followed Angelina's directions and found the bathroom with ease. She took care of business and spent a few minutes smoothing her hair and taking some "me" time. When she couldn't hide out any longer she exited and started her return trip. Halfway down the hallway she heard voices; Cristiano's she recognized at once. The other was a woman speaking.

"Cordelia stop," he said.

"Stop? Since when are you against a little foreplay?" The words teased, but there was an edge of anger beneath them.

"This is my mother's party…."

Cordelia's laugh interrupted the rest of his words. "We've had sex right in your bedroom down the hall."

"We were kids. We are not anymore."

A moment of silence stretched.

Damn, what can I do? Isabelle glanced around. There wasn't any other way to get from the hall to the patio. Do I make a bunch of noise so they know they're not alone?

"It's that woman, isn't it? The old Americana."

Cristiano laughed. "Isabelle is not old."

"But she is an Americana. Tell me, how did she get her hooks into you? You are usually so careful."

"And you would know, wouldn't you?"

"Don't flatter yourself, Cristo. I have no wish to marry, you or any other hombre. I hate seeing you break your mother's heart, though."

Isabelle drew in a harsh breath. She took a step forward. Stopped. What would his answer be?

"My mother will come around."

Cordelia laughed. "Are you sure? The woman…."

"Her name is Isabelle. Isabelle Allen."

"Fine. Isabelle is Americana, and what, twenty-years older than you? Your mama wants grandchildren. You are the eldest…"

"Stop," Cristiano said. "I don't think I desire children and if Isabelle does we can adopt."

"My God. You are serious about her. Where would you live? Do you expect her to move here with you? Have you even asked her?"

"San Francisco is not that far away."

"Cristo, think about what you are saying. What this will do to your mother?"

"Cordelia. I am thirty years of age, a man. I have lived away from home for many years. I do not live my life for my mother."

"You will leave your heritage behind, change jobs, or do you think your rich wife will support you?"

"Enough."

"Did you think I did not know about her money? All ready the talk starts. Cristiano a kept man….don't you turn your back on me. Cristiano, you come back here."

Their voices drifted away.

Isabelle leaned against the wall. The words hurt. What could their life be like? Could she stay here with him? Did she even want to give marriage another try? Marriage? They didn't even know each other. They'd met, what four days ago? You couldn't fall in love in four days…it was crazy.

She thought of his mother's uneasy looks when she looked at her.

"She'll never accept me," she whispered.

No. It would never work and she had to tell him so. Her home was in San Francisco, his was here. It's the only way to handle things. She took a deep breath and walked into the living room.

As she came through the courtyard doors, Cristiano came toward her with a slice of cake. "Thank you." Their fingertips touched as she accepted the cake, and a spark of awareness shot through her. "When will you be back on our beach?"

"In the morning. I am taking Institute Geological de Mexico's boat out …."

"I'd love to come along."

She watched his eyes widen.

"I'd like that very much, Isabella."

"When do you want me to meet you there?"

"Ten o'clock. We can spend the day together."

"What's this?" The words came from behind Isabelle and she turned.

Elena Casamiro stood there. "Mama, Isabelle and I are going out on the cruiser in the morning."

"How delightful." Her lips smiled, but her eyes were full of worry. She motioned toward her daughter. "Angelina, did you hear? Your brother is taking the company boat out tomorrow. I know how much you've wanted to get out to Isla Santa Maria."

"Mama…" Cristiano started to say.

"Don't worry, big brother. I know you want some private time with Isabelle. Besides, Stephano is taking me sailing tomorrow.""I see," Elena said. "My children keep very busy." She looked into Cristiano's face. "You will be joining us for family dinner on Sunday?"

"Of course, Mama. Perhaps Isabelle…."

"Look," Isabelle said. "Shar's waving at me. She and Brad must be ready to head home." She turned to Elena. "Thank you for letting us crash your birthday party."

"Crash? Oh, you mean come uninvited. You Americanos and your slang."

"They weren't uninvited," Angelina said. She cast a disapproving frown at her mother. "I invited them."

"Yes, yes. Of course you did. Thank you for coming." She held out her small hand. Isabelle clasped it and quickly let it go.

"I'll walk with you," Cristiano said.

"No, no," his mother cut in. "I need your help to take the cake into the kitchen…the bugs and all…"

"That's fine, Cristiano. I'll see you in the morning." Isabelle ignored his pleading look and hurried to Sharlee and Brad. "Let's go please. Now," she whispered.

"Brad, you get Magdalena. Izzy and I will be outside." Sharlee grabbed Isabelle's hand and pulled her toward the gate.

Chapter Twenty-Six

Magdalena waved goodnight to Isabelle, Sharlee, and Brad from her patio.

She went inside, stopped in the kitchen to light a candle and then walked to her bedroom. From Magdalena's bed Mira opened an eye, sat up and stretched.

"Ay, mija, it's been a long time since I've seen so many old friends."

Magdalena settled on the bed, stroked Mira's head and then ran her hand along the cat's spine. "The birthday party was elegant and very satisfying for me, Mira. It's late, but I think I will sit on the patio for a while. Will you join me?"

*****

"Sharlee, I'm going to take Sammi out. We'll head north on the beach, get some air."

"Okay, Sugar. I'm going to wash up and head to bed. I'll read for an hour or so, if you need anything…"

"I'm fine. I just need to stretch my legs and your friend does, too."

Sammi hopped in circles. Her tail fanning the air. Longfellow watched from the table, eyes half closed, tail twitching in annoyance.

"Wait a minute, Izzy…something I thought of earlier, what about your neighbor, what's his name? The jerk with the boat, is he still around?"

"Carl? I suppose he is. I saw him the other morning."

"You going to let him get away with what he did to you?"

"No. But I haven't decided what I'll do…I've been a little busy."

"He has to know you haven't forgotten. You be careful."

"You know what, Shar? He probably doesn't even remember it happening, he was so damn drunk. I'll be fine, you get some rest. I'll close up when we get back. See you in the morning."

Sammi-Sue waited for Isabelle to snap the leash before she stepped off the front ramada. San Felipe's lights glowed on the western horizon.

With Sammi trotting beside her, Isabelle walked to the shore and turned left. Sammi woofed, Isabelle unsnapped the leash and patted the sleek head.

"Yes, we'll be fine. I'm better all ready, but dang, just when I think I've got a line on things, something else jumps at us. You go ahead and have a run."

The basset hound dug in and flew down the beach. Isabelle heard her tags jingle away, circle back, fade again.

Isabelle felt tension lift from her shoulders. She'd never given much thought to a spiral being a sign of power. What would happen if she meditated inside one? In a clear space she traced a spiral with her walking stick and sat cross-legged in its center. Her breathing slowed and she closed her eyes. How long she sat there she didn't know, but when she opened her eyes she could see a pattern form in the air before her. Unseen hands wove shining strands on a glistening loom in the black sky. In the lower portion of the weaving, waves moved and pulsed, while stars flickered in its silken indigo sky.

Okay, is this real? Before this trip I would have said of course not, and blamed it on too much wine.

Isabelle leaned forward. She was surprised at her calmness. She lowered her chin toward her knees and stretched the muscles in her lower back. When she straightened, the weaving now completed, still hung in the sky. "So, it is real."

Sammi's jangling tags signaled her approach at a dead run. The basset hound's pace slowed, come to a stop. Isabelle watched Sammi who stood at the opening of the spiral, with head cocked, ears alert, listening. With a soft whine, the basset hound stepped into the spiral, and very un-Sammie-like, walked the three rotations of its path. When she reached Isabelle, she settled on the sand at her back. "You see it, too?"

Isabelle leaned against the warm dog bolster. The weaving danced in the air. The motion inside altered; the sky at the top and the flames at the bottom of the frame stabilized. Only the center moved, the waves marched toward the shore, their tops snowy with foam.

"So, now what? Somehow I don't think this is the end."

Isabelle stretched out on her back in the center of the spiral, the top of her head warmed by Sammi's heart. She closed her eyes and waited. The tide whispered at its ebb, sea gulls argued in the dark. She smelled fish and salt in the breeze that lifted the hair from her forehead.

A sensation of floating came over her and a high, sweet whistle circled. Isabelle opened her eyes. Above her, just below the weaving, a dolphin swayed. Stars shown through its translucent body. Their gazes locked.

"Isabelle, love is a precious gift, all creatures yearn for it. The warm enfolding of souls is ageless, forgiving. One must open to love, or it will wither, perhaps even perish."

"I gave my heart once and look how that turned out. I won't allow it to happen again."

"What makes you think you could be hurt again, Isabelle? Why can't you leave the past behind? Cristiano returns your passion. This is what has awakened the spirit of the Lost One. She hungers for what you two have now."

Isabelle felt warmth leach from her body and into the sand. She shuddered. "I'm not right for him."

"You refuse to let love grow anew in your heart? Learn from the anger and fear that stalks you."

Sammi started to growl. Isabelle sat up. Lightning flashed over the small caldera at the end of the island. The weaving in front of her intensified for a moment then vanished. A second weaving appeared. It showed the island's volcano, venting flaming gasses and spitting rocks from its mouth. They tumbled and bounced off one another. A small lagoon formed, surrounded by jagged red, black and tan lava boulders. The waters of the lagoon steamed and swirled. She heard the sound of sobbing.

"What the…?" Isabelle scrambled to her feet, whirled to face the dolphin, but the sky contained only scudding clouds.

With Sammi at her side, she walked toward the inflowing waves. The island loomed black against the horizon. Isabelle looked down at Sammi. The basset hound stared at the island, the hairs standing along her spine.

"Come on, let's get inside. Things will make more sense in the daylight."

*****

Isabelle slept on her back, arms out flung. Again she watched as large red and black forms rose high in the sky, fell into the sea. Sounds of tumbling lava boulders and hissing water filled her head.

"Isabelle? Izzy. Wake up, Sugar. Wake up."

She heard Sharlee's voice, felt her settle on the bed. She tried to roll to her side, but felt heaviness, as though she was being forced into the mattress. Isabelle fought against the pressure and tried to draw a deep breath.

"Longie, what is it?" She heard Sharlee say in sudden fear.

Longfellow hissed close to Isabelle's ear. Whiskers brushed her cheek. Isabelle felt a growl vibrate through him and the pressure that held her in its vice lifted.

Isabelle lurched up and gulped air.

"Izzy, you okay. You're as white as the sheet."

Her hand shook as she reached for the coffee mug Sharlee held toward her. "I—I think so. God, my head hurts."

"What was that all about?" Sharlee glanced down at Longfellow who paced beside the bed. His ears lay flat against his head and he twitched his tail back and forth.

"I was dreaming. I heard you call, but I couldn't move. Then I felt Longie growl…what time is it?"

"It's around 7:00, too early for me, by far. I want to hear all about the dream, but you've got to see this first…it all fits."

Isabelle sat up, swung her feet to the floor. "Shar, I'm heading home, day after tomorrow, if we can close up the house that soon."

"This has to do with the party yesterday? Doesn't it?"

"Yes and no. It made things clearer. I'll treat you to a day at the spa when we get to San Francisco, we'll have brunch wherever you say…I've got to leave."

"Well, maybe you do. And of course I'll help, but first I want you to come with me."

When Isabelle stepped out the front door, she looked first at the island, then to her left where Sharlee stood in front of the studio's open door.

"When's the last time you were in here?"Sharlee said.

"Not since the afternoon I arrived. Why?"

"Take a look."

Isabelle walked to the studio door, looked inside. "Oh, my God."

The boxes had been split open. Yarn covered the floor. Rugs were scattered, a chair tipped on its side, and in the center of the room was a square form outlined with hand-sized, quartz rocks.

Sharlee walked to the drafting table and picked up the framed photo of Isabelle in Hawaii. "Patricia's work for sure. What a mess. It looks like New Orleans after a Mardi Gras night."

Isabelle stared, shook her head. The weavings, the talk with the dolphin, the dream, and now this. Dizziness swept over her and she reached out.

Sharlee grabbed Isabelle. Guided her to the stool at the table. "Isabelle, here, sit down, Sugar."

"Hey, you guys in there?" Isabelle heard Brad call. He stepped into the studio. "What the hell happened?" His eyes went to the square formed by the rocks. "Would you look at that."

"Quite a display, isn't it?" Isabelle said and abruptly added. "Why don't you guys help yourself to some coffee?"

Sharlee looked at her. "You sure?"

"I need some time."

"Well, then okay."

They walked out of the studio.

A minute later Sharlee returned, bringing the phone with her. "Sorry, but it's Magdalena. She needs to speak to you now."

"Hello," Isabelle said.

"Good morning. I had a visitor last night. I'd like you to come and see what I found this morning."

A chill made the hair on the back of Isabelle's neck rise. "I had a visitor as well, Magdalena. I'm coming right over."

"I'll be on the patio."

Isabelle closed the studio doors and went in the house. "Sharlee, I'm going to finish getting dressed. Seems Magdalena also had a visit last night...."

"What?" Sharlee's eyes widened. "We're going with you."

Magdalena greeted them from the patio, Mira in her lap. "Good morning, come in, come in. Brad, there's a tray with coffee and pan dulce on the counter in the kitchen; without Andres here to help we seem to be short handed."

"We'll get it," Sharlee said. Brad held the door open for her and the two went into the house.

Isabelle pulled a chair close to Magdalena. "What did you find?"

"Tell me what was done at your house."

Isabelle gave a description of what they had found in the studio.

"I think the Lost One is attempting to communicate with us."

Isabelle stared toward the island. "There's more. Last night after we got back, I took Sammi for a walk. I don't know why, but I decided to see what would happen if I meditated inside a spiral."

Magdalena leaned in close. "And?"

"A dolphin spoke to me. She showed me weavings...."

Brad returned with the tray, Sharlee following behind him. He placed the tray on the table. While Sharlee poured coffee, Brad brought chairs for them.

"What did Marita show you?" Magdalena said. "For it had to be Marita; it seems my guide has become yours as well."

"I saw a weaving formed in the air. Sea and sky, with the island in the background, smooth and serene. The dolphin spoke to me. "Isabelle stared across Magdalena's shoulder for a moment remembering what Marita said about acceptance.

"And.?" Magdalena prompted.

"There was a second weaving, circular. A volcano erupted, flames and lava flowed into the sea. The water became hot and steam rose. It was somewhere on Isla Santa Maria."

Magdalena glanced toward the island. "I know the place you describe. Laguna Playa, the smaller caldera of the two that make up the island. There is a danger there for those on the sea, the rocks are close to the surface and the currents are strong. Within the lagoon, the water is calm and warm, a place of refuge. "

"Well, it wasn't calm last night." Isabelle said. "There was lightning above the island, and sobbing instead screaming and yelling."

"Isabelle, I believe the Lost One is speaking to us. Her figures…they are not spirals, but mazes. The spiral is an ancient symbol representing the, "life-death-rebirth" cycle. It symbolizes the sun. The ancients thought the sun died when it went below the horizon and was reborn each morning.

"Patricia with her mazes challenges, and promises we will never find a way to send her beyond."

"It fits. I don't think this is about Brad anymore," Isabelle said. " My dream was like the second weaving with the volcano and lava. When Sharlee came in to wake me, I felt like I was held down…I couldn't breathe. If Longie hadn't challenged…."

Magdalena turned to Sharlee, "What do you make of this, señorita?"

It still surprised Isabelle to hear Magdalena ask Sharlee's opinion on Patricia's behavior. There were certainly things about her friend she needed to learn more about.

"One weaving seems positive," Sharlee said. "The other…I don't know. The dream sounds like Patricia's making a point. If she can physically touch Izzy…then we need to get her away from here."

"I believe Patricia can only touch Isabelle when she sleeps, when she is open to the next plane."

"But what's she got against me?" Isabelle said. "Four days ago, she didn't know I existed."

"You were the catalyst," Magdalena said. "She was drawn to your creative soul, wanted to know more about you. Before Señor Collins' arrival Patricia believed she lived, that she waited for her loves' return." Magdalena sipped from her coffee. " Then I go with you to the island. I tell Patricia she is dead, something she does not wish to hear." Magdalena shook her head. "At the cove, Brad also tells her she is dead. Her reaction is yet more anger at his betrayal and it is you Isabelle, who has brought all of this upon her."

"I didn't know she was dead...I wanted to help."

"Patricia has fixated upon you. Destroy you and she destroys her pain."

"Well, like hell that's going to happen," Sharlee snapped as she pushed her chair back and stood. Her friend was in full protect mode. Isabelle heard it in her voice. She watched Sharlee pace the length of the patio and back.

"I'd like to see the maze she left you, Magdalena," Isabelle said.

"Of course, come."

They walked toward the side gate of the patio and went through. Outside a large triangle was traced in the sand; a labyrinthine path led to where three small, red rocks formed a tower.

They all stared in silence until the ringing of the phone made Isabelle jump.

"Brad, would you ...?" Magdalena said.

"Sure." He walked back toward the open patio doors.

"Could be Cristiano looking for me," Isabelle said, "He's taking the institute's boat out today. I'm going with him."

"Isabelle," Brad called, "it's Cristiano, for you."

Isabelle came back from the phone in time to hear Magdalena say, "Yes, I'm sure Carl is still here. But don't go to the house alone."

"No, of course not. Brad will you come with me?"

"Be happy to."

"Why would you go there anyway?" Isabelle said.

"We're going to have to go back to Isla Santa Maria," Sharlee answered. "I can't see how we can avoid it. I'm not going out there in some dinky row boat or even one of those pangas. We need a boat. As I see it, dear Carl owes you and he has a cabin cruiser."

"I don't want anything from him…except maybe a little payback," Isabelle said.

"Well, this can be it. He'll loan us his Bayliner and he won't have to worry about having a charge of attempted rape, or better yet attempted murder, leveled between his beady little eyes. What do you think?"

"We will have to return to the island to confront Patricia and a cabin cruiser would be nice," Magdalena added.

"Do I have a vote in this?" Brad asked.

"Of course you do," Sharlee said and tossed him a smile.

"Then I vote for the Bayliner. I'm not too crazy about going out onto that sea anyway. I haven't been in a boat of any kind since the accident."

Sharlee reached to touch his hand. "Well, then maybe you should stay…."

"No," Magdalena said. "Brad must be with us."

"But you said Patricia didn't care anymore that he's here…" Sharlee said.

"It is more for Señor Collins than for her."

Sharlee stood. "Then we get us a boat. I'm going over there right now."

"And I'm right behind you," Brad said. "Part of me hopes he'll try something. I'd like to knock him on his ass."

"I should come, too," Isabelle said. "Cristiano can…"

"Do you really want to see Carl…talk to him?" Sharlee said.

Isabelle shook her head. "I'd hate to say even one word…"

"Then you go meet Cristiano. Brad and I'll take care of this."

"I don't know." Isabelle frowned.

Magdalena patted Isabelle's hand. "Go with Cristiano. You have things that must be made clear between you. If for some reason we have to return to the island before you get back, we can contact you on the boat."

"I really need to get this over with."

Brad held out his hand to Sharlee. "Okay, let's make that little house call."

Sharlee twined her fingers with his and the two left, their hands swinging between them as they walked toward the line of houses. Isabelle thought they looked like newlyweds out for a stroll instead of one pit bull attorney bent on revenge and its handler.

Isabelle turned back to Magdalena.

"How is your coffee? Mine has chilled," Magdalena said. "There is more in the thermos. Will you freshen our cups?"

"Of course." Isabelle brought the tray to where they sat and poured for them. "I'm heading back to San Francisco."

"Yes, I know."

She had given up wondering how Magdalena seemed to know what was in her mind before she herself knew. "All this is getting to me; last night, the weavings in the air."

"Growth is usually a painful business, Isabelle. I have admired your determination from the beginning, but you are a different person now than the timid, conquered woman I met years."

"People change."

"Your dream. The weavings. It's your soul speaking to you. I feel something in you yearning to awake."

"Magdalena, I'm tired. I came here to find peace…do some weaving. "

"Perhaps your exhaustion comes from having chosen the wrong battle to fight."

"What?"

"You're still fighting Donald. Not accepting what is before you this moment. There is a man who loves you…"

Isabelle held up her hand. "Stop right there. Cristiano may have fooled himself and everyone else, but not me. Last night I met his family and the woman his mother has chosen for him. He loves his mother, all of his family. In the long run Cristiano will do what they want."

"Isabelle, how can you know? Why do you persist in flying your broken heart like a banner."

"I appreciate your concern-, but I'm closing the house and returning to San Francisco."

"What will you say to Cristiano?"

"What I have just told you."

"You will let your broken heart break another's?"

"I have to. That's what's best for me."

"Isabelle, the spiral has swept you up. The sooner you accept this, the better for you. Leave the past behind. You speak of San Francisco as a city. You did not call it home. You are needed here now." Magdalena reached for Isabelle's hand. "You are necessary to complete what began three years ago when Patricia Mullins' life was taken by the sea."

"And I'll be here until it's over, but then…Thank you, Magdalena, for all your help." Isabelle stood. "I'm going back to the house. Cristiano will be arriving soon."

"Very well, but please, Isabelle, listen closely and listen with your heart."

Chapter Twenty-Seven

Brad and Sharlee returned to Magdalena's patio ten minutes after Isabelle left.

"Carl was sensible, if not sober, Magdalena. He came to understand our position."

Brad broke in with a chuckle. "Our attorney here made things very clear to him."

Sharlee grinned, went on. "It seems he's had second thoughts about his behavior, wants to do something positive." She and Brad exchanged a smile. "The Bayliner is ours to use as often as we want and for as long as we need it.""Bravo, Señorita Sharlee." Magdalena clapped a flamenco riff, hands high.

"Isabelle has returned to her house. Cristiano is expected soon. I will call the hospital and check on Andres, then, perhaps some lunch and a siesta. I will think on how we can best go forward now."

"Carl's Bayliner is anchored out front of his place," Brad said. "My phone is on. Call us when you're ready and we can be on the water in fifteen, twenty minutes at the most."

"Do rest, Magdalena. We all had a late night. Brad and I will wait for your call," Sharlee added.

Magdalena watched them leave. She relaxed into the chair. Too late for coffee, too early for lunch. Mira jumped into her lap and soon the two dozed.

Outside the patio a pair of ravens walked the triangle labyrinth. Their clicks and low calls to one another became quiet as they neared the end of the path. Together in the terminus they examined the tower of red lava rocks balanced one atop the other; then launched with strokes of blue-black wings. After three circles of the ranch house, they lit upon the patio wall. Together they regarded the woman and cat, while from the peak of the island volcano, haunted eyes watched the beach.

Magdalena's mind's eye observed the campo from the center of a weaving of spiraling dolphins. On Magdalena's lap, Mira, stirred in her sleep, the fur on her tail came erect and her whiskers twitched.

Marita's mind joined Magdalena's.

The Lost One has reached out. She speaks to you in symbols. She desires to trust, but is fragile, filled with fear and confusion. My sisters and I have been to Laguna Playa. The treasure, guarded by Patricia's passion, lies there. You must come and see what has been discovered.

Sharlee and Brad stood on the beach in front of Carl's house. She pointed. "There she is, as promised." The cabin cruiser's white paint glistened in the afternoon sun. "What a beauty. I can't wait to get aboard and check her out."

"I'm surprised he can moor so close to shore," Brad said.

"That's a 340. She draws less than four feet of water."

"You seem to know your boats."

Sharlee glanced at Brad. "I've been on a few."

"Fancy looking and I'm sure the best money can buy, but is it safe?"

"It'll be like sitting in your favorite easy chair," Sharlee said. Brad laughed, but she heard the unease beneath it. "We'll be fine. The Bayliner is nothing like the little thing you guys were out in. She's top of the line."

"I'll walk with you back to Isabelle's," Brad said, turning away from the boat.

"You don't have to. I'm just going to grab a glass of tea and maybe try out the bed in the guest room."

"I'd like to do that, too," Brad said.

Sharlee faced him, smiled. "You want to try out that bed in the guest room, too?"

The color that flooded his face delighted her, but a part of her mind cautioned. What are you doing? This isn't fair to him. You've felt the connection between you. He'll want more than you can give right now.

I'll make him understand, she argued back. I want this. We need to be together again..in this life.

"Sharlee, are you listening to me?"

She tuned out her nagging conscience. "What?"

"Sheesh, you say something like that and then go away to God knows where."

"Well, what did you say?"

"I said that's not what I meant about the guest room."

"You wouldn't like to go to bed with me?" She placed her hands on her hips. "Why? I'm not your type?"

"Yes. I mean no. God, Sharlee, what are you asking me?"

"You know, Brad, sometimes talk is just plain overrated." She reached up, pulled his head down and took his mouth with hers. His lips were warm. Sharlee felt his body grow still. His mouth pressed against hers and his hands rose to grasp her hips. He pulled her tight against him and the ridge pressing into her stomach left no doubt she was indeed his type.

Satisfied, she pulled away. "Well, what do you say?"

He looked bemused. "I say I'd like to kiss you again."

She smiled. "That's a good start."

Brad shook his head. "I've never known a woman like you."

Yes, you have. Many women that were me, she thought. But, instead, she said. "There isn't another woman like me, Brad. I'm willing to bet there isn't another man like you." She reached to take his hand. "Come on. Let's walk."

They didn't hurry, they didn't talk, they just strolled along the tide line, hands swinging, letting the incoming waves bathe their feet.

Sharlee's pulse quickened as they neared Isabelle's casa. She caught Brad's eyes, shared a long look with him.

Sharlee opened the front door to complete silence and dread filled her. Where was Sammi? Had something happened? "Sammi-Sue."

The basset hound bounded from Isabelle's bedroom, looking somewhat embarrassed at being surprised.

Sammi wiggled in greeting, first in front of Sharlee, moved on to Brad and then looked beyond them.

"Nope it's just us," Sharlee said. She glanced at Brad. "How about that glass of ice tea?"

"Whatever you want," he said.

"That remains to be seen."

He took in a deep breath, turned and walked into the kitchen.

With a questioning meow, Longie sauntered from the living room. "Your momma will be back soon," Sharlee said. "I wonder how things are going with Izzy and Cristiano? I think she's making a mistake, but she's a big girl."

"Sharlee, your tea's ready," Brad called.

A tremble moved through her as she stroked Sammie's ears. "I've loved him so many times. And damn, I want this to be another life with him. It can't be, Sammie," she whispered. "I can't offer anything but the now…not until I find my answers."

She thought about the letter on the kitchen counter at home. Another dead end, but she couldn't stop searching yet. The new moon was coming and with it the visions would return. What did they mean? Who was the faceless couple who pleaded with her to find them?

Sharlee patted Sammi's head and turned toward the kitchen.

She really didn't have a choice. She'd have her now time with Brad, and head home. A humorless smile curved her lips. Now she sounded like Izzy. What a pair they made.

"Sharlee, your tea's getting warm."

"I'm coming."

"Not yet, you're not."

His words startled her, she grinned, and walked toward the kitchen with Sammi at her heels.

Brad sat at the table. He held his own glass of tea, hers sat across from him. He took a drink, licked his lips as she neared. He had a great mouth, and his hands, they knew just how to touch her.

She sat, picked up her tea and took a long drink, delighted at the extreme sweetness.

"Did I get it right?" Brad said.

"You did."

"I fixed it like mine. I wasn't sure. Some think it's over the top, that much sugar."

"And you used sugar, not the artificial stuff."

"Can't stand it. For me it's the real thing or nothing."

"Brad, what work do you do?"

"What?"

"I don't know anything about you, except you're sexy as hell."

He smiled. "I've never been called that before. Determined, a little pushy, but never sexy.

"Not even by Patricia?"

His smile faded and she wondered if bringing up his dead fiancé had been the right move.

"Patricia and I grew up next door to each other. Our families were friends. We went to the same high school, dated, went to the prom. Mom wanted us to be together. I proposed to Patricia right before my mother died."

"Did you love her?" My God, why was she pushing? She sounded like the lawyer she was, but she couldn't stop herself.

Brad took a long time answering. "Yes, I loved her. We would have been happy together."

Sharlee sat back, closed her eyes. "Maybe we shouldn't do this…"

"Is that what you want?'

She didn't hear him stand, or move, but suddenly felt his lips on the back of her neck. Her eyes flew open at the electric shock that shot through her. Brad pulled the chair back, lifted her from it and pushed it aside. He grasped her waist and pulled her back against him. His teeth nibbled the lobe of her ear and her knees quivered. His hands rose up along her rib cage, stopping below her breasts and for a moment she forgot to breathe.

"I want this, Sharlee. God, you don't know how bad I want this," he whispered into her hair.

Air rushed from her lips. She pressed back against him. Felt his hardness.

"Tell me now if you want to stop."

In answer, she placed her hands over his, drew them upward, onto her breasts. Against her back, she felt his groan move upward from his chest.

His palms grazed her nipples and she moaned. She turned in his arms. Their gazes locked, and he lowered his head and pressed his mouth against hers. Her hands went around his waist, she couldn't seem to get close enough to him.

Sharlee parted her lips, his tongue slipped inside her mouth and her knees buckled.

Brad lifted her into his arms. "Which way," he gasped.

"Down the hall. First door on the left."

He carried her. At the bedroom door, she reached to open it. They entered and he closed it behind them. From the other side of the door Sharlee heard a disgruntled whine. She couldn't have cared less.

At the edge of the bed, Brad slid her down the length of his body. Her knees shook, but held. His fingers found the bottom of her tank top and lifted it over her head. He stopped, stared at her lace-trimmed, strapless bra. She watched his tongue lick his lips and heat coursed through her. She reached behind herself, undid the hooks and let the bra fall to the floor. Sharlee felt her nipples pucker. A groan came from Brad and he reached for the zipper on her shorts.

"Wait," she said. "My turn."

Her fingers made quick work of the buttons on his shirt. She pushed it from his shoulders, down his arms, tossed it across the room. His chest was tan with a nest of blonde hair. Her eyes lowered to his flat stomach and she knew even before she looked she would find a small brown cone-shaped birthmark above his hipbone.

"Sharlee, if I don't touch you, I'm going to die right here."

"Well, we can't have that." She stepped toward him.

His hands didn't go to her breasts, but instead he traced her lips with the tip of a finger.

Oh, dear God. In how many lifetimes has he touched me like this?

Her stomach quivered. His hand moved from her mouth, trailed across her chin, throat, and stopped at the upper curve of her left breast. He had to feel her pounding heart.

Sharlee shifted restlessly, took a step closer. Brad's palm now lay flat against her skin. It felt like a brand and when he lifted his hand the imprint would remain above her heart.

She lifted her hand and placed it on his chest above his racing heart.

With his hand above her heart and hers above his, they stood. Nowhere else did their bodies touch. Her gaze locked with his, she saw a strange expression cross his face. *Does he remember? We've stood like this many time before.*

Holding her captured gaze, Brad slid his palm down the slope of her breast. Sharlee felt a rush of heat flood her core and she gasped against his lips. She rose up onto her toes and arched her back, aching for his touch. She moaned when his hand at last slid across her sensitized nub.

He had her whole body trembling…and she still had her shorts on. She would explode before much longer if he continued with his mind-blowing torture.

Sharlee felt his fingers at the button of her shorts. His other hand left her breast and trailed a fiery path down her stomach. Brad slid her shorts down her legs and cool air bathed her fevered skin.

He stepped back; his eyes moved across her. "You are so beautiful." What his control cost him was evident in the hoarseness of his words.

Good, she thought. I'm not the only one about to lose it. He's dry kindling waiting for a spark and I'm about to supply it. Her gaze dropped to his erection pressing against his shorts. And with a smile, she stepped forward and ran her fingers along the length of the bulge.

Brad gasped and all control fled. Greedy hands and lips, both hers and his, seemed everywhere at once. She couldn't touch enough of him, soon enough. Their remaining clothes disappeared. Their bodies entwined on the bed, coming together, separating, then coming closer still, as if they wanted to crawl into each other, become one soul. They sought for, raced toward release and found it as deep shudders moved through them.

Brad collapsed upon her and she gloried in the weight of him. Sharlee murmured in protest when he rolled from her.

"I'll squash you."

"No. You're fine. Don't leave me."

"I'm not going anywhere." She felt his fingers entwine with hers. "That was amazing," he said.

It always is, she thought. Sharlee ignored the wrench of pain she felt inside and forced herself to laugh. She took a deep breath, turned on her side to face him. "You never did say what you do for a living."

He glanced at her, returned to examining the ceiling. "I don't want to tell you."

"Why not? Let me guess. You're a gigolo. You make your living having sex."

Brad laughed. "Not hardly."

"Well, you could. I'd sure pay you."

He stared into her face until she was the one to break eye contact. "If you really want to know. I write romance novels."

"You do what?"

"I write romance novels....Colleen Bradley at your service."

"My God! I've read your books. *Bayou Madness* is one of my all time favorites. No wonder you're so damn good in bed. Some of those scenes...."

"It's fiction, Sharlee. It's all in my head. I've never had a real life experience like what I write...not until now."

Oh, yes, you have. Now she knew why that one scene in *Bayou Madness* had seemed so real to her. She rose onto her knees, straddled him. "That scene in *Bayou Madness*, when they're in the canoe, do you think we can try that?"

He rested his hands on her waist. "This isn't a canoe."

She moved against him, felt his response. "We can improvise."

And they did.

Sharlee lay with eyes closed. Brad snored beside her. They'd have to get up soon, but maybe they would have time to take a shower together. She turned and looked at his face, felt a tug at her heart.

She kicked the sheet aside, stood, and what felt like icy fingers raced along the back of her neck. Her arms erupted with goose bumps.

What the hell?

Beside her, Brad moaned. She reached to touch his arm and an enraged scream shrilled. Sharlee gasped and covered her ears with her hands, but it did nothing to dampen the sound. She looked at Brad. He slept on. Isabelle's words came to her, what she'd said about the screams at the cove.

The scream came again, followed by harshly sobbed words she couldn't make out. It didn't take a genius to figure out the problem…she, Brad, hot sex, and maybe even awareness of the emotions tugging at her heart.

Shut up, Patricia. He was mine way before he was yours, and besides, you're dead. We're alive.

I am not dead. The words seared into Sharlee's brain.

Bitch. Whore.

Across from her, the striations snaking within the stone walls moved. A face formed. Black eyes glared. The mouth moved.

I had begun to trust Isabelle's words. I was stupid. You have stolen what I love. Now I will take from you.

"What? What do you mean?"

You will ache, Bitch, like me. Where your heart should be you will feel nothing but pain and a cold that never ends.

Sharlee began to tremble at the words spit from the mouth.

"Oh," she said, then forced a smile before going on. "From what I hear then, you haven't changed all that much."

The stone lips thinned to a sneer.

You speak bravely, but that will change when you hold your friend's dead body against your heart.

Sharlee ran to the wall. "You leave Izzy out of this. She's done nothing to you."

Nothing? It is all because of her.

Patricia laughed wildly, then the face was gone.

"Sharlee?" Brad's voice came from behind her. "Who are you talking to?"

"We've got to go to Magdalena right now. Patricia's going to do something to Isabelle."

Sharlee grabbed her clothes and began pulling them on.

Chapter Twenty-Eight

In dolphin form, Magdalena swam with Marita and the dolphin sisters. The group flew through the water above the island's roots. Amongst and around volcanic boulders, hardened lava flows spread along the sea floor. The dolphins moved northwest, along sandy beaches, past the ancient smoothness of the island's original volcano. They glided by the islet where Magdalena and the sisters first experienced the fury of Patricia .

We travel to the key, Magdalena. The key to the chains that bind the Lost One's heart. It is there you will find the missing pieces.

When they arrived at the end of the island, the group of dolphins spread out.

The volcanic flow ended here. A line of shredded black and red lava rocks extended two hundred feet north into the sea. Sharp, irregular shards reached toward the sky.

Magdalena swam at Marita's flank.

Move carefully now, sister. We must go one by one. Stay near me. The rock is unforgiving, the water's surge powerful, yet beyond, all is calm.

Magdalena and the dolphins swam through a corridor two dolphins wide and six long. The passage twisted and turned, opened into a lagoon. The sisters formed a spiral around her. She looked down upon scattered bones.

Here the Lost One lies, Marita said.

The dolphins descended, the spiral formed and reformed around Magdalena. Her belly whispered against the sand. The bones swirled as she passed.

Staccato beeps of her phone jerked Magdalena back to consciousness.

"Hello?"

"Señora Fuentes? Dr. Arguelos here. We have Andres' written permission to proceed with treatment. This means we will operate to correct the fracture of his left tibia. The procedure is scheduled for seven AM tomorrow. His cousin, Margarita, is here. Would you like to speak with her?"

"Si. Thank you, Dr. Arguelos, for calling." Magdalena said and then the husky voice of her niece came through the phone.

"Tia, how are you?"

"Margarita, it's good to hear your voice. When did you arrive in San Felipe?"

"Just this morning. Mom called and told me about Andres. I cleared my calendar, and I'm going to stay until poor old Andi is on his feet again."

"Oh, mija. I'm so relieved. I'm well and so is your friend Mira. Greet Andres for me. I send him my love; please stay in touch."

"Of course, Tia. Bye for now." And the call ended.

Magdalena put the phone down and ran her fingers through her hair. She walked to the sofa, sat and began to weave her hair into a French braid. Andres was on the road to recovery and she had a boat at her disposal.

With Marita's guidance and the discovery of Patricia's remains, she knew she must venture once more to Laguna Playa. Her fingers stilled their movement and she stared into space. Laguna Playa--where her daughter was conceived. Laguna Playa--where she sat for days with Rodolfo's urn. Laguna Playa--the youngest, most active caldera on Isla Santa Maria.

"Magdalena, are you there?" Sharlee called.

Magdalena watched Brad and Sharlee hurry across the patio."Yes, come in. I am almost ready." She leaned over, pressed her forehead against Mira's. "I am off to the island. Please watch the house. We will return soon."

"We've got to find Isabelle and be quick about it," Sharlee said.

"What has happened?"

"It was my turn to have a visit from Patricia." Sharlee glanced at Brad. "She's not very happy with me. She threatened Isabelle.

Magdalena grabbed her bag, put it over her shoulder. "I see. Let's go."

"You know I'm not going to be much help," Brad said.

"No problem," Sharlee said. "You can be my first mate."

They topped the berm, started toward the shore.

Brad cursed under his breath. "That bastard Carl has had the last word. He's left the dinghy tied to the Bayliner. I'll go out and bring it in for you, no need for us all to get wet."

Magdalena and Sharlee waited at the shore.

"Patricia's plenty pissed at me," Sharlee said.

"I imagine she is. I sense a difference in your relationship with Señor Bradley, Sharlee. Perhaps your siesta was not all restful sleep."

A blush crept up Sharlee's face. "Patricia treated me to a screaming fit. She said I'd taken her love, now she would take from me someone I loved."

"We will not let that happen. " Magdalena looked toward the island. "I also had an informative siesta. We must go to Laguna Playa."

" No," Sharlee protested. "We've got to find Izzy."

"Patricia must be dealt with first. Stopping her removes the threat. The answer to sending the Lost One on lies at Laguna Playa. Trust me in this, Sharlee." Magdalena looked toward the sea. "We will go to Laguna Playa. There we will find answers. Come, Brad is ready for us."

Sharlee wanted to argue more, instead she pressed her lips together and gave a curt nod. They walked down to the shore and Brad helped them aboard the runabout and then unhooked the mooring line.

In the main cabin, Sharlee set a course for the south end of the island.

"Magdalena," Brad said. "I'm starved. I'm going below to see what we've got for groceries. Anything special for you?"

"I would love some tea, thank you."

"What about you, Sharlee?"

"A bottle of water with a slice of lime would be great."

"Coming right up."

The afternoon was warm and the sky clear. After a few minutes, Brad came topside carrying a bottle of water. "Carl must have bouts with his conscience after all. There was a complete tea chest. I've started some green tea for us, Magdalena." He walked to Sharlee and held out the water.

Magdalena watched Sharlee drink from her water bottle and then said. "Sharlee, have you thought that perhaps both Patricia and Isabelle are simply progressing to the next level of their individual development?"

"What?"

"Perhaps the two of them are evolving and we are only bystanders to the events. Perhaps Isabelle is merely a catalyst."

Brad sat down next to Magdalena. "You think so?"

"Patricia Mullins does not accept her death. There is a strong communication between Isabelle and Patricia. The two circle each other, neither willing to give way. It can't go on." Magdalena stood. "I think perhaps I'll go forward and have my tea. I find the light very bright this afternoon. Sharlee, please call me when we pass between the islands."

"I'll do that."

Magdalena poured a mug of tea and went forward into the captain's berth. She tasted the tea, sat the mug on a railed shelf next to the king size bed, stretched out and lay quietly among the cushions and pillows.

Patricia is one of the most grasping women I have ever known. But she was so young when she lost her life; I must make allowances. Yet, I so regret she has drawn me back to Laguna Playa. Tears slid down her face.

On the other side of the thin fiberglass hull, the sounds of Magdalena's soft crying reached Marita and her sisters. They rode the bow wake beside her, their communication stilled in respect.

After a while, Magdalena's eyes closed.

On Isla Santa Maria, Patricia watched as the Bayliner neared and she smiled.

In the main cabin, Brad skimmed a yachting magazine. He could see Sharlee's tanned feet and legs swinging as she guided the boat and monitored the electronics. Lethargy flowed through him and in moments his eyes drifted shut. The magazine fell from his hands.

Sharlee set a new heading as the Bayliner cleared the southern point. Now familiar with the controls, she relaxed a little. The Bayliner was easy to handle and the sea calm. The sun and the gentle movement of the boat lulled her. Her eyes grew heavy and she shook her head.

The glare on the water seemed to intensify and she adjusted her baseball cap.

"Brad. Magdalena," she called. But no one answered. Where are they? Guess I'm on my own.

She yawned, shook her head again. She hummed and sang aloud, but couldn't overcome the sudden drowsiness. Her head fell forward and rested on the wheel. The Bayliner headed toward the rocks where the sea swirled and waves glowed green in the sunlight.

On the island, Patricia's smile widened.

Chapter Twenty-Nine

The institute boat was moored one hundred yards off shore. Isabelle had planned to swim later and had pulled white shorts over the bottom of her red tankini.

At the shoreline Cristiano picked her up.

"What are you doing?" she said.

"No sense you getting wet, Isabella."

"It's only what? Three-feet deep where the boat is." She pointed. "And I'm dressed to get wet."

He kissed the tip of her nose. "Silence. I wish to do this."

His arm beneath her legs seemed to brand her where they touched. He pulled her closer, pressing her breasts against his bare chest.

Isabelle felt her heartbeat quicken. I should tell him now, save us both some pain. But I want this day. Maybe it's selfish…hell, it is selfish. I'll tell him later. Make him understand, it's for the best.

Isabelle looped her arm around his neck and leaned in closer yet to Cristiano.

The walk through the sea was all too short.

"Isabella," Cristiano called from the helm, "you are turning pink."

273

"What?"

"You require sun screen. I cannot have you hurting, unless it is for want of me." He tossed a grin at her.

"I've got sun screen in my bag." She stood, crossed the boat, fished it out and flipped the cap open.

"No. Come here. I will help you."

"You're driving."

"You can take the helm. The way before us is clear of danger."

Cristiano stepped to the side and Isabelle slid between him and the wheel. The wood of the helm was warm and she felt the hum of the boat's engine in her fingers. "What do I do?"

"Just hold her steady." He stood so close his breath caressed the back of her neck.

Salt spray coated her face and she licked if from her lips. Wind teased her hair from its braid and whipped it out straight behind her. The deck vibrated beneath her bare feet, the beat rose into her thighs. She laughed into the wind. "This is wild."

She felt his lips touch the nape of her neck. "It only gets better, my Isabella."

He stepped closer still. She felt his erection press against her lower back and the throbbing of her heart dropped to meet the shudder that moved up her legs.

His finger tips grazed the nape of her neck as he untied the halter strap of her bathing suit and let it fall forward across her breasts. The sun screen was cool against her skin, his fingertips delicious and abrading as he spread the lotion along her shoulder, across her back.

His fingers went down her spine and she caught her breath as they slipped beneath the waistband of her shorts.

"Cristiano." The word came out a hoarse gasp. "There are rocks ahead."

He laid his hands over hers on the helm. "We change course, so." She felt the muscles of his arms and chest slide against her as he guided the boat around the jagged volcanic mounds.

The movement of his arms had worked her tankini top low upon her breasts. "I'd better tie my top before I lose it again," she said.

"I much prefer you as you were the first time we met."

Isabelle ducked beneath his arm, stepped from him as she forced a laugh. "I must have been a sight; wet, bedraggled and cold."

"You were vulnerable, beautiful and magnificent."

Her face heated. "Very gallant of you to say, thank you." She turned, looked toward the island. "We're getting close."

"We are near. In the basket beside you there is a scarf. Tie it around your eyes."

"What?"

"I wish the site to burst upon you…all at once."

"Oh. Okay." Isabelle found the green silk scarf. She tied it around her eyes and instantly entered a different world. She felt how the sun shone warmer on different parts of her body. The scents of the ocean became more intense, briny with the smell of clean decay. She shook her head. Clean decay? Yet somehow it fit. The boat rose and fell beneath her feet, her stomach dipped with it and she swallowed. Over the dull roar of the engine she heard the sharp cries of arguing gulls. Beneath her fingertips she could feel each ridge of the side rail. The flood of sensations made her reel and she lifted her hand to untie the scarf.

"No, we are almost here," Cristiano said.

The boat slowed, she felt its bow sink lower into the water, the engine cut off. She lifted her hand toward the scarf again.

"One more minute. Okay. Now."

Isabelle untied the scarf. For a moment, even behind her sunglasses, the sudden glare blinded. She blinked, lifted her hand to shade her eyes. "Oh," she whispered. The scene before her was a jumble of light, sound, and texture. Mountains of red and black lava-rock formed walls to each side of a flowing inlet. The sea beat against them, a sonorous roar, sending misty plumes of water skyward in endless patterns.

Beyond the entrance to the lagoon it was as if a line was drawn from rock wall to rock wall. The water smoothed, looked like a sheet of glistening blue-green glass. "I have to put this in a weaving."

"And where will you put the flame?" Cristiano said from behind her.

Isabelle closed her eyes. She could see the design in her head…the scene exact as it was before her, but coming from the sky would be slender fingers of pale flame, like the sun was caressing the waves with its hand. "The passion will be there," she said, turning to him.

He held two glasses. "I have dropped anchor. Champagne?"

"Thank you." She accepted a glass.

"I also have strawberries. I love the taste together." He drank from his glass, licked his lips.

Isabelle couldn't tear her gaze from his mouth.

"You don't like champagne?"

She lifted her eyes to his. "What? No, I love it."

"But you are not drinking."

She felt her face heat as she gulped champagne. "Are we going into the lagoon?"

"Yes. We will swim, but first." He took the glass from her, sat it aside and reached for the scarf she forgotten she still held.

Isabelle felt her eyes widen. Her stomach fluttered in anticipation. "What?"

"Do you trust me, Isabella?"

She swallowed and nodded.

Cristiano set his glass of champagne next to hers, walked behind her. She felt his warm lips graze the back of her neck, and the scarf again blotted out her sight. Something cool and smooth traced her lips.

"Open your mouth."

She did.

"Bite."

The sweet taste of strawberry flooded her senses. She chewed, swallowed.

"Drink."

Tart champagne tickled her tongue, made her groan with delight. "Cristiano?" She lifted her hand, reached out and her fingertips touched warm, bare skin. She took a step forward, laid her palm against him. His heart pounded beneath her hand and she felt a moan move through him. The boat rose and fell, the motion of entwined lovers.

"Finish your strawberry." Cristiano spoke hoarsely.

She felt the fruit against her lips and lifted her hand to push it away. "I don't want…"

"Patience."

She took the strawberry into her mouth. Chewed quickly and swallowed.

His soft laugh reached her ears. "More champagne?"

Isabelle nodded, then tensed when the glass did not touch her lips.

His hand removed hers from his chest, placed it at her side. "Cristiano?" Her ears strained. She heard the sigh of the wind and the faint cry of seagulls. Then Isabelle gasped as cool, wetness, dripped onto her left shoulder, trailed down her shoulder blade. "What?"

"Oh. It seems I have spilled some champagne." His words came from behind her. "Do not worry, my Bella. I will remove it from you."

Warmth licked away the coolness and her knees trembled. "Oh God."

She felt him circle her. More wetness. This time flowing across the top of her breast and moving downward. Her breath caught in her throat with expectation.

"How clumsy of me."

His mouth followed the champagne's path. Isabelle gasped when he tongued her nipple through the thin nylon of her tankini.

"This must go. Lift your arms."

She felt him remove the offending top. Air kissed her skin and warmth having nothing to do with the sun, heated her core.

"Bella, you are beautiful. Your skin is like cream. And then there are these berries."

He breathed warmly against her right nipple and drew it into his mouth. Pleasure arced through her. She wound her fingers in his hair and held him against her.

Cristiano's hands rested on her hips. Without taking his mouth from her breast, he skimmed her shorts and tankini bottom down her legs.

His hands, his mouth, the sun on her naked body and the motion of the boat…it was like no other experience in her life. Her legs trembled. Cristiano's arm went around her waist. He pulled her against him. And it irritated her to feel clothing between them. Isabelle's hands rose to the waistband of his shorts, found the button, the zipper and unfastened both.

She heard his quick intake of breath and smiled. Two can play at such torture.

She pushed his shorts down his legs, gasping when she felt his swollen flesh graze her stomach.

Cristiano trailed wet kisses to her other breast and Isabelle moaned.

"Enough of this," she said and pulled the scarf from her eyes. They were both naked now. He lifted his head. Isabelle wound her fingers into his dark hair and urged him forward.

His lips were warm with the slight taste of salt. Her mouth parted and his tongue slipped inside. Isabelle pressed against him. It was if she couldn't get close enough. They dropped to the deck. They moved in unison with the motion of the boat, faster and still faster, until with a loud cry Isabelle shuddered and collapsed against him.

She lay unmoving, her ear against Cristiano's heart. It's thudding slowed and she could hear the cry of sea gulls. The heat of the sun on her back registered. We should go below. Neither of them needed sunburns, but she hated to move.

Beneath her, Cristiano stirred.

"Bella."

She felt the word rumble through his chest.

"Hmm?"

"We should…."

Isabelle sighed. "I know." She rolled from him and stood. Her gaze swept his body. He was so damn beautiful. She looked at him again, slowly, wanting to burn his perfection into her brain.

"Bella, what is it?"

"What?" She met his eyes.

"You looked so sad."

"No. No I'm fine. I was just admiring the view."

"As am I." His lips spread into a slow smile.

She reached a hand toward him. "You need some help getting up?"

His smile changed to a grin. "I don't know. You be the judge." He gestured, her eyes followed the movement of his hand.

Heat flashed into her cheeks at the sight of him, ready again. She let her hand drop. "That isn't what I meant."

Cristiano rose to his feet. "See I am up."

"Yes, I can see that."

He reached to take her hand. "Shall we go below and continue this conversation?"

Isabelle sighed in contentment. She lay on her stomach, her cheek against her outstretched arm. Cristiano slept beside her, his arm a delicious weight across her waist. She smiled reliving each moment of their passion, filing it away in her mind.

She'd had some rough times on this trip, but these moments with Cristiano made it all worthwhile. She clamped down on her thoughts, refusing to go any further down that path. She and Sharlee would get the house closed up tomorrow and be on the road to San Francisco Monday. It had to be that way. To wish otherwise was crazy. Cristiano and Cordelia would be married. The thought made her stomach clench, and she carefully slid from the bed. Cristiano murmured, but did not wake.

Naked, Isabelle went topside. The sun felt wonderful. She turned looked back. He makes me feel beautiful. My butt isn't too big and my breasts are fine. "Thank you." she whispered.

Isabelle walked to the side and looked up at the sheer rocky cliffs of the island. "I understand Patricia. I get it. It must be hell remembering love and passion and not be able to have it. But you have to move on. Your time here is over. You're going to go crazy hanging around, only seeing, never experiencing. Life will never be yours again. And from what I've seen, neither will Brad."

"Bella, to whom do you speak?"

Isabelle turned. A naked Cristiano stood behind her. "To Patricia. I thought I'd try some reasoning, maybe a little female bonding. Nothing else seems to work."

He shook his head. "I believe our Patricia has a different mindset."

"But she has to see. This isn't her world any longer."

"Does she, my love? Does she?" He held out a shirt toward her. "No matter how much I enjoy the sight of you as made by God, you are turning pink."

Her body warmed. "Thanks." And in her mind she added, for much more than the shirt. She reached for it, but Cristiano shook his head and held it open for her to slide her arms into. When she had, he smoothed it across her breast and began to slowly button the shirt, starting at the top and going downward. The shirt ended just above her thighs and she swore her heart stopped for a moment when his fingers grazed her as he finished with the last button. Good God. How can I walk away from this man?

"What about you?" She managed to say. "I'm sure you can get too much sun also."

"I can, but I will be fine for a few moments more." Cristiano pulled her into his arms and she rested her cheek against his heart.

"About tomorrow," he said. "I want you to be with me when I go home for family dinner."

Isabelle stiffened. Here it was. She felt a shiver move through her.

"Bella, you are cold. Come, we will go below and dress." He stepped back, took her hand.

"Cristiano, I can't come with you tomorrow. Sharlee and I are getting the house ready for us to leave."

His hand tightened on hers. Isabelle kept her eyes on the boat's deck. "We're heading back to San Francisco on Monday. It's been a great vacation, but Sharlee reminded me of appointments I have on Wednesday."

He released her hand, stepped back. It was only a few inches, but it felt as if miles were between them. "I see," he said.

God, I can't face him and do this. I can't. She whipped around, stared across at Isla Santa Maria, blinking eyes that were suddenly full of tears. Isabelle swallowed. "I hope we can get together my next visit. Although I really don't know when that will be." She spoke quickly, running her words together, until she ran out of air, took a deep breath that made her ache all the way to her toes.

His words came quiet and controlled. "This time has meant nothing to you."

"Oh, of course it has. It's been great, well, almost all of it, but vacations end, we go back to real life."

"I see," he said again. "I will start the boat."

"The lagoon. Aren't we going in?"

For a moment Cristiano said nothing, then he snorted a laugh. "Why not? We want to complete your vacation experiences, don't we? Let's start with this." He grabbed her shoulders and turned her around.

"Cristiano…"

His mouth smothered her words. The rough kiss stole her breath. And she felt her knees buckle. His hands clamped upon her hips and he pulled her against his body. Cristiano's mouth left hers, trailed down her neck. She groaned as she leaned back in his arms. His kisses stopped on the slope of her right breast.

"Is this what you want? Too bad we do not have a camera. You know what they say? A picture saves a thousand words, or something so." His cold words were like a frigid shower.

Isabelle's hands rested on his shoulders. "Stop."

"Stop?" He licked her nipple. "Are you sure?"

She pushed against him. "I'm sure."

"As you wish, señora." He stepped back.

Isabelle looked into his face. A white line etched Cristiano's lips. "Don't you see? It would never work. Your mother…Cordelia…."""

"Do I look as if I cannot think for myself?"

His controlled words hurt worse than if he'd screamed them at her.

Isabelle clenched her hands into fists. "I have to protect me. How soon before you grow tired of…? I won't go through that again."

"Your heart knows I am not Donald. Why will you not let your mind accept also?"

In silence, she looked down at her feet.

"You do not trust, you have no faith…."

Isabelle jerked her head up. His words sounded like pained acceptance, a swift panic flowed through her. He turned, walked from her. *No.* Her one word scream filled her mind. She took a step toward Cristiano—the boat surged and dropped from beneath her.

Isabelle landed on her hands and knees on the deck. The boat rose again, dropped. Cold water flooded over her, a roar filled her head.

"Isabelle," Cristiano screamed. "Remain where you are."

The boat bucked. She slid across the deck, came up hard against the side. Water filled her mouth. She coughed, spit. They weren't far off the rocks. Would the anchor hold? The boat rose, fell, and her forehead slammed against the deck.

Isabelle screamed and a shrill cry of triumph filled her head. *Patricia*, she thought as her vision grayed at the edges.

The boat heaved again. She felt a weight across her body and turned her head. Cristiano lay beside her. "It's easing. One moment more. Hold on."

Isabelle's hand searched for and found his. She held her breath, waited for the next wild ride, but it didn't come.

Cristiano pulled his hand from hers. She turned her head to face him, a protest on her lips. He rose onto his hands and knees, waited a moment and stood.

"It's over. Are you hurt?"

Isabelle took stock. Her wrist ached. She knew she must have a lump the size of an egg on her forehead, but nothing seemed broken. She rolled over onto her back and sat up. "I'll live."

Cristiano's fingers traced the lump on her forehead. "There is pain medication below. I will get it."

He turned away. "Cristiano?"

He glanced back. "What?"

"Some clothes," she suggested.

He looked at her, down at his nakedness. "Si, some clothes."

Chapter Thirty

"A four point five, judging by the instrument panel," Cristiano said. They were both clothed and sipped from cups of hot, green tea.

Isabelle's pain medication had kicked in, and she felt wrapped in a soft cloud of complacency.

"In a moment, we will lift anchor and start back to your beach. You are sure you are okay?"

"I'm fine. I'll be sore tomorrow, though."

"You may have to postpone your trip home."

She glanced at him, but his face told her nothing. "I know that was a sea quake, but…." She looked toward the island.

"What?"

"I heard Patricia laughing."

"You did?"

She looked at him, saw nothing but concerned speculation in his face. "It seemed to be directed at us."

"Why?" Cristiano said.

Isabelle rubbed her wrist. "I'm beginning to think she doesn't like me."

He set his cup aside and stood. "I'll bring in the anchor."

Isabelle watched him walk away. I don't think he likes me anymore, either. Tears filled her eyes. She didn't try to

286

stop them, and they felt warm upon her cheeks. Doing the right thing sucks.

She stood where she was and listened as Cristiano engaged the anchor motor. It's over. Isabelle wished she could blame the dullness she felt in her heart on the pain medication, but she couldn't. A grinding noise sounded from behind her and she turned. Cristiano swore.

"What's wrong?"

"The anchor is fouled." He walked to the front of the boat and looked over the side. "I'm going to have to take a look."

"Down there? What if there's an aftershock?"

"I won't be long." Cristiano stripped down to his skin. "I guess getting dressed was a waste of time."

She watched dumbfounded as he dove into the water. She ran to the side, looked down in time to see him take a deep breath and disappear.

It seemed like forever before he reappeared. "Rocks have it buried. I might be able to dislodge one and cause a small slide." He dove again.

Isabelle counted to herself. If she reached one hundred and he wasn't back, she was going in. He resurfaced at eighty-five, swam toward the ladder.

"Isabelle, lean down."

"What?"

"I found something. I need to pass it to you."

She leaned over the side of the boat. One-handed, he climbed three rungs, then reached. Without thinking she took what he held, straightened, and backed from the boat's side.

Isabelle looked down. When her mind registered what she saw, she almost tossed it back into the sea. It was a white skull, worn smooth by sea and sand.

A shudder moved up her spine, made the hair on the back of her neck rise. "Dear God." She frantically looked around. I'm holding a skull...someone's head. Her stomach clenched.

"Isabelle, give it to me," Cristiano said from behind her. She whipped around, thrust it toward him.

"Where did you find it?" she said as he took it from her.

"When I moved the rock to try and free the anchor. It was in a grave of sand."

Isabelle swallowed. "Do you know who it is?"

"Of course I do not. I'll take it to the authorities in San Felipe." He frowned. "Can you stand to hold it one moment more? I think there is a field sample bag below."

"Okay." She held out her hands and he placed the skull into them.

"I won't be but a minute."

She watched Cristiano disappear into the cabin. The skull in her hands seemed to warm. Her fingers trembled. It's not alive. It's a skull. It's not getting warmer.

Cristiano returned with a small green canvas bag. She noticed that while below he'd taken a minute to slip on a pair of tan shorts.

He held the bag open. "Put it in here." Isabelle obeyed. "I'll take it below."

She sighed in relief to see the skull and Cristiano disappear into the cabin.

"No. Mine. You will not."

The sudden shriek filled her head.

On the island, rocks tore free and bounded and bounced toward the sea. A cloud of dirt rose. A rock landed on the deck beside her. Another. A smaller one struck her shoulder and she cried out.

"Isabelle," Cristiano screamed.

Something pushed her, she stumbled to the side, turned. A fist-sized rock struck Cristiano's head. He swayed, another hit his shoulder and he went over the side.

"Cristiano." Isabelle ran to the side of the boat, looked down, saw nothing but churning water.

She dove.

The chill of the water took her breath away. She looked around wildly. Where is he? Dear God. Where is he?

In front of her a dolphin leapt. Magdalena's dolphins? Did she send them? Can they understand me?

A dolphin leapt again.

"Help me. Help me, please."

The dolphin dove. Seconds seemed hours. He's gone. He's gone.

In front of her two sleek backs appeared. Cristiano's head broke the surface. A dolphin swam beneath each of his arms.

He coughed, spat water.

Alive. Thank God. Thank God. Isabelle looked up at the boat. She would never get him aboard. The lagoon was their only hope. She faced the dolphins. "I can't do it without you." Isabelle swam to Cristiano. "Turn on your back. I'll hold your head."

He stared into her face.

"Cristo, please."

He turned, let his legs float out from him.

Holding Cristiano's head above water they started toward the beach.

Time had no meaning as she fought to keep his head above water and to breathe herself. Twice she cried out in panic for the dolphins to stop so she could draw a deep breath without water.

The current grew stronger. Rocks of wall surrounded them…and then they were inside the lagoon. The water calmed. The dolphins angled to the right, toward the beach.

She hooked her arm around Cristiano's waist. "I can take it from here." The dolphins dove. Taking a deep breath, she swam with Cristiano the last few feet to the sandy beach. Grabbing him by his shoulders, she dragged him forward, and collapsed beside him.

Cristiano's moan roused her. *My God. How long was I out?* She sat up, looked at him. A raw gash across his forehead made her gasp. That needs stitches. There's a first aid kit on the boat and my cell phone. She looked toward the lagoon's opening. It's not that far. And the boat's just beyond. She stood on trembling legs, stumbled into the water.

I can do this. I have to do this. Isabelle stroked in time with her thoughts. She looked toward the lagoon entrance. She was only halfway. Something brushed her leg and she screamed. A few feet from her a dolphin's head broke water. The dolphin swam alongside her and Isabelle grabbed a fin.

Within minutes, they were at the side of the boat. Isabelle climbed the ladder. With trembling arms she pulled herself up and fell into the boat. "Thank you. Thank you. Thank you"

She crawled to the cabin, found her bag and cell phone. Punched in Brad's number.

***

A dolphin whistled a high warning and leapt across the bow of the cabin cruiser. It's shrill call of alarm grew louder.

Sharlee felt the sound, lifted her head, stared through the windshield and screamed.

Brad jerked awake. "What? What, Sharlee?"

"We're practically on the rocks. Good God, what happened? I'll get us out of here, but grab hold of something, this is going to get exciting." She stood. "Check on Magdalena."

Magdalena awoke to the dolphin's cries of distress. She sat up on the lush bed, disoriented and alarmed. She felt the boat turn rapidly, got up and rushed through the door.

"Hold on to something, Magdalena," Brad shouted.

The boat pitched forward. His feet went out from beneath him and he landed in a tangle on the deck. Magdalena lurched backward. Her head hit the wood framing of the companionway, blood flowed.

"Hang on, hang on," Sharlee yelled. She pushed the throttle forward; her other hand gripped the wheel. The twin diesels roared and Sharlee bent her knees with the motion of the boat. She moved the wheel in a tight turn, heard the props hit rock, the boat dug in and they leapt away from the shoals, bow high and diesels pumping.

"Whoa, what happened there?" Brad said. He and Magdalena were on the settee, a first aid kit between them on the cushion.

Magdalena winced as Brad cleaned the cut. "I believe the Lost One distracted us almost to our ruin."

"The glare is the last thing I remember. We were damned near on the rocks," Sharlee said. "We need to be up top. Brad, when you're finished, come here and stand by while I go up on the bridge. I can see better from there."

"And someone should be forward in the bow too as we near the lagoon. I'll go," Magdalena said.

"Are you sure," Sharlee asked. "You took a good hit."

"I'm fine. I'll call out the course when we get near."

Magdalena went forward and sat in the bowsprit; her hands on the stanchions on each side. Her feet swung over the water. Below, Marita and the dolphins danced in the bow wave.

Magdalena, currents push. Rocks cut. Water strong.

Brad stood behind and to the side, in front of the forward windows, his hand braced on the deck above. "The water is clear as glass."

"I see this place in my dreams often. It's where I have marked each of my life's changing moments. Yet, never have I seen the water so." Before them one of the dolphins jumped higher than the others. Magdalena smiled. "Marita welcomes us to her home."

"How you doing up there?" Sharlee called.

"We're getting close," Magdalena said.

"Slowing down then." The Bayliner fell from its plane. "Will I see the opening to the channel when we get there?"

"The entrance to the channel is difficult to see," Magdalena replied. "The dolphins and I will direct you. It's around the point."

Brad's cell phone rang. "Brad here." He listened for a moment. "Are you okay? Yes, we're just on the other side of the island in Carl's boat. Where are you?" He frowned. "Okay, hold on. We're almost there." He flipped close his phone. "There's been an accident, Cristiano's hurt."

Chapter Thirty-One

Isabelle's legs trembled as she walked to the end of the boat and looked down at the runabout. *Can I?* With a sigh she turned away. *I don't know how to operate it. If I try we could end up in a bigger mess.*

She ran back to the boat's ladder, climbed down and dropped into the water.

Isabelle felt the current's tug grow stronger as she neared the passage between the rocks. She kicked and stroked harder, but knew it would be a battle to get into the lagoon before the waves batted her against the rocks.

She closed her mind to the thought of failure. She would make it. She had to.

Isabelle stopped, treaded water, looked toward the jagged rocks. She'd get by them and into the lagoon even if it required leaving skin behind. Her best bet was to let the current take her and angle away at the last minute.

She stretched out, let her body flow. It felt great not to fight, for at least these moments. She moved faster now, struggled to keep the water out of her mouth. How close? How close? But she couldn't raise her head against the rush of the water.

Swim now, Isabelle. Swim. Her arms and legs felt weighted. She angled left, stroked against the current. The water yanked her back. No. She kicked harder. Felt the

293

scrape of rock against her hip, suddenly as if a gate dropped the water smoothed.

Isabelle's heart pounded as she swam toward the beach. At first, she didn't realize when her fingers scraped bottom. She stood, stumbled toward Cristiano and dropped to his side. He looked as if he hadn't moved since she left. But it had only been minutes, not the hours her heart felt.

She watched his chest. It rose and fell. The gash on his forehead still oozed blood. Shouldn't he have come around by now?

"Cristiano. Cristo, can you hear me? Brad's on the way. We'll get you to the hospital."

Isabelle turned, looked toward the lagoon's entrance, back to him. "I'm stupid and a coward. I love you. I don't care if we've only known each other five days. It seems like I've looked for you my entire life."

She settled back, drew her knees to her chest. "I want to spend the rest of my life with you. I don't care if it's thirty days or thirty years."

Isabelle pushed dark hair away from Cristiano's forehead. "Come on, Cristo, speak to me."

His lips moved.

She leaned in close. "Cristiano?"

His eyes opened. "Isabelle. What...?"

"You're hurt. Just lie there. Brad and the others are on the way."

Chapter Thirty-Two

Brad snapped the phone shut. "I'm calling Gustafson. Looks like we're going to be doing another med-evac."

"As soon as we clear the point, we should see the institute boat," Magdalena said.

"I see it," Sharlee called. "I'm going to get us positioned and drop the anchor." She slowed the Bayliner. "How does the bottom look Magdalena?"

"It's perfect, not too many rocks. We'll be safe here."

Sharlee backed the boat, hooked the anchor and shut down the diesels.

Brad pulled the dinghy to the swim step. Sharlee hopped in, started the motor. He glanced at her. "You sure about all of us leaving the boat? What if Patricia starts tossing rocks around…"

"I'm going," Sharlee snapped. "If you think someone should stay here, then you do it. I'm sure Magdalena can handle the institute's runabout."

As Brad lifted both of his hands in surrender, a shout of laughter echoed from the island's highest peak. As one, all three turned and glared at the mountain.

"I'll motor us over to the runabout. Brad can take it into the lagoon," Sharlee said. "We'll try Gustafson again from the beach."

Magdalena looked at Brad. "Are you sure? You and the sea…?"

His lips tightened, but he nodded. "I can do it."

In a short time, they were at the side of the institute boat. Brad stood, reached for the ladder. Sharlee watched him take a deep breath and climb upward. Aboard the boat he glanced down. "See. Piece of cake. You two go ahead. I'll be right behind you."

Sharlee looked from him, toward the entrance to the lagoon and back. God, she had never felt this torn, two people she loved. If something happened to Brad. One look told her the current running through the channel flowed strong.

"Sharlee, get your ass moving," Brad called. "I'll be fine."

She nodded, pushed away from the boat and headed toward the lagoon.

As she and Magdalena entered the lagoon, Sharlee saw Isabelle scramble to her feet. She waved. Behind them she heard another outboard and knew Brad had entered also.

The runabout and the dinghy arrived at the same time. Brad jumped from the runabout and tugged it higher on the sand. Magdalena didn't wait for Sharlee to pull the dinghy higher; instead she sprang into the water and waded ashore.

As Sharlee cut the motor and lifted the outboard, Brad joined her. "Here, let me help."

She jumped into the water beside him and the two of them dragged the dinghy higher on the sand.

With a thankful smile, Sharlee turned and ran to Isabelle.

Magdalena had Cristiano sitting up. "I think some of these cuts are going to need stitches. Okay, tell us what happened. No, not you." She pointed a finger at Cristiano. Let Isabelle."

"The anchor snagged on something and Cristiano dived to clear it."

Brad held a water bottle toward Cristiano who took a long drink.

Isabelle glanced at them. "He found remains."

"What did you find?" Magdalena said.

"A skull."

"You found a skull?" Brad said.

"I believe it could be a woman's," Cristiano said. "Magdalena can tell us. I'm feeling better," he added at Magdalena's frown. "The skull is on the institute boat." He took another drink. "I placed it in a sample box. When I came back on deck, all hell broke loose. Rocks were flying."

"Cristiano was hit and fell overboard."

"My God," Sharlee said. "Isabelle, how did you get him here?"

"The dolphins," Magdalena answered and nodded at Isabelle. "Right?"

"Yes," Isabelle said. "With their help, I got him to the beach. They helped me get back out to the boat, too. "

"Cristiano, you've taken a hell of a hit. I've tried to reach Gustafson, but so far no luck. I'll try again." Brad flipped open his cell phone. "Got him." He spoke quickly into the phone. Listened. "He'll bring the chopper." He glanced at Cristiano. "You want the institute boat moved to its mooring?"

"Yes."

"I'm going with Cristiano," Isabelle said.

"What's with the dolphins?" Sharlee pointed.

They circled just off the beach. Magdalena turned to look.

"Gustafson says don't worry, he'll bring Elisio to take care of the boat."

A humming filled the air and they turned toward the mountain. It simmered and glowered above them, sheet lightening flashed.

"Quite a show," Sharlee said.

Brad stood, walked to the edge of the beach. He stretched and with hands on hips looked over the water.

Magdalena moved to him and put her arm around his waist. "This is nearly finished, my friend. There is one more thing we must do today."

Brad turned to face her. "What?"

"Once Cristiano is on the way to the hospital I will tell you."

Twenty long minutes later, the whomp, whomp, whomp of the helicopter sounded.

Magdalena watched the helicopter land on the calm water of the lagoon and move toward the beach. A man hopped out and waded toward shore. He went straight to Cristiano.

"I'll give them a hand," Brad said.

They got Cristiano aboard and Isabelle climbed in.

Sharlee, Brad and Magdalena watched Gustafson take the helicopter up.

"I'll get the runabout. Move the institute boat to its mooring," Elisio said.

Magdalena looked again at the still circling dolphins. "There is unfinished business. Sharlee, we will take you to the Bayliner. Brad and I must return to the lagoon. My dolphin sisters have shown me where the last of the Lost One's remains are."

"Hold it. Why can't I stay with you?"

"The boat is too small for all of us and the diving gear. It will be best to have you on the bigger boat. Be ready to leave quickly."

"Magdalena," Brad said. "Let's get this done."

Sharlee frowned. "How are you going to do it?"

"It is time to close the circle of Patricia's life. I will dive."

"Not without a partner. I'll go with you," Brad said.

"My dolphin sister, Marita, is here. You stay with the boat. She and I have explored the area many times. We'll be back before you know we're gone."

"Are you sure?"

"Of course, rest and gather your thoughts. I'll go down and be back up quickly."

They moved the boat closer to the rock tumble at the north end of the lagoon. Magdalena lit sage, saluted the directions as she would an old friend. She put on the scuba gear, tied a dive bag at her waist and rolled over the side into the clear water. The dolphin was at her side in an instant.

Brad stared at the spot where Magdalena disappeared beneath the water.

"The skull is yours, isn't it Patricia?" he murmured. "If only I could have gotten back to you." The scent of Magdalena's sage swirled around him. "We searched and searched, but you were gone. It's over. We'll take you home to San Diego. At last, your parents will know."

*****

Magdalena and Marita circled toward the floor of the lagoon and drifted above a mound of ten or twelve bones. Two dolphins joined them.

Sisters, we must be quick. I breathe from the tank.

Magdalena, we are with you.

Their light movements stirred the sand and the bones shifted on the sea floor. She saw what looked to be part of a rib cage, a bit of spine and an arm with the hand still attached. Something glittered. Magdalena picked up the arm bone and felt a blow between her shoulder blades. A rock dropped beside her. A warning, Patricia? It will not stop me. It must end. She put the bone in the mesh bag.

Magdalena, the Lost One is not pleased.

Magdalena winced as more rocks bounced off her tank. Pain lashed the length of her thigh.

She looked down. The falling rocks had landed deep in the sand. She couldn't see the bones. Patricia, why do you fight me? Magdalena checked her regulator. She couldn't believe what she saw. How can this be? I have maybe five minutes left. She remembered the blow against the middle of her back.

She looked at Marita. *Quickly, querida. The tank...my air is low.*

They turned and sped toward the channel. The rain of rock slowed and then stopped. Her regulator stuttered. Magdalena twisted the instrument more firmly into the air line.

The dolphins' clicks rose to a whistle and the four rose toward the surface. The water churned around them. Magdalena looked toward the small, pitching boat.

She heard Brad shout. "Patricia, stop."

Magdalena spit out the mouthpiece and took a deep breath of fresh air. The three dolphins surfaced. She watched Brad fling his arms wide.

He shouted again. "If you love me. You won't do this."

The conflicting currents began to settle.

Sisters, we must return. The man speaks to her. We will collect the bones and leave this place.

They kept to the surface until they were again over the bones of Patricia Mullins and then dove.

With Marita above her and the others at her sides, Magdalena scooped the bones into the dive bag.

Brad looked up as they cleared the surface. In moments, they were at the side of the boat.

"Brad, here. Take it. Hold it close." As she lifted the dive bag the water swirled, pulled the boat against the anchor line. "She does not give in easily."

He took the bag from her.

The dolphins rose from the water on their tails and then dropped and sped away.

"Speak to Patricia again, picture her at her most beautiful, tell her you love her. Make love to her. I'll get us out of here." Magdalena pulled the starter rope three times before it caught.

She turned the boat toward the lagoon channel.

In her hands, the tiller jerked and the dinghy angled toward submerged rocks.

"Magdalena," Brad cried.

"I see them." The small boat began to buck, swirled in a powerful circular motion. She gave the outboard more throttle, for a heart-wrenching moment the motor sputtered, and then they were through.

On the Bayliner, Sharlee had the engines at an idle. When Brad and Magdalena were aboard, she raised the anchor. They swung around the line of jagged pinnacles powered up to avoid the tidal swirl and foam, and headed toward their campo.

They arrived at the beach as the lowering sun neared the top of the peaks in the southwest. Without comment Magdalena took the dive bag and field sample box from the boat.

"Magdalena, shall I call when Isabelle gets back," Sharlee asked.

"Please do." Magdalena faced Sharlee and Brad. "It is time for Patricia's remains to be brought together." She touched Brad's arm. "You will do this."

Magdalena sat the dive bag on the sand in front of him. "Sharlee, the field sample box. Place it next to the bag."

Sharlee did.

Brad took a deep breath, opened first the box, then the bag. He stood, stared at the white bones, then picked them up and placed them around the skull in the box. Tears filled his eyes, ran down his cheeks. With hands that shook, he closed the box. Brad swallowed, turned to Magdalena. "How can I thank you?"

She patted his arm. "Peace for all is thanks enough."

When Magdalena arrived back at her house, Mira was solicitous and attentive.

"Ay, Mira." Magdalena carried the field sample box to the table. "At last, here is the Lost One. Not all of her, but enough to send her on her way." She brought a small glass of brandy, sprigs of lavender and put them beside the box.

She sat heavily in a chair. Mira jumped into her lap at once.

Magdalena stroked the silken fur, her gaze lingered on Isla Santa Maria. "We will have some fruit and bathe and then it will be time to rest ourselves, but first, the sunset waits for us. Shall we?"

She unbraided her hair as the two walked onto the west patio. The sun lowered below the horizon and a haze of lightening shimmered for an instant above Laguna Playa. She breathed a prayer, ran her fingers through her hair, and walked back into the house.

"Mira, my heart, I want you to stay near me. We'll eat on the patio. Give some peace and comfort to our Patricia."

Magdalena started the tea kettle, piled fruit into one bowl and fish into another. While the kettle heated she brought a scarf from her room and draped it over the box on the table. She poured a thimbleful of brandy for herself, lit a small candle and toasted Patricia.

Mira sat on a stool, watched her every move. Magdalena scooped tea into the pot, put everything on a tray. She turned out the overhead lights and carried the tray to the patio, Mira at her heels. Through the window she watched the candle on the table flame up, waver, nearly extinguish, then lower and burn steadily.

The raven pair glided in and lit under the branches of the palo verde tree. "Bienvenidos, my friends." Magdalena paused for several heartbeats then whispered, "The Lost One rests inside. She will go to the sky at sunrise. You have flown many miles, watched over us all and we are grateful." The pair seemed to bow then turned to one another with low vocalizations. "You have been more than generous."

She and Mira ate their small meal, then Magdalena went into the house to her bath. Before she stepped into the water she sat on the edge of the tub and lit her pipe. Magdalena waved some of the smoke over her and puffed her fragrant mix. She put the pipe on the counter next to Mira and stepped into the tub.

When her bath was finished, Magdalena removed the blue and green scarf from the top of the box. She crossed to the music system and loaded it with three drum chant discs. "Come, mija. We'll go to the patio."

She moved a side table opposite her meditation chair, placed the tray upon it. She kindled a small fire in the pit, smudged the patio, and then sat in her chair between the fire and the fountain. The fountain, the fire pit, Magdalena's chair and the table that held the remains marked the four directions.

The ravens watched from above.

Magdalena relaxed into her trance. Time stopped, forms dissolved. Patricia Mullins stood in front of her. Magdalena rose from her chair to face the young woman. The bruises were gone from her face, her blond hair lay on her shoulders, glowed against the blue of the simple gown she wore.

"My heart, you've come to us."

It seems I've been here forever.

"It's true. Now it is time to say goodbye to this place and go to your rest."

Tears flowed down Patricia's face. Her hair swung forward and her shoulders slumped. *I didn't have time. Time for my art, time for my love, it's not fair.*

"Surely it seems that way to you now. The soul has its own idea of time, mija, its own concept of growth. The part of you which has raged and suffered is finished now."

What other part can there be?

"Oh, my dear one, the soul has many facets, as does a precious gem. To know them all is not our task, only to grow and learn. Time is of no concern to the soul."

But I want my time. I want my life back. Patricia raised her head."

"I suppose you do. We all want what we want. Sometimes we are able to have it, other times not. It is time for you to go."

How? How do I leave?

"We will help you. Tomorrow at sunrise we will send you on your way."

With a nod of her head, Patricia faded from sight.

Magdalena slowly came out of her trance. She exhaled and raised her arms, palms together over her head. The ravens spoke to one another and lifted from the wall, soaring to the roof of the house.

"Let's go in, Mira. In the morning, the sun will light the way for Patricia's soul to travel to its reward."

The cat stretched, then bounded toward the house.

Chapter Thirty-Three

Brad and Sharlee walked hand in hand. Brad turned to her and opened his arms. She went to him and felt the shudder that ran through his body. She stepped back, her hands on his shoulders. "C'mon sweetie. I'll run you a bath and check in with the hospital."

The sun set as they continued their walk toward Isabelle's house.

Sammi-Sue woofed and hopped in circles when they entered, while Longfellow stood in the entrance to the kitchen and glowered.

"Tell ya' what, Shar. I'll take care of my own bath. Sammi wants to go out and it looks like Longfellow needs some attention." Brad walked to Longfellow and leaned down to scratch between his ears.

Sharlee opened the door and Sammi-Sue bounded out. She sniffed her way toward the high tide line. Sharlee strolled behind the basset hound and kept her eyes away from the island.

Brad hung up the phone as Sharlee and Sammi returned. "That was Isabelle; she and Gustafson are leaving town now. Cristiano's okay, but he'll stay overnight in the hospital. I'm getting in the tub."

Sharlee was in the kitchen making a salad when Brad came back down.

"I've called Magdalena," Sharlee said "She's on her way over.

"Can I help?"

"Why don't you open us a bottle of wine? Far, bottom cupboard. Glasses are on the top shelf."

"I can do that." Brad headed toward the cupboard.

Sharlee glanced at the clock. "How long does it take to get here from San Felipe by helicopter?"

"About an hour and half with a good tailwind."

"Then they should be here within the next twenty minutes."

Brad opened the wine. "A glass for you?"

"Why not."

Brad was telling Sharlee and Magdalena about the plot for his next book, when Sammie jumped up and raced toward the door.

"They must be here," Sharlee said. She met Isabelle at the door.

"Sam headed home," Isabelle said.

"Sugar, you're all done in." Sharlee wrapped Isabelle in a hug. "You want to take a shower and change? I'll pour you a glass of wine."

"Let me duck in and out of the shower," Isabelle said.

"You hungry? I've made a salad and we can throw some leftovers together."

"Maybe. I'm too tired to know."

"You take your time."

Isabelle waved at Brad and Magdalena and walked toward her room with Sammi-Sue at her heels.

In her bedroom Longfellow had a look in his eye. "Give me a minute, then it's some special time for both of you."

Isabelle stripped and stuffed her blood-splattered clothes in a laundry bag. She folded herself down, cross-legged, on the rug beside the bed. Sammi hopped, complained and rejoiced at the same time, while Longie stretched out on the bed and purred and chirped in her ear.

"Oh, my friends, what a day. It's changed me and I hope it will bring some major changes for you, too." Sammi-Sue settled beside Isabelle. "You knew Cristiano belonged with us all along, didn't you?" The basset hound stared into Isabelle's face for a moment and woofed. Isabelle reached up to stroke Longie's head. "We'll still have to go back to San Francisco, close the house, but the City by the Bay, will have to get along without us until fall." Isabelle smiled, stood, gathered up clean clothes and slipped into the bathroom.

She joined Magdalena, Brad, and Sharlee. "Cristiano's in a room with Andres. He called his family. How are you guys doing?"

"Mija, we all need a meal and a good night's sleep. I think tonight will be much calmer than the last few have been," Magdalena said.

"Thank God for that."

Magdalena stood, walked to Isabelle and placed her arm across her shoulders. "There is something you should know. In the lagoon, there were some bones…"

"The skull…"

"… had been washed away from the others."

Isabelle glanced at Brad. "They're Patricia's, aren't they?"

"I am certain," Magdalena said. "She tried hard to keep me from retrieving them."

Isabelle felt a tremor move through the other woman. "What happened?"

Magdalena stepped away, shrugged. "Patricia was being Patricia."

"Tell me," Isabelle said.

Magdalena sighed and told the three of them what had happened below the sea.

"She could have killed you," Sharlee said.

"She fought hard for what she thought she desired," Magdalena said.

Brad raked fingers through his hair. "Tomorrow she goes on her way. It's past time; Patricia was always a bit stubborn."

"Damn straight," Sharlee said. "Then we have a party, you can even call it a wake if you want."

"A party," Isabelle said. "Sounds good. Let's make it later in the day so Cristiano and Andres can be here." She smiled down at the floor. Maybe she and Cristiano would have some news to share? Isabelle yawned. "What time do we do this send off?"

"Sunrise on the beach in front of my casa," Magdalena said. "Brad, before we sit down to eat, step out to the patio with me, will you?"

"Of course, let me refill our wine glasses."

"Izzy and I will get the food on the table, take your time," Sharlee said.

Brad brought their wine glasses out to a small table on the front patio and dusted off the cushions. He held the chair for Magdalena, then sat beside her.

"A toast," Magdalena said. "To our work today."

They raised their glasses and both glanced at the island.

"This has been a difficult time for you. And while it is nearly over, it is not yet completed. Tomorrow morning at sunrise we will gather on the beach and say our final farewells to the spirit of Señorita Patricia."

Brad's response was a sigh and a slow nod; he placed his glass on the table and leaned his forearms on his knees.

"But now, there is something I must give you." Magdalena reached into her pocket and withdrew a small velvet bag. Brad sat up and Magdalena handed it to him. "The item in the bag was among the remains."

Magdalena sat and listened to her heart echo in her mind. She looked at Isla Santa Maria and remembered..her love and her loss. Her own farewell to Rodolfo at Laguna Playa. She breathed deeply for a space of time to honor Patricia Mullins. She turned and looked at Brad. He sat silent, his gaze on the sea, the small bag in his hand.

With a deep breath, he opened the bag and withdrew the ring. The wide platinum band sheltered a perfect emerald cut aquamarine. It was if the piece was fresh from the jeweler's hand, the platinum glowed and the gem reflected the colors of the sea beyond.

Brad cleared his throat and turned to her. "I gave it to her that morning. We had chosen the stone and met with the jeweler to design the piece. She loved the aquamarine for the colors of the Sea of Cortez. Patricia was happy here. Look, we had it engraved." He leaned close and held the ring for Magdalena to see.

It was inscribed.

B.C.& P.M. Forever

"It's wonderful, Brad."

"She was a lovely woman, talented and bright. We liked to visit here and even talked of perhaps building a home one day." He cleared his throat again and went on. "Patricia and I discovered our hearts together. I was her first lover and she was mine as well. It seems a million years ago."

"It might as well have been, mijo." Magdalena patted Brad on the back. "My heart goes out to you. You have my respect and my love. You are welcome in my campo any time." She stood and said, "Now we will join Sharlee and Isabelle. We will eat, then we will rest. Tomorrow at sunrise we will send Patricia on her way."

Brad looked up at her and for a brief moment he thought he saw a flicker of light surround her before she turned and walked into the house.

The four friends ate quietly.

"Ladies, the soup is delightful, do I taste a bit of lemon?" Magdalena said.

"You do," Sharlee answered, "I always add a little lemon when I'm using chicken stock. I'm glad you like it."

"The salad greens are from a friend, a chef, who has a garden on the roof of his restaurant in the city," Isabelle said. "He gave me quite a lot. I'll serve the rest tomorrow for dinner. Brad, be sure and ask the Gustafsons to join us, will you. Cristiano will bring Andres. Cocktails at five, dinner at six."

"Sounds good," Brad said.

They all joined in clean up. By the time they were finished, each covered yawns.

"Until tomorrow morning then. Sleep well my brave hearts," Magdalena said. "The sunrise will begin at six-thirty. I will meet you on the beach in front of my house; we will say our farewells to Patricia. Buenos noches."

"I'll join you, Magdalena. Sammie would like a walk. I'll close up when I get back," Isabelle said. Sammie-Sue danced and hopped toward the door.

"Don't be long, Sugar. I'll make some chamomile tea and leave the thermos in your room," Sharlee said.

"Brad, you're certainly welcome to stay the night if that's what you'd like to do," Isabelle said.

"I think I'd like that, thanks."

Isabelle followed Magdalena to the front door. Sammie-Sue was two steps ahead of them.

The three stepped off the front patio onto the sand, into the soft starlight. The tide swished gently as they walked toward the shore. "It's a beautiful night." Isabelle said.

"Oh, yes. And calm. Perhaps tonight we will see florescence in the water. Often in spring and fall, the microscopic life of the Sea of Cortez glow as they come ashore. It's biology, of course, but I prefer to think of it as a kind of blessing."

They walked the rest of the way in comfortable silence. At Magdalena's door, the two shared an embrace.

Isabelle stepped back, waited until Magdalena walked inside and slapped her leg. "Come on, Sammie. We sure got more than we bargained for this little trip, didn't we? It's had its ups and downs, but I hope tomorrow will make it all worth it."

Everything about the beach seemed calm. Occasionally a seabird called, the breeze was light and warm, with a hint of lavender.

By the shore, the soft waves that lapped at her feet glowed green as they splashed her toes.

At their house, Isabelle rinsed both hers and Sammi's feet in the bucket on the patio before they went in. Longfellow greeted them at the screen door and asked in no uncertain terms for his midnight snack. Isabelle fed him and then walked to her bedroom.

Isabelle lit the trio of candles on the counter. She opened a drawer to take out her vitamins and toothbrush, caught her breath and pulled her hand back as she heard a sound inside.

She flicked on the light over the sink and breathed out a whoosh of air as she watched the cricket scramble for cover. "Ah, it's good luck to have a cricket in the house," she whispered to the small, black insect. "But I'm taking you outside."

She scooped it up, walked to the rear door, and stepped out. "Maybe I should keep you until after my talk with Cristiano. No, that's silly. Everything will be fine."

She released the cricket into the desert-garden planter behind the studio, turned and went back inside.

Chapter Thirty-Four

It was still dark when Isabelle walked into the kitchen the next morning, looking for coffee. A glance at the clock told her the time hadn't changed more than twenty minutes from the time she 'd stumbled out of bed. Five A.M., and still too damn early, unless you were some hungry bird.

Sharlee leaned against the island counter, with a mug in her hand. "Izzy, it was thoughtful of you to extend the invitation to Brad," she said. "The poor boy was exhausted and just about wrung out. Thank you, Sugar. He's gone over to the Gustafson's to change and brush up. He'll drive us to Magdalena's."

"Good. Coffee. I need it." Isabelle poured herself a cup

Sharlee brought a bowl of melons, grapes, mango and papaya from the fridge. "I forgot to bring the fruit out for dinner; have some." The two ate from the bowl with their fingers.

Brad entered the kitchen. "Morning, beautiful ladies. Thanks again, Izzy. Don't know if I could have made it back to Gus' last night. Gus says they'll be here around five and bring a little dessert tray. Here, they sent over some cinnamon rolls." He put a waxed-paper wrapped package beside the fruit. "How's the coffee?"

"Great, help yourself." Isabelle smiled. She glanced toward one of the kitchen windows. "Still dark out there. Guess we've got a few minutes before we have to leave. I'll have to drag Sammi outside this morning. She was still snoring when I got dressed." Just then the basset walked slowly into the kitchen yawned and then stretched. "Well, that's that, I guess," Isabelle said. "We'll be right back."

The sky was beginning to lighten over the point. Sammi pulled against the leash, but Isabelle shook her head. "No baby, just a short walk for now. We'll have a good long one when I get back." Isabelle heard a motor start and turned back toward the house. "Sounds like they're ready."

*****

Magdalena's hair swirled around her shoulders. She had been on the beach for hours. She was warm enough, dressed in layers, but she felt cold from the inside out. On the sand beside her sat a long, narrow ceramic box. Herb bundles and the remains of Patricia Mullins mingled within a silk scarf inside. She'd taken all from the field sample box and placed them inside the other this morning.

The day before the family left, after the accident that had taken Patricia's life, one of the relatives had visited her patio. The woman was in a daze, said Patricia's mother had at last slept. They wanted Magdalena to accept the gift of the box in remembrance. It was the latest in a series Patricia had been working on, a series she'd developed especially honoring the Sea of Cortez, which she loved. Magdalena had accepted the lovely ceramic piece and placed it on the mantle.

She watched a light waver and swirl through the sky over the island. An echo? An aurora? A breeze gusted, pushed and pulled the flames. The constellations swung along their sky paths as Magdalena tended her fire.

She dipped into the bag in her pocket, filled her pipe, lit it and smoked as she stirred the fire. She meditated and breathed. She remembered and forgot. She shivered and burned. She might have slept, but if she did, she hadn't rested. Now the sky was lighting. She put a small piece of juniper wood on her fire. In the sea, one lone dolphin jumped. Aye, Marita, this has been a time. The Lost One is found. Our home will again be clear.

Magdalena tossed sage leaves and lavender flowers into the fire. She pulled her sleeping bag around her and rocked side to side, following a rhythm in her mind. She heard Brad's truck arrive, a moment of conversation then Brad and Sharlee's approach. Magdalena moved the box closer to her side and turned to greet the couple.

"Come and sit with me," she said

"It's beautiful here now. Thank you, Magdalena, for helping us," Brad said. He spread the blankets, helped Sharlee settle beside Magdalena.

"Morning dear," Sharlee said. "I've been watching the sky since I got up. The lights I saw over the island were so like an aurora. I haven't seen them for a while."

"Yes, the energy is calming, diminishing I think. Not yet completely at rest, but headed in that direction. You feel the energy, don't you, señorita?"

"I do and I have since I arrived. The energy has been strong around Isabelle ever since the cove, and I think it's starting to take a toll."

Brad sat beside Sharlee. "We're all about used up."

Isabelle joined them.

"Welcome, Isabella. What we're going to do now, we each must do each in our own heart," Magdalena said.

"We are here beside one another and each will help the other. At this moment, Patricia is here with us also." Magdalena lifted the sea colored box from its place on the sand at her side. "Here are the earthly remains of Patricia Mullins. This is her work, given to me by her aunt. I now give it to you, Brad. Place it between yourself and Isabelle, and if any of you have something to say aloud or to place in the container, this is the moment. Soon we will be silent, each going into their heart and bidding Patricia safe passage, sending love and acceptance. Wishing her well. When I speak again, we will be finished here and Patricia will be on her way."

Isabelle lifted the lid and placed a piece of hand woven lace inside. "I know you were an artist like me. I wish we'd been able to get to know each other in this world."

Isabelle looked at Sharlee. Her friend placed a short strand of rose quartz beads inside the box. "Brad said this was your favorite color."

Brad removed the velvet bag containing the platinum and aquamarine ring from his shirt pocket. He kissed it, put it with the other offerings and then replaced the lid.

As the sun lifted above the horizon, each of the four deepened their meditation. The fire was down to coals and the sun's rays touched the top of Isla Santa Maria. A light breeze swirled and as the disc of the sun rested on the horizon, the dolphin saluted the new day in the rose colored light reflected in the calm sea.

Isabelle watched as Magdalena swayed side to side across from her. The breeze rose, spinning among the four seated about the fire ring. Then it dipped into the ashes and lifted them, spiraling them up to disappear in the early morning light until all that was left was an empty circle of stones.

Brad held the ceramic box in his hands, and each of the four exhaled and seemed to slump toward the circle.

***

Isabelle sipped from her glass of wine and smiled. She fought to keep her eyes from wandering toward the front door. Her ears strained for the sound of a knock. The party was in full swing and a success, but she'd expected Andres and Cristiano an hour ago. Were they all right? Had they decided not to make the drive?

"Izzy, you're like a cat ready to pounce on a rat," Sharlee said. "Quit staring at the door."

Isabelle's face heated. "Obvious, huh?" She smoothed her hair. She'd left it unbraided and it felt strange brushing her bare shoulders. She'd also chosen to wear the dress she'd worn to Magdalena's birthday party. Cristiano had liked it.

"What's going on in that head of yours? You've been quiet all night," Sharlee said.

"They're late." Isabelle glanced toward the door again.

"Cristiano and Andres?"

"You don't suppose they had car trouble?"

"Maybe they didn't get discharged, or one of them was too tired."

Isabelle's stomach tightened. She turned toward the telephone. "I'll call."

Sharlee touched her arm. "Izzy, give them a few more minutes. You know how that road is."

Isabelle nodded.

"Now, let's go play hostess. I spy at least one empty glass."

"Maybe I should take Sammi out…?

318

"So you can stand outside and stare toward the road. No way." There was hint of exasperation in Sharlee's voice. "Izzy…"

"You're right. I'm being silly. They'll get here when they get here."

Isabelle turned, walked to Magdalena. Forcing herself to stand with her back to the door, she said, "Some more wine?"

Magdalena looked into Isabelle's face for a long moment before shaking her head. "I am fine."

Isabelle traced the rim of her wine glass with a finger." I am so glad everything turned out fine for Patricia."

"It must be a relief for you."

"Oh, yes it is. I feel much more at ease."

"I can see that." Magdalena smiled.

Isabelle sighed. "Am I as transparent as cellophane?"

Magdalena took Isabelle's glass from her and sat both of their glasses on a side table. She reached to clasp both of Isabelle's hands. "Love's path sometimes twists and turns. What is important is to know when it is time to accept the preordained ending."

Isabelle felt a sudden chill and rubbed her bare arms. "What do you mean?"

"We don't always get what we want, when we want it."

"Don't I know that?" Isabelle forced a laugh. "I can be so stubborn..isn't that what you told me? People change…"

"Sometimes when it is too late," Magdalena said.

Isabelle pulled her hands free. "I won't believe it's…I can't…."

Sammi-Sue barked and headed toward the door. Isabelle's heartbeat spiked, but she forced herself to remain where she stood, although she did allow herself to turn to see who entered.

Andres hobbled in on crutches, alone, wearing a boot to immobilize his leg. It felt like her heart dropped into her stomach. He didn't come? Why wouldn't he? Isabelle closed her eyes for a moment. *He doesn't want to see me. It has to be.*

Cristiano walked through the door. He looked tired and bruised even from where she stood.

He stopped. His eyes searched the room, they swept over her, his head jerked back and she felt her heartbeat surge again.

"Go, Isabelle," Magdalena said. "Follow your path."

Isabelle started toward Cristiano, but before she could get there, well-wishers surrounded him.

That's okay. I have time.

She turned and walked back to where Magdalena had placed her wine. She picked up the glass and emptied it in one long swallow.

The next hour went the same way. Every time she started toward Cristiano, someone beat her to him. She could have joined whoever he spoke to, but she wanted him alone long enough to arrange some private time.

Isabelle poured herself another glass of wine.

"You're drinking more than I have seen you do before." Andres' voice came from behind her.

She turned. "Am I?" Isabelle grimaced. "How many glasses have I had?"

"Two in the last hour. What is it?"

"Nothing."

"You have not spoken to me or Cristiano since our arrival."

"I've been trying. He's been constantly surrounded." She heard the frustration in her voice and looked away.

"I," Andres emphasized the word, "am here now."

Her cheeks heated. "How are you? You look great."

"My body will be fine in time. Yet…." He shrugged.

"What's going on with you?"

"Too much time to think, but what else can you do laying flat on your back in a hospital bed." Andres frowned.

She touched his arm. "Thinking's over rated."

"I'm leaving San Felipe."

"Where are you going?"

"I don't know. I know I have to leave." Andres drained his glass of wine.

She decided to play devil's advocate. "How will you live?"

"What do you mean?"

"I mean, what do you do for a living? I've never known. I don't think flamenco dancing would pay all that well."

"I have a B.S. in Nuclear Engineering."

"Whoa. Really?"

Andres grinned. "Really."

"Okay then. You're coming to my house San Francisco," Isabelle said. "It's so simple. I should've thought of it before."

"Isabelle. I was not…"

"I know. But there's plenty of room, and you and San Francisco, it seems a natural match. Who knows, maybe who, or what, you're looking for is there."

And you can take care of the house for me.

Emotions played across Andres' face: hope, fear, and then excitement. "You are sure? It would not inconvenience you?"

"Not in the slightest. It's settled. You are going to live at my place. No more discussion. Right?"

"Si. Si. I must pack. You are returning home soon, right?" Andres' smile lit up his face.

Isabelle avoided answering his question by asking one of her own. "You mean you haven't all ready?"

"I only decided for sure on the drive to here, but tomorrow I will begin." Andres' wobbled on his crutches.

"Hey, let's find you a seat." She looked around. The chair next to the sofa was available. "Over there." Isabelle followed him to the chair and stood at his side, ready to offer help, while he settled into it. "You let them come to you," she said. "Need anything?"

"No. No. I'm fine." He stuck his leg straight out in front of him. "As long as no one thinks this is a roadblock."

His voice sounded a trifle testy to her. This was only day number three with him wearing the boot. She could see it only getting worse. Isabelle thought of something. "How are you going to get to my place? You can't drive."

"I will fly. if someone will take me to the airport and if someone will pick me up in San Francisco." He slapped the arm of the chair. "It gets more and more complicated. Maybe…"

"No. We'll make it work. No more thinking about it. Just sit here and let folks cater to you."

Andres scowled. "Fine. Fine."

"Is my grandson again complaining?" Magdalena said from behind her.

Isabelle turned. "Only a little. If it was me, it would be worse."

Magdalena smiled at Andres, then looked again at Isabelle. "Have you spoken to Cristiano yet?"

"No…"

"He is alone now."

Isabelle looked, but did not see Cristiano anywhere.

"He went into the kitchen."

"Thanks.

Cristiano stood in front of the sink, staring out the window.

"Hey," she said. "Great party huh?"

He straightened, but did not turn. "Si. It's also a beautiful night."

"How are you feeling? "

Cristiano shrugged. "I am fine. A little sore. I haven't thanked you for my life."

Isabelle shook her head. "You don't…"

"But I must."

She held up her hand. "I'd rather you didn't. Besides it was more the dolphins than me. We can both thank them later."

He looked as if he would say more, but then turned and looked out the window again. "This party, it serves a dual purpose?"

"What?"

"A remembrance and farewell to Patricia Mullins, and for you to also say a goodbye to Baja."

Okay, here it is. She'd prefer not to say this to his back. "I'm not saying adios to Baja."

"Well maybe not goodbye, just so long for awhile. You made that clear on the boat."

Isabelle frowned. "A lot of things happened on the boat, as well as in the lagoon." Damn. Please turn around and face me, she silently begged. "Cristiano, let's go for a walk on the beach."

"That wouldn't be polite. You have guests."

"They're not just mine. Sharlee can handle everything. I'd like to talk to you about something."

Cristiano faced her. They'd done a good job of fixing the gash above his right eye. The scar would be a small one. She winced at the sight of a bruise in all of its black and blue glory marring the skin above his left cheekbone, but it was his closed expression that made a shiver of unease move up her spine. It'll be okay, she told herself. Everything will be fine after I tell him.

"Si, Isabelle, we will walk."

She followed him out the door. He hesitated, then turned right and headed toward the beach.

Cristiano didn't hurry his steps, but neither did he reach for her hand. In fact, he seemed to be making an effort to keep a good twelve inches of space between them.

They walked in silence, until she gauged they were far enough from her place for their voices to remain unheard.

Isabelle reached to touch Cristiano's hand. "Let's stop here for a moment."

He stopped, stepped back from her and turned to face Isla Santa Maria. "Patricia has left?"

"Yes. This morning. It was beautiful and sad at the same time."

Cristiano glanced at her. "Si. Saying good bye is always hard."

She took a deep breath. "About that…saying good bye. On the boat…"

He turned from her again. "You made yourself clear. I respect your choice."

Isabelle moved closer to him. "Would you look at me, please."

He faced her. "Why, Isabelle? I don't want to hear, it was great while it lasted. Don't say to me, let's be friends. I can't be your friend."

"I know. I know. It's not like that." She licked her lips. Her mouth felt as dry as the sand. "When you were hurt in the lagoon…when I thought you would die…I realized how much I loved you."

Cristiano's eyes narrowed. "Stop."

She reached toward him. "No. You were right. What does it matter our ages; the future? We could die tomorrow. What's important is now…this minute. One day…one week…whatever time I have left, I want to spend it with you. Here, San Francisco, or someplace different, I don't care."

He slowly shook his head and it felt as if her heart clogged her throat. That wasn't what she'd expected.

"No," he said in a hoarse whisper.

Isabelle lowered her arms. "What? What do you mean no? You love me, you said so, and I love you."

"I loved you like I had no other woman. I offered you my heart…you refused it."

"But Cristiano…"

" I can no longer trust you. I have no faith in your love or your words. Yesterday you did not love me…today you do. What will tomorrow bring?"

"No. I did love you, I was afraid. I…Donald…"

"Yes, he hurt you. Refused your love. I know how it feels. The pain filled me as I lay in that hospital. No drugs help here." He touched his heart. "I will never let you do so to me again."

"Cristiano, I was wrong. It's worth it to take the chance, you're worth it."

He shook his head. "But you are not."

His words were like blows. Isabelle hugged her stomach. Her knees shook. She stumbled back, turned away from him. Tears filled her eyes, ran down her cheeks. "Go," she choked out.

She didn't hear him leave, but when she dared to look up, he was gone. "Oh, God. Oh, God." How can I hurt so much and still be breathing? Her legs gave out and she collapsed onto the sand. She drew her knees to her chest and ignoring the fact that her dress's hemline had hiked up to her waist, she rocked and stared with blurred vision toward the island.

"Izzy. Isabelle."

She heard Sharlee's worried voice calling, but she didn't answer. Instead, she tried to muffle her sobs against her bare knees. And wasn't successful.

She felt Sharlee drop to the sand beside her. "What is it? I saw Cristiano come back into the house. He said something to Andres and Magdalena, then left."

Isabelle shook her head. "It hurts. It hurts."

Sharlee wrapped her arms around her and pulled her against her breasts. "Tell me."

She couldn't get the words beyond the sobs, so Sharlee held her, let her cry, until the sobs became quiet hiccups, and then at last slow shudders.

Isabelle drew back, rubbed at her hot, wet cheeks.

"Better," Sharlee asked. "Can you tell me now."

Isabelle blew out a shaky sigh. "I blew it. I waited too long. I was afraid. I didn't...couldn't trust what I felt."

326

"Cristiano?"

"I told him on the boat, right before all hell broke loose, we were through."

"Ah, Izzy…"

"I know. " She pushed her hair back from her face. "But when I thought I would lose him, I realized how stupid I was being. I told him so…" Her voice cracked. She swallowed, more tears threatened and she blinked her eyes. "But he said it was too late. He'd never let me hurt him again."

"Oh God. I don't know what to say."

Isabelle faced her. "There isn't anything to say. Cristiano is right. You don't toss someone's love away. No matter what." She glanced down at herself. "Would you look at me. Covered in sand and showing my ass to the world. What would my mother say?" She stood, smoothed her dress down and brushed sand from her hands and arms. Isabelle glanced back toward her house. "Some hostesses we are."

"Brad's there and Magdalena, everything's fine."

"Hey," Isabelle said. "I hurt, and I will for a long time, but I'll survive."

"Love is such a bitch," Sharlee said.

"She can be, but one thing, I don't regret it, any of it. Now I know what the real thing feels like." Isabelle took a deep breath. "Okay. It's back to the house." She reached out, gave Sharlee's hand a squeeze. "I'm calling it a night. You tell them anything. I just can't…."

"I understand. I'll handle it. You take a hot shower, try to sleep. Tomorrow will be better."

Isabelle turned away without answering.

***

"Well that's the last of them," Brad said, stacking the box next to the others. "Not bad at all, considering you're taking some of Andres' stuff too."

"A little crowded for Sammi-Sue in the back, but we'll be fine," Sharlee said.

"About that," Brad said. "I could give you a ride back in the helicopter. At least to San Diego. You could meet up with Isabelle and Andres there."

She touched his cheek. "That is so nice of you, but I need to spend this time with Izzy. You know with the Cristiano stuff and all."

"I get it, I just thought with Andres.."

"I need to be with Isabelle for me," Sharlee said.

"Will you be over-nighting in San Diego?"

"Probably not. It depends on what time we get started in the morning. Why?"

"I thought maybe we could get together, I'll be there by five this evening."

Sharlee reached, took his hand. "Let's walk."

They headed down to the shoreline, stopped where the waves played out. She lifted her hand to shade her eyes and looked across the water toward Isla Santa Maria. It looked no different, but inside her she felt its change. There was a serenity that hadn't been there before.

Brad squeezed her hand. "She's really gone."

"Yes."

"I know she died three years ago, but it's only now I can accept it."

Sharlee looked into his face. "What are you feeling?"

"Sadness at what we might have had together. And relief at finally being able to say good bye to her."

"Yes, it's another ending. You realize how many beginnings and ending there have been in this stretch of

Baja," Sharlee asked. "Isabelle's love for Cristiano began here."

"Looks like it ended here, too," Brad said.

"Magdalena scattered the ashes of the man she loved in Laguna Playa. Another ending."

"And Andres, he had a ending and a beginning here," Brad said. He took her other hand. "What's it going to be with us? Beginning or ending?"

Sharlee closed her eyes for a moment before answering. "Both."

His hands tightened around hers, then he let them both go. "I see. Is there a why?"

"There are things in my life right now...I can't get involved, not until I get them straightened out."

"What things?"

"I'm adopted. I'm searching for my birth parents."

"That shouldn't be that hard."

Sharlee smiled. "You'd think not, but I keep running into walls."

"Let me help. I'm good at research."

She stared into his face. Could they be together again? The thought made her stomach tighten. "But, your writing?"

"I can do that anywhere. Besides I think you would only be an asset." He grinned. "Not so much fiction anymore. A little hands on experience."

Sharlee felt her cheeks heat. "Brad, I don't..."

"I'll be in San Francisco in two weeks to meet with my publisher. Why don't we have dinner? See how things stand. Maybe what we're feeling is because of all of this." He waved his arms toward the sea and islands. "A vacation induced infatuation."

She knew it was much more. Seeing Brad again would be letting him into her life. But she had two weeks to make the decision. "Sure. Why not. Give me your cell phone."

He did and she typed in her home number into his phone.

"Call me. Unless you come to your senses, of course." Sharlee smiled.

"Oh, I'll call, Sharlee. You can count on that."

"We should get back," she said. "I know Isabelle's anxious to see this beach in her rearview mirror."

Chapter Thirty-Five

In San Felipe

"I couldn't find us a room," Sharlee said. "But the front desk clerk at…"

"No. No. No," Andres said shaking his head. "We will stay the night at my old place."

"Andres, are you sure?" Sharlee said.

"Miguel has insisted. He will be with a friend until morning. It's much better than a motel room, especially for Sammi-Sue and Longfellow."

Isabelle smiled at him in the rearview mirror. "Thanks so much."

"It is my pleasure. We will settle, then go to Baja Indigo to fill our stomach with food, cerveza and admire some Flamenco. The performing troupe is good, although not as talented as me." Andres clapped his hands above his head. "And I have decided it will all be on me."

"Now, that I won't have," Sharlee said. "I pay my share or I'm not going."

"I have all ready seen to payment. You, Miss Sharlee can pay somewhere along our journey to San Francisco."

Andres sounded smug and Isabelle couldn't help but grin.

"Where is your old place?" Isabelle said.

"I will direct. Ahead turn left."

They were there within minutes.

Andres opened the back car door, swung his booted leg out first.

Sharlee already had the back hatch open. "I've got the overnight kits."

Sammie woofed in excitement and did a little dance. "I know," Isabelle said. "New place equals new smells. I'll have you out in a second." She picked up Longfellow's travel crate, sat it beside her and then motioned Sammie forward. "Okay. Your turn."

With Sammi-Sue on the ground, leashed beside her, and Longie's crate in hand, she headed toward Andres' apartment.

*****

On San Felipe's main street, Isabelle drove by an office building . The meal had been great. She'd kept to one beer. She was only holding it together through sheer will-power, and alcohol wouldn't help. The Flamenco dancers had been superb in her opinion, but then she wasn't a professional. Andres had labeled them mediocre.

Isabelle could tell from the modern design the building was a new addition. She wondered what had been demolished to make room for it. It was close to midnight, but one light glowed through a window's blinds.

"That's the Geological de Mexico's building," Andres said.

"Cristiano's office?" Isabelle said.

Andres nodded. "Most likely the one with the light still on. Judging from when we last spoke, he will be working many late hours for a good long time."

Isabelle glanced back at him. "What did he tell you?"

"Only that you were returning to San Francisco." She felt his hand pat her shoulder. "Not a smooth break up, right?"

For a moment Isabelle could not get words beyond the lump in her throat. "No," she managed to say.

She heard his sigh, then his mutter of, "Stubborn. Stubborn. Stubborn. Too much pride."

Isabelle almost asked who he spoke of, but then decided she didn't want to know.

A car's horn honked behind her and she jumped. She hadn't realized she'd stopped in the middle of the narrow street.

Swallowing, she started the Suburban forward again. They passed Casa de la Playa and a wash of pain made Isabelle gasp.

"Izzy," Sharlee said. "Why don't I drive for awhile?"

Isabelle pulled the Suburban over to the side, and then leaned her forehead against the steering wheel.

"Madre Dios," Andres said. "Do you love him?"

"He doesn't want…" Her voice cracked.

"Doesn't he? You are both being stupido." Andres' voice rose with frustration. "I would give my eye teeth to love someone and have them love me!"

"I screwed it up. "

Andres' hand clamped on her shoulder. "Make it right, Isabelle."

"Izzy, Andres has a point. You don't give up on something you want, that's not you."

"But what about you two?" Isabelle said.

"You take us back to the apartment," Andes said. "Tomorrow we take a taxi to the airport and fly to San Francisco."

"Better yet," Sharlee said. "We call Brad and he flies us to San Francisco."

Isabelle hesitated. "He would?"

"He offered, but I wanted to spend the time with you," Sharlee said.

"Oh, Sharlee." She looked into each of their faces. "Even if it doesn't work out with Cristiano, I'm not coming back. Not yet."

"Say what, Sugar?"

"I just decided. I'm going back to the beach. I can't leave yet. I don't know when I will. I came to Baja for something, and I don't have it yet. If it's not Cristiano, then it's something else."

"Izzy…"

"It's not so far away, Sharlee. You can come visit anytime. And I'll be back. I just don't know how soon."

"Well, damn, Isabelle Allen. This isn't what I expected," Sharlee said.

Isabelle smiled. "What did you think would happen if I can work it out with Cristiano?"

She watched as emotions scrolled across her friend's face.

"I guess I really didn't think. I was too busy just feeling." Sharlee glanced toward the lighted window. "Well, you go get your man, Sugar. I'll call you when we get Andres settled into your old place."

"Isabelle," Andres said. "Your home…"

"Not home. House. It doesn't feel like home anymore," Isabelle said.

"But…?"

"I'll take care of everything, or my lawyer will." She glanced at Sharlee.

"Piece of cake." Sharlee snapped her fingers.

Isabelle pressed down on the gas pedal. "Then let's do it."

Isabelle walked up to the front door, then stood there. What do I do? Knock? If Cristiano answers he could shut the door in my face. She looked at the doorknob. If its unlocked, I go in. If locked, I get in the Suburban, go back to the apartment, pick up Sammie and Longie, and we all head to the beach.

Isabelle placed her hand on the knob and turned. It was unlocked. She pushed the door open. The room was dark, except for the lights from outside. She made out a desk and some office chairs. A square of light and the sound of raised voices came from a room on the far side. She walked toward it. Stopped beside the door. One of the voices belonged to Cristiano, the other was male and one she'd heard before.

"Uncle Ramon, I know what I am doing. It is for the best."

"The best? You lock yourself in this office. You do not come to dinner with your family, as promised."

"Momma didn't need to send you. I'm fine. There is much work I need to catch up on."

"Cristo, you must listen to your heart. We are a proud people. But sometimes a tree must bend, or it will snap."

"Tio, Uncle. I cannot love what I cannot trust. Isabelle was right. We are not for each other. And it has nothing to do with age or skin color."

"I never believed it did," Ramon protested.

No, Isabelle thought. Those were my words.

"Cristo, stop. Look at me."

Isabelle heard the rustle of papers being shuffled.

"Fine. I am looking."

Ramon laughed. "You sound so sulky. Like when you were a nino."

"Uncle, what is it. I need to finish this report tonight."

"Tonight? It is all ready tomorrow..yes, yes. I will say only one more thing, then I am out of here. Actually it is a question. Do you love Isabelle? You notice I do not say, did you love. I am asking do you love? And do not spout that trust bull shit. I know trust is important. But trust is also something you feel in your heart and soul. So, look into your heart and answer me."

Isabelle felt her breath catch. Her fingers dug into the side of the doorway.

"Uncle," Cristiano said.

"There is only me and you. In fact, do not answer. I will leave. Answer to yourself."

She heard footsteps coming toward her. Isabelle stepped back as Ramon came through the door. He stopped at seeing her, then opened his arms. With a smothered sob, she walked into them. He held her close for a long moment, then still in silence, he stepped back and motioned with his head toward Cristiano. She nodded and Ramon walked from her.

Isabelle faced the office door and took a deep breath. She walked to it, stood just inside and waited.

Cristiano sat at a glass and chrome desk. A computer took up half of its surface, papers lay before him in three neat stacks. The window from which she'd seen the light from the street was to the back of him. There were framed pictures of different islands on the walls. In some of them volcanoes belched smoke.

He muttered, frowned and raked fingers through his hair. He still wore the same clothing as he had at the party.

Has he been here ever since?

336

Isabelle licked her lips, searching for words. They had to be the right ones. So much depended on it.

Suddenly as if shocked by an electric current, Cristiano jerked his head up. Their eyes met, held. For an instant, she saw a look of joy on his face, then it fled, replaced by an expression of remote coolness.

"Miss Allen. I would have thought you would be across the border by now." His strained voice branded his cool expression a lie, and her hopes rose.

She walked into the office. Stopped in front of a photograph on the wall. "I'm not going. I've decided to stay."

"For how long will you grace San Felipe with your presence?"

"This is Isla Santa Maria, isn't it?"

"Si."

"These others, have you been to see them?"

"Si. Isabelle…"

She faced him. "Now it's Isabelle. What happened to Miss Allen?"

He looked down, shuffled papers on his desk.

"We need to talk," she said.

Cristiano didn't look up. "I am very busy right now. Perhaps you can call for an appointment. If the time you are staying permits it."

"I have the time, but I don't think that would work."

He lifted his eyes toward her. She walked toward him. Cristiano stood, then took a step back from his desk. "Miss Allen…"

"We are back to Miss Allen. A moment ago it was Isabelle. How can it be Isabella again?"

He shook his head. "I must keep my heart safe from Isabella."

She stood at the edge of the desk, across from him. "Too late. I have it, and you have mine." Isabelle watched him swallow. "Let me make this clear, I'm not going to San Francisco. Sammie, Longfellow, and I will be at the beach casa for a very long time. And all three of us love you."

His words came soft. "Sometimes love isn't enough."

"Yes, I heard what you said to your Uncle. Trust is very important to you. It's important to me, too."

Cristiano's eyes narrowed. "You heard us speaking?"

Isabelle picked up a crystal dolphin from his desk. "He didn't wait for the answer from his last question." She looked up. "I am."

"What?"

"I'm waiting for the answer. What did your heart tell you?"

"Isabelle…"

"Wait," She held up her hand. "On second thought, words can be lies." She smiled. "I of all people know that." She circled the desk, stood in front of him. "In fact, talking is overrated." She leaned into him and pressed her mouth against his.

He stood, unyielding for a moment, then she felt his groan against her lips. His hands gripped her waist, pulled her hard against him.

It was if his kiss sucked her soul from within her, and in return offered her part of his. In her heart, she accepted it with no reservations. This was marriage, mating. As far as she was concerned, no words said by priest or whomever could bind them any closer .

He lifted his lips from hers, looked into her eyes.

"I love you," she said. "I won't walk away. I can't promise we'll never make each other hurt. You have that power over me. I don't care how much time we have with each other. I'll take every second."

"Isabella."

She smiled. "Say it again."

"Isabella, my Isabella."

"Yes, yours forever. Now kiss me again."

Barbara M. Hodges lives on the central coast of California. She shares her life with her husband Jeff, two basset hounds, Ophelia and Hamlet, and a ginger-striped tabby cat, Wallace. Barbara is the author of eight novels - three in her young adult Daradawn fantasy series, ***The Blue Flame, The Emerald Dagger*** and ***The Silver Angel.*** Her fourth, ***Magical Stew*** contains three pieces of her shorter fiction. Her fifth novel, ***Shadow Worlds,*** is a science fiction novel co-written with Darrell Bain. Her sixth novel**, *Ice,*** is co-written with Randolph Tower, as is her seventh novel, ***One Last Sin****,* due for release from Coastal Dunes Publishing, the summer of 2012.

When Barbara is not writing, she enjoys going to or watching NASCAR on television, as well as decorative painting.

Maggie Pucillo retired from Pasadena Unified School District as an Early Childhood Education Specialist. She moved to California's Central Coast thirty minutes later. She lives there with husband Ricardo and Jack the Gypsy Cat. Her hobbies include dreaming on Baja's beaches, gardening and lots of reading. Her latest short story **The Lady in the Valentine Sweater** is part of the Santa Maria California Word Wizards' anthology **Scattered Hearts.**